Kings & Carnage

Aventine University Book Three

Sadie Hunt

Blackthorn Press

Kings & Carnage

Aventine University Book Three

Sadie Hunt

Part One

Chapter 1

Willa

I was floating on a dark sea. The tide flowed gently under me, lapping at the shore of a distant beach. There was no moon, no stars. Just the dark sky overhead blending into the black fathomless waters.

And then, a crash.

Metal on metal.

I tried to right myself, hoping to tread water while I looked for the origin of the sound, but my body was paralyzed. I was frozen, a prisoner of the water that held me captive in its dark embrace.

The sound grew louder, accompanied by the guttural growls of an unseen monster.

Panic clawed at my insides. Where this dark place? Why couldn't I escape? Why couldn't I see anything? I tried to flail my limbs to no avail, attempting to force my eyes open as the sounds in the distance grew more recognizable as shouting.

Someone — or something — was with me in the great sea.

And then, little by little, a sliver of light appeared.

I wasn't floating after all. I wasn't even in the water. I was lying down on some kind of bed.

My relief at being able to open my eyes was short-lived. The light was piercing, its brightness like a power drill in my brain, and I closed my eyes quickly against the pain before attempting to open them again.

"She's waking up," a woman said from the other side of my closed eyelids.

"What's taking security so long?" another voice — this time a man — said.

"I don't know, but keep him out of here," the woman said.

I tried again, forcing my eyes open against the pain shrieking in my brain, and was blinded by fluorescent lighting shining down from a white ceiling.

"Willa? You're okay," the woman said. "You're in the hospital, but you're okay."

I blinked again and she came into focus above me, a middle-aged woman with brown hair and creases around her comforting blue eyes.

"What's happening?" I asked.

The commotion in the background was getting louder, a deep voice angry and insistent.

Animalistic.

And now that I was awake, I knew that voice.

I knew it in my blood. In my bones.

Neo.

Then I remembered: leaving the island with Oscar, Rock, and Neo. Driving with Rock to meet my mom, to tell her the truth about Roberto.

I remembered something else too. Gurneys being rolled past me in a long white hall, blood seeping through the clothes of the unconscious men on them.

My men.

I tried to sit up and winced at the pain that shot through my sternum. It was so powerful it took my breath away and I sucked in air as I fell back onto the pillow.

"The airbags in the car and your seat belt saved your life," the woman (doctor? nurse? I didn't know) said. "But you got pretty bruised up."

The pain was enough to make my eyes water, but now that I remembered what had happened, nothing mattered but them.

The Kings.

My Kings.

"My... friends... Rock..." I remembered seeing Oscar and Neo being rolled past me in the hospital hallway right after the accident.

But I didn't remember seeing Rock.

"Your friends— " It was as far as she got before the door to the hospital room flew open.

I lifted my head from the pillow and tried to make sense of what I was seeing.

Neo, his massive frame somehow looking vulnerable in a hospital gown, looming in the doorway like a raging bull, his amber eyes lit with chaotic fury.

His gaze landed on me and relief washed over his eyes.

"Willa... thank god." He started through the door and headed for the bed but he only got a few steps in before two security guards grabbed his arms and started pulling him back.

I started to protest but didn't get very far before Neo's roar tore through the room.

"Get the fuck off me!" he bellowed, shrugging one of them off like he was nothing but a fly. The guard stumbled backward. "You can't keep me from her! No one's going to keep me from her!"

"It's okay!" My shout was feeble but desperate. I needed to see him. Needed to know he was okay. Needed to know what had happened to Oscar and Rock. "Let him in! I want to see him! Let him in!"

The security guards looked at the woman still standing by my bedside and she nodded her approval.

They let go of Neo with a scowl and he lurched toward

my bed, unsteady on his feet, as if he were drugged, a vicious gash above his left eye.

He seemed to reach me all at once, pulling me into his arms gently but ferociously.

He lowered his head to my hair. "Thank god," he breathed. "Thank fucking god."

I wrapped my arms around him and sank into the solid feel of his body.

He pulled back and held my head in his hands, studying my face. "Are you okay?" He ran his hands carefully down my shoulders. "Are you hurt?"

"My chest hurts." The pain had disappeared into the background in the wake of my relief at seeing Neo, but it was still there, a throbbing ache that started on the left side of my chest and radiated through my upper body. "But I think I'm okay. What about you?"

I studied him for signs of an injury other than the cut that had been stitched above his left eye.

"I'm good," Neo said.

The nurse bustling around us snorted and I narrowed my eyes at Neo.

"Why don't I believe that? And where are Rock and Oscar?"

"Drago took a bullet to this thigh and— "

"A bullet?!"

"He's okay," Neo said. "But..."

"But?" My heart was hammering in my chest and my brain beat out a rhythmic plea.

Please let them be okay, please let them be okay, please let them be okay...

And then, just one word.

Please.

Neo hesitated, then took my hand in both of his big ones.

It was such a tender gesture, so out of character from his usual roughness, that the drumbeat of fear beat even louder, threatening to block out everything as my head filled with a strange buzzing sound.

"Rock has a head injury," Neo finally said. "He hasn't regained consciousness."

Chapter 2

Neo

S he was bruised and battered and the most beautiful thing I'd ever fucking seen.

There had been a team of people around me when I'd woken up in the trauma unit but all I could think about was her. I'd fought the doctors and nurses investigating my chest wound. I'd wanted to get up, to find Willa, because I'd known — I'd fucking known — my father hadn't just sent men to kill Drago and me.

The real fun for Roberto was taking the people who mattered most to me.

My mother.

My brothers in all but name.

And most of all, Willa.

After that, they'd given me something to make me sleep and I'd woken up in recovery from the surgery that had saved my life.

It had taken a while for the drugs to wear off, but when they had, finding her was priority number one once I'd found out she was alive.

Now she was looking up at me with tears in her big green eyes, fear written all over her face.

"I need to see them," she said.

I nodded and got to my feet, because I was making it my personal mission to give Willa Russo everything she needed as long as she'd fucking let me.

"You can't get up until you see the doctor," the nurse said to Willa.

The two security guards who'd tried to keep me from her still hovered near the doorway.

Like they could stop me.

"I need to see my friend," Willa said. She licked her lips and straightened her spine. When she lifted her chin, she looked straight into the nurse's eyes. "I'm going to see my friend."

There was something new in her voice, an undercurrent of steel that had only been hinted at before.

The nurse sighed and grabbed a blood pressure cuff. "Let me check your vitals at least."

Three minutes later we were shuffling past the security guards. They glared as we made our way out of the room and I resisted the urge to give them the finger.

My chest fucking hurt. The doctor told me in recovery that the bullet had missed my heart by less than half an inch and I was now the proud owner of twelve stitches across my left pec.

"You okay?" I asked Willa, holding on to her as we made our way down the hall. "I can get you a wheelchair."

"I'm fine," she said. "You're the one I'm worried about. I feel like there's more under that hospital gown than you're willing to admit."

I tried for a grin, just to ease her mind. "There's more all right, but you might want to rest before you start thinking about that."

She rolled her eyes and a smile teased the corners of her mouth. Even now I wanted to press her against the wall, kiss her until she couldn't breathe.

"You're going to have to tell me the truth eventually," she said. "I'll find out anyway."

Her meaning was clear and I had a flash of memory: Willa naked and gleaming next to the fire in the house on the island, leaning back against Rock, his cock buried in her ass, Drago's dick in her mouth, her sweet little pussy taking my dick.

Fuck. She was the only girl in the world who could get me hard after major surgery.

"It's this one," I said, slowing my steps outside Rock's room. I held her back "He's... He doesn't look good."

She sucked in a breath and nodded, then opened the door.

Rock was as still as he'd been when I'd checked on

him on my way to Willa's room. All the color seemed to have drained from his body in the twenty-four hours we'd been at the hospital, and cords and IVs snaked from his arms and chest to the machines beeping quietly at his bedside.

One of his arms was in a cast and his face was a mess of cuts and bruises.

Drago was sitting in a chair next to the window. He got to his feet when he saw Willa and lurched toward her. I knew he'd been shot in the thigh, but the wound was covered by his hospital gown.

"Are you okay?" he asked, pulling Willa into his arms. "Are you hurt?"

"I'm fine," she said against his chest. "Just a little beat up."

He pulled back to look at her, studying her face like I'd done when I'd gotten to her, like she was a rare piece of art that had been carelessly handled.

Because she fucking was.

"Nothing broken?" he asked. "They didn't shoot at you?"

"Oh, they shot at us," she said. "But we shot back, and then the car went off the road and..." She squinted, like she was trying to see what had happened from a distance. "It's fuzzy, but I think the car rolled a few times. Then I was in a helicopter. That's all I remember until I got to the hospital and saw you being brought in."

"They had to cut Rock out of the car," Drago said. "He's got some kind of head trauma."

She turned her attention to Rock. "How bad is it? What do the doctors say?

"The doctor came in while Neo was looking for you," Drago said. "She doesn't know much yet, but he definitely has a concussion and maybe some other kind of head trauma."

Willa walked to Rock's bedside and took his big hand in her two small ones. "Can't they do... I don't know, an MRI or something?"

"Apparently an MRI will tell them more if Rock's conscious. They're going to do a CT scan," Drago said. "The doctor said his reflexes are working though and there's no sign of paralysis."

Willa stared at us with wide eyes. "Paralysis?"

"Relax, Jezebel," I said. "There's no sign of paralysis remember?"

It was a relief to fall back on our old dynamic. Patronizing Willa was a lot easier than thinking about the fact that I almost lost her.

If she took offense at the old nickname, she didn't show it.

"This is all my fault," she said.

"The fuck it is," Drago said, sitting next to her at the edge of Rock's hospital bed.

She shook her head. "No, you don't understand. This is

really my fault. I told my mom about the lighthouse when I called her for Christmas."

"What lighthouse?" I asked.

"The red one," Willa said. "Across the water from the island."

Drago tucked a piece of gold hair behind Willa's dear. "Still not your fault, tiger."

A shot of jealousy rocketed through my aching body. I envied how easy Drago was with her. For me, being with Willa felt like walking through a field of land mines.

Don't be an asshole.

Don't say anything too revealing.

And for fuck's sake, don't tell her how much you fucking love her.

"I knew Roberto was dangerous," she said. "I knew it and I was just so happy to be having a normal conversation with my mom that I practically drew him a map to us."

"Look at me," Drago said to Willa. I felt like I should leave. Like I was witnessing something intimate, something that hurt me to watch because I wanted to be the one comforting Willa and instead all I could do was tell her to relax and call her Jezebel while I tried to silence the screaming in my head at the thought of something happening to her. "The only person to blame for what happened to all of us is Roberto. He's already done enough damage. Don't let him make you feel guilty on top of everything else. Don't give him the satisfaction."

She drew in a shuddering breath and nodded. "You're right. It doesn't matter now anyway. All that matters is that we're all okay." She glanced at Rock, who looked about ten years younger in his sleep. "That Rock is okay."

"The doctor said the next twenty-four hours are critical," Drago said. "She said if he wakes up by then, the odds of a full recovery are good."

"Then we'll wait," Willa said. "And he'll wake up. He has to."

I didn't want to hear the note of desperation in her voice. Would she be as worried about me if I were in Rock's shoes? It wasn't like I'd done anything to deserve her concern. We'd fucked — although it would never be just that for me — but I didn't know how to take care of her like Rock, didn't know how to talk to her like Drago.

"I'm just so fucking glad you're okay, tiger," Drago said.

Willa looked from Drago to me. "What happened to you? Did they try to run you off the road too?"

"Tried and succeeded," I said, glad to be back on safer ground. Feelings weren't my strong suit. "Not sure they were happy to get what they wanted though."

"What do you mean?" Willa asked.

"Neo nailed one of them in the head before he even got out of the car," Drago said.

"You... killed him?" Willa asked.

"Yeah Jezebel, I killed him. That tends to be my gut reaction when someone's trying to off me."

"How many of them were there?" Willa asked.

"Two," Drago said.

"Same with us I think," she said. "What about the police? Won't they ask about the dead guy?"

"He was in the car with the other one," Drago said. "He drove off when a car stopped to see what was going on, but you're right about one thing — the cops have already been here."

Alarm was written on Willa's face. "At the hospital?"

Drago nodded. "We told them we had no idea who the other men were, but they'd already run our names. They definitely didn't buy it."

Drago was underselling it: the cops thought we were full of shit. And who could blame them? We were both sons of notorious mafiosos — my father was the New York boss for fuck's sake — who'd just been involved in a roadside shooting.

The movie practically wrote itself.

"So what now?" Willa asked. "Will they be back?"

"They'll definitely be back," I said. "They told us not to leave town."

She stood. "We have to get out of here. Like... as soon as Rock is awake and the doctors say it's okay."

I'd never been fucking prouder. The rule-following wallflower Willa had been wearing as a disguise was dissipating before our eyes.

She was remembering who she was.

And she was right. The more the cops dug, the greater the risk one of us would be arrested. If that happened, we'd be sitting ducks.

My father had people everywhere.

Shouting sounded from the hallway and we all turned to look at the door to Rock's room. Together, we were the eye of a never-ending fucking storm, carnage following us wherever we went.

If there was trouble, it was safest to assume it had something to do with us.

My suspicions were confirmed a few seconds later when Celeste Russo Alinari burst through the door in head-to-toe Gucci, her garishly made-up face contorted in outrage.

Chapter 3

Willa

I shouldn't have been happy to see her. She'd told Roberto — intentionally or otherwise — where to find us. Neo and Oscar were obviously injured (I didn't buy their macho bullshit, I wanted to see under those hospital gowns) and Rock was in real trouble.

We could have been killed.

But what can I say? I'd just been through something traumatic. I'd woken up in a *hospital*.

And she was still my mom.

"Where is my— " Her gaze landed on me and she heaved a sigh of relief. "There you are! Thank god!"

She clicked toward me on a pair of gold stilettos and yanked me into her embrace.

I winced, my body still sore from the car crash, and allowed myself a few seconds to sink against her silk cheetah-print blouse.

But it wasn't right. Her favorite perfume had been replaced with something new and probably a lot more expensive and her once-curvaceous body had been punished into a whiplike version of herself that felt completely unfamiliar.

She pulled back to look at me. "I can't *believe* it took them so long to notify me. I'll be filing a complaint with the police department in this hodunk town."

"I'm not a minor anymore," I said weakly. "They wouldn't call you unless I asked and I was unconscious until about an hour ago."

I didn't know why I bothered defending the police department in this *hodunk town*, wherever that was. I had no idea where they'd brought us after the accident, but my mom thought any small town was hodunk if it was shabby. If it was cute she called it quaint.

"Absurd!" she declared before looking me over. "You look all right. Are you all right? What happened?"

I looked from her to Neo and Oscar, standing next to Rock's bed like a couple of bodyguards. Neo had a vicious scowl on his face, and I couldn't say I blamed him. After what had happened — what Roberto's men had done to us — it was obvious we were at war.

I didn't believe my mom had known what would happen if she told Roberto where we were — she was oblivious, not pathological — but once I told her the truth, she would have to pick a side.

"Let's talk somewhere else," I said. I didn't know if Rock could hear us, but I didn't want the stressful energy in his room.

"I'll come with you," Neo and Oscar said in unison.

I stared them both down. "No, you won't. We're in a hospital. I'll be fine."

It was time to have the conversation I'd been on the way to having when Roberto's men had started shooting at Rock and me. It wasn't going to be easy, and my mom deserved privacy when she heard the truth about her new husband.

I led her out into the hall and headed for a group of chairs set up near a bank of windows.

I had to blink against the bright December light streaming in through the wall of glass. Just yesterday we'd left the island and parted ways with Neo and Oscar in the marina parking lot, but it felt like a lifetime ago.

"I'm sorry I didn't come sooner," my mom said, taking a seat in one of the chairs and dropping her giant designer bag in the one next to her. "I waited at the restaurant and then tried to call when you didn't show."

"It's not your fault." I lowered myself carefully into the chair across from her and winced as pain tore through my upper body. Whatever painkillers they had me on were wearing off fast. "But this — all of this — is why I was coming to meet you."

She frowned. "What do you mean?"

"There's no easy way to say this, so I'm just going to say it." I drew in a breath, wishing we'd been able to have this conversation yesterday, minus the whole shot-at-and-run-off-the-road thing. "Roberto is involved in Emma's disappearance. And not just Emma's disappearance — the disappearance of other girls from Bellepoint too."

I didn't know what I'd expected, but it wasn't the utterly blank expression on her face. "I honestly can't imagine what you're talking about, Willa."

I wished we were on the other side of the windows where I could suck in the cold winter air, or at the very least, near a coffee machine so I could down a coffee or three.

Anything to clear the cobwebs from my brain so I could find the right combination of words that would make my mom believe what I was about to say next.

"I've been trying to figure out what happened to Emma ever since I got to Aventine," I said. "Turns out, she's not the only girl who's gone missing from Bellepoint over the years."

"Get to the part about Roberto," she snapped.

"Someone was sending me creepy letters, threatening me if I didn't stop looking for Emma. Then I got a different kind of letter, one that told me to go to a cabin in the woods if I wanted to know what had happened to her," I said. "So I went, but when I got there, two men tried to kill me. One of them was Dean Giordana."

Now I had her attention. She sat straighter, her forehead furrowed as much as her Botox would allow. "Dean Giordana is dead."

"I know. He died that night, the night he tried to kill me, along with another man who got away," I said. "The Kings — Neo, Oscar, and Rock — saved me, and then they told me Emma had come to them for help before she died."

"What kind of help?" The sunlight slanting in through the windows was harsh. It made my mom look older and tired, and I suddenly wished I didn't have to be the one to tell her that her new husband was a killer.

She'd been through enough.

"She'd been looking for the missing girls and she needed help. The Kings thought she was in some kind of trouble, and I started wondering if the same person who'd been threatening me had been threatening her. And the thing is, Mom, I know who that person is now. I know because the same person who's been threatening me — the one who sent me the letter telling me to come to the cabin — sent people to run Rock and me off the road, shoot at us, do the same to Neo and Oscar."

She stood, two bright spots of color standing out on her cheeks. "You need to tell the police!"

I was relieved to see the alarm on her face, to hear it in her voice. Alarm meant she hadn't known, and deep down I'd been worried she might, that she might have known it was Roberto all along and covered for him to protect herself and her new lifestyle.

Now I knew that wasn't true. My mom wasn't above lying, but she'd never been very good at it. She really was as oblivious as she seemed, and while I didn't love that about her, it was better than covering for a killer.

"It's... more complicated than that," I said. "That's why I was coming to talk to you."

"I don't see what's complicated about it, Willa." Her trademark disapproval was back in her voice. "If someone is trying to hurt you, it's time to call the police, especially if you know who that someone is."

I blew out my breath, trying to get up the guts to just spit it out. "I did some digging and it turns out that cabin? The one where Dean Giordano and the other guy were going to kill me? It's owned by Roberto."

Okay, I was stretching the truth a bit. We didn't know for a fact that the cabin was owned by Roberto, but come on: it was named after Neo's probably dead mother. It was way too much of a coincidence and I needed a compelling argument to get my mom away from her psychotic husband.

She blinked like I was speaking a foreign language. "I don't understand."

"Roberto owns the cabin where those men were going to kill me, and the Kings have suspected for a long time that he was involved with the missing girls. I was coming to warn you when we were run off the road. You have to leave him. You're not safe with him."

Skepticism was written all over her face. "I think you hit your head harder in that accident than the doctors realize, Willa. You sound insane."

"I know," I said, trying to throw her a bone. "But it's all true. You can't go back to him. You have to leave town for a while, hide out somewhere or something."

"Why would Roberto hurt those girls?" she asked. "Why would he hurt Emma?"

"He hurt Emma to keep her quiet," I said. "The other girls... I don't know yet. We're still figuring out the details."

I hated to admit it, to give her any opening to discount what I was telling her, but it was the truth, and telling her that maybe there was no motive, that maybe Roberto was just a psycho fuck who liked to hurt people, seemed like a bad idea.

She tipped her head at me like I was a little girl with crumbs on her lips claiming not to have raided the cookie jar. "Willa, you can't seriously expect me to leave my husband over some half-baked accusation with zero proof and even less motive."

"I expect you to believe me," I said. "I'm your daughter."

"That doesn't mean I have to buy in to some ridiculous conspiracy theory about Roberto."

"Tell me one thing," I said, switching tactics. "Did you

tell Roberto where we were? Did you tell him about the lighthouse?"

Her gaze slid away from mine and for the first time, I thought maybe I was getting through.

"It sounds to me like you ran into some crazy driver with road rage," she said.

"A crazy driver who shot at us in two different locations?" I asked. "What does that sound like to you? Because it sounds like a hit to me."

I was the daughter of a Mafia boss and the granddaughter of a Mafia boss.

I knew a hit when I saw it.

She picked up her bag. "I'm not going to listen to this nonsense."

"I think you mentioned the lighthouse to Roberto," I said hurriedly, sensing the moment slipping away. She was shutting down, getting ready to walk out so she didn't have to think about what I was telling her. "You told him and he sent someone to kill us, to keep us quiet. And I get why this is hard to hear, but I'm asking you to choose me. Just..." I blinked away the tears stinging my eyes. "Just this once, choose me."

"Don't pull that card," she snapped. "You're being dramatic, as always. This was an unfortunate incident. You were in the wrong place at the wrong time. I'm not going to blow up my life — both our lives, because in case you've forgotten, Roberto is paying your tuition at Aventine — to indulge your hysteria."

My shoulders sagged. I knew when I'd lost.

"You're making a mistake," I said.

She planted a stiff kiss on my cheek. "You need rest, Willa. We'll talk when you're feeling better."

I stood next to the windows and watched her walk away, her heels clicking on the hospital floors as she made her way to the elevator.

Chapter 4

Oscar

I watched Willa sleeping on the bed next to Rock and thought about the mess we were in. Across the room, on the other side of Rock's hospital bed, Neo had finally fallen asleep.

The room was dimly lit by the machines monitoring Rock's vital signs, the sky dark on the other side of the room's windows. One of the nurses had tried to make us leave only to be told, "We're not leaving," by Neo, Willa, and me in unison.

Willa was determined to stay until Rock woke up, determined that he *would* wake up, and that he would want to see her when he did.

I couldn't argue the point. She'd been the first thing I'd wanted to see when I woke up.

Neo and I wanted to be there for Rock too, but there

was a darker reason for our vigilance that neither of us wanted to share with Willa.

Roberto.

His men had failed to take us out. Worse, we'd sent one of them back with a bullet in his brain.

Roberto wasn't done with us. Not by a long shot.

My bet was on another attempt on our lives sooner rather than later, probably even before we could leave the hospital and go into hiding.

Which we would abso-fucking-lutely have to do.

Not forever. There was no running from someone like Roberto, and even if it had made sense, I wouldn't want to do it.

He had come for us.

Had fucking come for *Willa*.

I felt sick every time I thought about it. We could have lost her.

I could have lost her.

Roberto would have to pay for that eventually. Would have to pay for all the things he'd done and that one most of all.

I tried to piece it all together — the girls from Bellepoint, Emma, the cabin in Roberto's name — but it felt like I was missing something and I was too fucking tired to make sense of it.

I watched Willa instead, because watching her, knowing she was alive and breathing in the world, made me feel like I could breathe too. Her long blonde hair was tangled around her shoulders, her full mouth parted slightly in sleep.

I would have taken a picture if I hadn't left my Nikon behind when the EMTs arrived on the scene.

I wanted to watch her forever. Wanted to protect her forever.

Not that we'd done such a bang-up job of that the first time around. So far she'd almost been buried in the woods surrounding Aventine and had been shot at and run off the road.

We had to do better, had to find a place where she would really be safe, because keeping Willa safe was the only thing that really mattered.

One thing was certain: we couldn't rely on Willa's mom for support. Willa's tear stained face when she'd returned to Rock's room after talking to her mom had said it all.

Celeste hadn't believed her.

I wasn't exactly surprised, but I'd hoped for better. Willa had already lost her dad and Emma. With her mom squarely in Roberto's corner, she must have felt like she had no family left.

Fuck.

I shifted in the uncomfortable hospital chair and took a drink of the bitter stale coffee from the vending machine in the hall. It was so bad it was actually offensive.

It would have pissed Rock the fuck off.

I was so zoned out I didn't notice right away that Rock's eyes were open.

I stood and moved toward the bed, wondering if the dim light in the room was playing tricks on me. But nope.

He was awake.

"Hey," I said quietly, not wanting to startle Willa. "How are you feeling?"

"Is she okay?" he asked.

I nodded. "She made out better than the rest of us, thanks to you."

"*She's* right here," Willa said. She sat up and looked at Rock, then burst into tears and threw her arms around him. "You're okay!"

His good arm came around her and I almost envied the asshole for getting to see how much Willa cared about him.

"What the fuck is wrong with my other arm?" His words were muffled by Willa's hair.

Willa laughed and sat up, tears staining her cheeks. "It's broken, but it's your head injury the doctor was worried about."

"What head injury?"

"The one that had us worried fucking sick," Neo said, standing next to the bed.

"Aw, you were worried about me?" he asked.

"Worried we'd have to haul your unconscious ass out of here on a stretcher," Neo said.

Rock started to laugh, then winced. "Ow. Fucker. Stop making me laugh."

"I wasn't joking," Neo said. "We need to get out of here."

"Where is *here*?" Rock asked. "I mean, a hospital obviously. But where?"

"The name of the place isn't as important as the fact that it's got a population of about a thousand people," I said. "The hospital serves a few towns like this in the area, but it's small."

"I take it security leaves something to be desired?" Rock asked.

Willa was snuggled up next to him on the bed, for the moment unconcerned with our conversation.

Neo snorted. "That's an understatement. More like nonexistent."

"Fuck," Rock said. "Then you're right, we do need to get out of here."

Willa sat up and looked down at him. "You remember."

"I remember being shot at by Roberto's thugs," he said. "And I remember the car flipping."

"That's more than I remembered when I first woke up," Willa said.

"It's enough to know we can't stay here," he said.

"You have a concussion," Willa pointed out. "And maybe even more serious head trauma than that. Plus, your arm is broken."

"I'm fine," Rock said, sitting up.

Willa got off the bed. "We don't even have a car. And I don't know where our clothes are."

There was a note of desperation in her voice as she tried to convince him we couldn't leave.

"Those are solvable problems, Jezebel," Neo said, heading for the door of Rock's hospital room.

She glared at me when Neo disappeared into the hall. "This is insane. You're all hurt and— " she raised her voice to talk over me when I tried to protest, "don't even try to tell me you're fine because I can tell from the way you and Neo are moving that you're hiding something under those hospital gowns and it's not just the good stuff."

I laughed in spite of myself. How did this fucking girl know us all so well? "It doesn't matter, tiger, because if we stay we're going to be a lot more than hurt — we're going to be dead. Do you really think Roberto is going to let us watch reality TV while we recover in the hospital? That he's going to let us saunter off into the sunset?"

"Of course not," she said. "But it'll take time to... I don't know, assign the job to someone else, send them back up here."

"We were all out of it for a while remember?" I asked. "We've already lost more than twenty-four hours. Even with the six-hour drive, he's had more than enough time to regroup."

Rock took her hand. "He's right, kitten. And I think you know it. We have to get out of here. No discharge papers, no announcement, just a quick and quiet exit."

An internal war played out across her beautiful face, but she didn't have time to say anything else because a second later, Neo stepped through the door holding a stack of light green scrubs.

"Solved problem number one," he said, tossing the scrubs on the bed. "Let's go."

Chapter 5

Willa

This was a bad idea, but it was the best one we had, because the Kings were right: Roberto wasn't going to let us walk off into the sunset. I didn't know what we'd do or where we'd go once we left the hospital — it didn't seem smart to go back to the Kings' house — but we were sitting ducks in the hospital.

The Kings stripped off their hospital gowns then and there, like it was impossible a nurse or doctor would come in any second and see them bare-assed — and I did mean bare-assed — because there was no underwear under the gowns.

But it wasn't their bare asses that got my attention — it was the bandages covering what were obviously serious wounds.

I gaped at the one on Neo's chest, right over his heart. "Oh hell no. We are not leaving this hospital. You didn't tell me you'd been hurt!" I frowned at Oscar, who had a similarly large bandage on his right thigh and a giant bruise on his chest. "I'm not surprised Neo would lie to me, but you? I expected better."

"First of all," Neo said, "we didn't lie."

"It was a lie of omission," I said, "and you know it."

"Second," he continued, like he hadn't heard me, "it's fine. They fixed it in surgery."

"In surgery?"

"Yeah, me too," Oscar said. "Took the bullet right out."

"See?" Rock asked. "We're good to go, kitten."

"You shouldn't be saying a word," I said, reconsidering the whole thing. "You have a head injury. You shouldn't even be out of bed."

"I feel fine," Rock said. "I just have a little headache."

I glowered at the three of them, half-naked and covered in bruises and gauze. "This is a terrible idea."

"You got a better one, Jezebel?" Neo asked, slipping one of the scrub shirts over his bare chest.

"Stay here and recover? Hope for the best?"

"Not an option," Neo said. "And you know that."

Rock bent to kiss my head. "Don't worry. It's going to be fine. We'll find a place to rest and recover, one where Roberto can't find us. Now get your sweet ass dressed."

I sighed and stripped off my gown, weirdly self-conscious to be naked under the harsh lights in such a weird scenario.

It was dumb. After our hot Christmas night together, the Kings knew every inch of me.

And I did mean every inch.

But this was a whole different kind of intimacy.

I slipped off my hospital gown and was surprised to see the Kings staring at me.

Actually, it wasn't the staring that surprised me. I was ass-naked in front of them and their voracious sexual appetites were well documented.

It was the expressions on their faces that took me by surprise — not lust but a kind of still fury that sucked the air out of my lungs.

"What?" I looked down at my naked body and understood. I was covered in cuts and bruises. There was the big one on my chest, the one caused by my seat belt that made it hurt when I moved or even breathed. But there were countless others too, and the Kings looked absolutely murderous at the discovery.

"I'm going to kill him," Neo said quietly. "Long and slow."

"Same," Oscar and Rock said at the same time.

"It looks worse than it is," I said. "I'm okay. I mean, yeah, this bruise on my chest hurts like a mother, but the nurse told me it'll heal."

"Maybe we shouldn't leave," Oscar said.

"Yeah," Rock agreed, "you need rest."

"You don't need rest after being shot and having a head injury but I need it with a few scrapes and bruises?" I shook my head. "No way. You were right when you said we have to get out of here. It's more dangerous to stay than to leave."

I pulled on the scrubs left on the bed and tried not to wince from the pain that zinged through my body with every move. It was worse now than when I'd first woken up, probably because back then I'd been too worried about the Kings to focus on my own pain. Plus, I was pretty sure the pain meds they'd been pumping into my body while I was unconscious had worn off.

Now I knew the Kings were okay and my body was making it clear that it had been through some shit, but I didn't want to give the Kings' rage any more fuel. We needed to focus on getting somewhere safe. Revenge would have to wait.

Sic temper tyrannis.

The words drifted through my mind and I clutched at my throat, feeling for the birthday gift the Kings had given me the month before. "My choker's gone!"

"We'll buy you another one," Neo said, heading for the door.

I shook my head. "I want... I want that one."

Neo scowled.

"It... it was a gift," I said.

His expression softened, as much as Neo's expression

could ever soften. "We'll check your room on the way out, but if it's not there, we leave without it."

I nodded. I couldn't expect them to turn the hospital upside down just because I was feeling sentimental.

Rock moved toward the cabinet against one wall of the hospital room. "Fuck yeah," he said, reaching inside. He held up his wallet and looked from Neo to Oscar. "Want to go back for yours?"

"Not worth the risk," Oscar said. "You have access to everything anyway."

I didn't know what it meant but it seemed to satisfy Rock, who nodded and slipped his wallet into one of the pockets of his scrubs.

He stuck his head back into the cabinet and emerged holding his shoes.

"They kept my shoes!" he said, slipping them on.

"Congratulations," Neo said, moving toward the door of Rock's room. He cracked it open to look in the hall.

"Are you sure we can't just sign ourselves out?" I asked no one in particular. I didn't like how clandestine it all felt, like we were criminals when we were the victims. "It's not like they can force us to stay."

"Can't afford the time," Oscar said. "They'll want Rock to stay, and even after we make it clear we're leaving, the discharge papers will take forever. It's too risky to wait."

"Fine," I grumbled. "It just seems dumb to leave

without our clothes and our things when they're right in the next room."

"They probably cut our clothes off our bodies," Rock said, "but you can take what you find when we go for your choker."

"All clear," Neo said, glancing back at us. "Act like you belong."

"Why are you looking at me?" I asked.

Neo rolled his eyes. "Because you're the one who wants to sign out like a good little girl."

Why did it sound hot when he was basically calling me a nerd?

We slipped into the hallway, Neo in front, me behind him, then Rock and Oscar. They were like a military unit, changing formation depending on the circumstances, and I knew Neo and Oscar were protecting not only me but Rock, who was more compromised than the rest of us even if he wouldn't admit it.

The hall was quiet and we passed the three rooms between mine and Rock's without seeing anyone, although the background of beeping machines and murmuring voices made me feel like someone was going to stumble upon us any second.

I told myself it didn't matter — we were allowed to leave — but I knew the Kings were right: having to explain ourselves would take time and draw attention and I had a sinking feeling we couldn't afford either.

Back in my room, I moved to the cabinet against the wall and found a plastic drawstring bag labeled with my name. My clothes weren't there, but I found the choker and — bonus — my purse and the lug-soled boots I'd been wearing when we'd left the island.

"Yes!" I said, removing the bag from the cabinet. I started to reach inside for the choker but Neo stopped me with a terse command.

"Bring the bag."

Right. We were in a hurry.

"I'm putting on my shoes," I said, bending to slip my boots onto my feet. "I'll be able to move faster."

I slipped my wrist through the strings on the bag and we made our way back into the hall.

We were halfway toward the elevator at one end when a voice sounded behind us.

"Excuse me."

I froze, then turned on instinct toward the commanding female voice. She was young, and her white lab coat told me she was a doctor. She looked at Rock with recognition tinged with disapproval. "You shouldn't be out of bed."

"Yeah..." Oscar began. "We kind of have somewhere to be, Doctor."

She frowned and started toward us, her footsteps brisk. "The only place this one needs to be," she said, gesturing at

Rock, "is in his bed, recovering from his head injury and waiting for the results of his CT scan."

"That sounds nice and all," Rock said, "but my friend here is right, we have someplace we have to be."

"There's nowhere you could be that's more important than—"

She stopped short, her gaze drawn to something behind us. I didn't know what it was, but I knew from the expression on her face that it probably wasn't good.

The Kings noticed it too and we pivoted toward the elevator. I understood immediately why the doctor looked so alarmed: the four men exiting the elevator and walking purposefully toward us clearly weren't at the hospital to visit a sick relative.

They were Roberto's soldiers, as recognizable to me as family even though I didn't know their names.

They were big, wearing the combination of jeans and leather jackets that were favored by street soldiers. They thought it made them blend into the rest of the population, but to anyone who was a member of the family, they might as well have been wearing a sign that said *I'll kill you for a hundred bucks.*

The biggest one was nearly as tall as Neo. He reached under his jacket and withdrew a gun.

Neo reached back and grabbed my hand. "Run!"

Chapter 6

Willa

He didn't have to tell me twice, partly because he was already dragging me behind him and partly because I had no desire to come face-to-face with the four men moving toward us.

Neo shoved the doctor toward the wall as we passed. "Get down and stay down!"

Then we were flying past her, Rock and Oscar a blur of movement on our heels.

I had no idea where we were going or where we were supposed to hide. At the end of the hall, the door was open to a hospital room, the curtain drawn around what I assumed was a bed, the TV mounted near the ceiling blaring a game show.

I was grateful for my boots as we rounded the corner into another long hall. If I'd been in socks, I would have slid into the wall at the speed Neo was pulling me along.

I had only a second to worry about the gunshot wound in his chest, Rock's head injury, the bullet hole in Oscar's thigh. A second later, two shots sounded behind us, embedding themselves with a thunk into the wall to our right.

"Fuck!" Neo said, scanning the doorways on either side of the hall for an escape.

We were coming up on another corner, and I was starting to understand that the hospital was laid out in a series of hallways that met to create a square. If we could get around two more corners we'd be back at the elevator, although waiting for it to arrive didn't seem like the best idea.

A couple of nurses and an older man in a hospital gown appeared in the hall, drawn out by the commotion.

"Get back! Get back!" Oscar screamed as we ran past.

We were approaching the end of the hall when I spotted a small metal plaque next to a closed door.

Stairs.

Neo must have seen it too because he pulled me toward the stairwell. He opened the door and practically threw me through it and then waited while Oscar and Rock followed.

Halfway down the first flight of stairs, I glanced back and saw the three of them pounding down the stairs after me.

"Go go go!" Oscar shouted from the back.

I hit the second flight of stairs and heard the door open above us, followed by the sound of heavy footsteps.

The aches and pains that had been so noticeable twenty minutes earlier were gone, my body flooded with adrenaline as I went into full-on fight-or-flight mode. I could only hope the same was true for Neo, Oscar, and Rock, that they weren't feeling the pain of their injuries, which were a lot more serious than mine, and especially that Rock would remain conscious and that he wasn't doing further damage to his head by fleeing the hospital instead of resting like a not-insane person.

Roberto's men had apparently given up on being quiet because shots were fired above us, echoing through the confined stairwell and making my ears ring with the sound of metal on metal.

I had no idea how many flights of stairs we'd descended when we hit one of the landings and I saw a sign for the second floor next to a door leading out of the stairwell.

We were almost to the ground floor. Roberto's men were still right on our heels, but if we could just make it into the lobby we'd have somewhere to run.

"One more!" I shouted, hoping the Kings could hear me over the noise of clanging footsteps on metal stairs and the shots that rang out every few seconds.

Roberto's men were obviously just hoping to get lucky

and slow us down because there was no way they had a clear shot in the stairwell.

Relief swelled in my chest when I saw the sign for the first floor. I flung the door open and held it for Oscar and Rock. Neo burst through the doorway a second later, then stopped running.

"Get her to the parking lot," he said to Oscar and Rock. "Find a car."

It hit me that he was telling us he wasn't coming. That he was going to stay behind.

I clutched his arm. "No! We're not leaving you!"

"You better not fucking leave me," he said, kissing me hard and fast on the lips. He shoved me toward Oscar and Rock and held on to the levered handle of the door leading to the stairwell. "I'm just going to slow these guys down long enough for you to find a car. I'll be right behind you."

I wanted to argue. There was safety in numbers and I had never felt safer than with the Kings. Even more than that, I didn't want to leave Neo to face Roberto's men alone.

But arguing would be a too stupid to live moment.

There was no time.

"If you don't come I'll kill you myself," I said, turning to run.

"Have that fucking car ready when I get out there," Neo shouted at us.

I heard the men banging on the door as we ran through the hospital lobby, then the sound of more gunshots coming from the stairwell as Roberto's men tried to shoot their way out.

The people milling in the lobby screamed — some ducking and hiding, others running — as the gunfire rang through the hospital. The scene devolved into chaos in less than five seconds, security hurrying toward the sound, people running every which way in a panic, which had probably been Neo's idea.

Once he let go of the door, he could run with the crowd. It would be harder to identify him.

Harder to shoot him.

He might make it to the car in time.

"Wait," I said, breathless as we pushed through the doors into a clear frigid night, "how are we going to get a car?"

"Don't worry about that, tiger," Oscar said, pulling me toward the parking lot, seemingly oblivious to the cold pavement under his bare feet. "Just help us find an older car. Something that needs a key."

I glanced back as we raced past the first few rows of cars. People were streaming from the hospital with panicked expressions on their faces. Some of them put distance between themselves and the building and then turned to watch the commotion. Others headed straight for the parking lot, clearly wanting to GTFO.

"We need to hurry," I said.

I didn't think anyone was going to take the time to file a police report if they caught us stealing a car, but I didn't want the owner of our eventual ride to catch us red-handed either.

"There," Rock said, pointing at a sea-green sedan parked under a tree.

Upside: it was parked under a tree in the shadows, away from the streetlamps that illuminated the parking lot.

Downside: it looked like it had been driven off the factory line before my mother was born.

Also, it was huge. Not exactly the fast getaway car we needed.

"This will work," Oscar said. I noticed he was limping and bit my tongue. They'd been right to insist we leave the hospital when we did. If they hadn't, we might all be dead, and that eventuality still wasn't off the table.

Oscar's limp was something to worry about later.

He checked the driver's side door, found it unlocked, and breathed a sigh of relief. "Fuck yes. Get in."

Rock eased into the backseat while I climbed into the front. Neo would need a quick getaway — Rock could open the door for him while Oscar drove.

The car was huge, so big I didn't even have to pull my knees in while he dug around in the glove box emblazoned with the word *Impala*.

"This baby has a V8," Oscar said. "Not a fast pickup, but a lot of power. We could have done worse." He rummaged for a few more seconds until he found a screwdriver. "Yes!"

I had no idea why someone would have a screwdriver in their glove box, but it was a good thing I guessed?

I jumped as shots rang out — and this time they weren't coming from inside the hospital.

I turned to look and saw that Rock was doing the same. Neo was running barefoot through the parking lot in his scrubs, using the cars as cover while his father's men tried their best to hit a moving target.

It might have been funny if I hadn't known he could be killed at any second. My heart clutched at the thought and I didn't have time to think about what it meant that the thought of losing him — of losing any of them — made me feel like I couldn't breathe.

I'd already come close. Way too close.

Please, I prayed silently to anyone who would listen. *Please*.

"They're out," Rock shouted at Oscar. "Neo's exposed. Hurry the fuck up!"

"Working on it," Oscar said calmly, like he was washing the windows instead of trying to hot-wire a car while Roberto's men shot at Neo.

I tore my eyes away from Neo and looked at Oscar. His head was bent, gaze inches away from the ignition of the car, which had been pulled out to expose a jumble of wires in varying colors.

He sifted through them, found two he liked, and used his teeth to strip the plastic coating from the ends.

More gunfire, this time even closer.

"Fuck!" Rock said. "What's our ETA on this thing? Because I'm about ready to go out there and give them another target just to make their job harder."

"Almost..." Oscar said, "there."

The engine roared to life.

"Get ready to open the door," Oscar said, putting the car into gear.

It lurched forward and I reached for my seat belt only to realize there was no shoulder belt, and if there was a lap belt it was tucked into the long bench seat Oscar and I shared.

Perfect.

Oscar hit the gas and the car chugged as it picked up speed. I held on to the dash as we came to the end of a row of cars and turned hard, then sped down the aisle.

Neo was crab-walking behind the cars on the next aisle, Roberto's men moving through the parking lot with guns drawn, scanning for him.

"Next aisle over!" I shouted.

"Got him," Oscar said, making another hard turn at the end of the aisle and speeding up the next one.

I held my breath as we got closer to the car where Neo was hiding, my attention ping-ponging between the top of his head and Roberto's men, now running toward Neo —

toward us — as they realized they were about to lose their prey.

Rock flung open the back door at the same time Oscar screeched to a halt in front of the giant pickup truck Neo was using for cover.

Shots sounded behind us and I heard the clang of metal as they hit the car's bumper.

Please not the tires...

"Get the fuck down!" Neo shouted at me. He dove into the backseat, his feet hardly off the pavement when Oscar gunned the engine.

I ducked under the top of the bench seat just as the rear windshield burst, shattered glass falling like crystal rain as Oscar floored it.

Chapter 7

Rock

We'd been driving for two hours when Drago finally pulled off the road and into a massive truck-stop complex with gas pumps and an attached diner. I'd lost track of where we were a long time ago, Drago navigating the Impala through a series of backroads in an effort to stay off the highways.

And it didn't matter anyway. There was only one thought in my head, only one thing that mattered.

Willa had been hurt on my watch.

I didn't bother saying it out loud. Drago would tell me not to be dumb, Neo would tell me to stop feeling sorry for myself, and Willa would rush to explain all the reasons it wasn't my fault she was covered in cuts and bruises.

None of it would change the fact that she'd been with me when the car rolled, when Roberto's men shot at us. If some random driver hadn't stopped when the car rolled, forcing Roberto's men to take off, Willa would be dead.

I couldn't think about it without wanting to scream.

She'd moved to the backseat, and I looked over at her, the bruises on her pretty face visible even in the shadowed interior of the car. Nothing felt more important than keeping her safe.

And I'd failed.

"Are you sure it's safe to stop?" Willa asked, eying the busy parking lot, teeming with long-haul truck drivers and tourists on road trips. A series of massive semitrucks with attached cargo trailers were lined up on one side of the parking lot, some of them idling, others dark, their drivers either asleep inside or stretching their legs and grabbing food from the mini-mart or diner.

"Define *safe*," Drago said, cutting the engine.

She lifted her eyebrows. "Any environment where Roberto's men aren't going to show up shooting?"

"No guarantees," Drago said, "but unlikely. We left the hospital ahead of them and have been off all the major roads. I haven't spotted a tail, and there were plenty of stretches where I would have."

"Okay," she said. "I'll go in, get us some clothes, then we can all go grab food and stuff."

"We'll all go," I said. I wasn't about to let her out of my sight.

She tipped her head like I was short a few screws. "Seriously?"

"What?" I asked.

"Look at us," she said. "We're in scrubs, Neo and Oscar don't have shoes, and we're totally beat up. If we all go in, someone's going to call the police."

She had a point, and I fought against the burst of maniacal laughter that threatened to explode from my throat. I'd been in a lot of weird situations — in the States and in Sicily working for the family — but none of them came close to sitting in the darkened Impala with three of the four people I cared about most (I needed to contact Sophia, check in, make sure my little sis was safe), all of us in stolen scrubs, debating the merits of a late-night shopping trip in a truck stop in the middle of nowhere.

"I'll go then," I said.

Neo rolled his eyes. "You're the last person who should go. You shouldn't even be walking around. What if you pass out or something? We won't be around to get you out of there. Drago should go."

"Why Oscar?" Willa asked.

"Because I scare the fuck out of people even when I'm not trying," Neo said. "And everyone will think you need help. Plus, no fucking way I'm letting you go in there alone."

"Seconded," I said.

"Thirded," Drago said, then added, "Is thirded a

word?" He looked up, like he was trying to figure out the answer, then shrugged and twisted in the driver's seat to look at Rock. "I'll go. Give me your credit card."

"If we use credit, they'll be able to track us," Willa said.

"Not for a while," Neo said. "And we don't have a choice right now. We need to get clothes and food, switch cars and plates, and find a place to regroup."

"He's right," I said. "By the time Roberto's men track my card — if they even bother — we'll be long gone. Once I get inside, I'll use the Wi-Fi to access our offshore accounts and have money transferred to the numbered account in Aruba."

Willa shook her head. "Wait, you have... offshore accounts?"

Drago held out his hand for my credit card. "We've been preparing for this for a long time, tiger. We just didn't count on having our hideaway compromised."

"I'm sorry," Willa said, misery written all over her face.

I reached for her hand. "Stop apologizing. Nobody blames you. We just need some time to figure things out. Money will help us do that."

I gave my credit card to Drago and he reached for the door.

"I wear an extra-large in everything," Neo said.

"I know," Drago said.

I could almost see him rolling his eyes.

"Don't you need to know my size?" Willa asked.

Drago glanced back at her with a smirk. "You think I don't know your size, tiger?"

It was dark in the backseat but I was pretty sure Willa blushed. It was one of the most adorable things about her. It wasn't like she was some kind of sheltered virgin. She'd been through hell and back, had traveled the world alone and had probably had a few hookups along the way.

Not that I liked to think about that. In fact, I tried really fucking hard not to think about that because it was one of very few things that made me want to smash something. I wasn't naïve. I knew Willa had been with other men before us — I just didn't like to think about it.

But even with all of that, she could still seem shy and I couldn't help but find it hella cute.

Drago shut the door behind him and we watched as he made his way toward the truck stop. He'd parked away from the streetlamps that illuminated the parking lot but when he finally made his way to the light that emanated from the complex, I saw how bad it looked.

I didn't know if Drago had been limping when we'd raced through the hospital and out into the parking lot, but he was limping now, obviously wounded, hair askew and looking like he was coloring with a few crayons short of a full box.

It didn't look good. and I sighed and sat back against the seat, hoping he could get in and out before drawing too much attention to himself.

Willa slid across the long backseat and pressed against my side. She touched my head gently. "Are you okay? How are you feeling?"

I put my arm around her and drew her close, savoring the feel of her body against mine even as shame twanged through my body like a bad chord. "I'm just fine, kitten. Don't worry about me. How are you? We haven't had much time to talk."

"I'm fine too," she said. "Thanks to you."

"Thanks to me?"

"You were the one driving when they came after us," she said. "Neo and Oscar both got shot. You kept me alive."

I shook my head. "Can't take credit for that. If those people hadn't stopped..."

I only vaguely remembered the moment right after the car rolled, but I remembered a white minivan stopping at the top of the embankment, the driver peering over the edge, my relief as Roberto's men sped off right before I sank into unconsciousness.

"But they did. And you were the one driving and giving orders while they were shooting and trying to run us off the road," she said.

It was a paltry contribution to her safety but it wasn't her job to soothe my wounded ego.

I kissed the top of her head. "I'm just glad you're okay."

"We should split up when we get inside," Neo said from the front seat. "We can't afford to take anything for granted, and Drago is drawing attention in there whether we like it or not. It'll be better once we're all in real clothes, but someone might remember him and we're going to look suspicious as fuck."

"Agreed," I said.

"You and Willa grab all the food you think we'll need for the next couple of days," Neo said. "I'll find first aid supplies and Drago can get toiletries and burner phones."

"Willa should go with you or Drago," I said.

Willa shifted and looked up at me. "Why? Someone should be with you."

"I don't need a babysitter, kitten." I kissed the top of her head to soften my words. I wasn't mad at her. I was mad at myself, and I didn't trust myself to protect her anymore. "And you'll be safer with Neo or Drago."

Her luscious mouth turned down in a frown and I bent my head to kiss her. I was all kinds of fucked-up, my head pounding like someone had taken a jackhammer to it, my body aching, my broken arm starting to throb.

And that was just the physical stuff.

"It's not up for negotiation," Neo said. "Willa stays with you."

"Fine," I muttered. I didn't feel like myself and I wasn't up for trying.

I watched people come and go from the truck stop, envying their freedom. The complex was a hub of activity with cars pulling up to the gas pumps and leaving only to be replaced by other cars and a steady stream of customers heading into the truck stop and emerging a few minutes later with bags in their hands. Illuminated by the artificial lights that surrounded the place, it was an eerie oasis, a beacon in the darkness of wherever the hell we were.

Finally Drago emerged along with several other people. He was carrying two plastic bags in one hand, limping past people laughing and talking, carefree in their knowledge that no one was hunting them and willing to gun them down in public.

He looked so out of place, so obviously *wrong*, that I half expected someone to stop him during his journey across the long stretch of pavement between the truck stop and where we were parked, but a minute later he was there, opening the driver's side door and sliding into the car with a loud exhale.

"Fuck," he said.

"What?" Willa asked.

"I tried not to draw attention but— " he said.

"You drew attention?" I asked.

"More or less," he said.

"Did you find us all some clothes?" Neo asked.

"More or less," Drago said.

Neo glared at him. "Give me those bags."

Chapter 8

Willa

"I can't fucking believe this," Rock grumbled on our way across the parking lot.

"I don't want to hear it," Oscar said. "You were all in on me doing the shopping."

"Yeah, because I didn't know you were going to get me a dress," Rock said.

"It's not a dress, it's a caftan," Oscar and I said in unison.

We'd already had this conversation in the car. Oscar had been torn about what to get Rock because of his arm, so he'd chosen a flowy caftan with a tropical print, thinking that Rock could keep his arm on the inside.

Rock hadn't argued the logic, but that didn't mean he was happy to be entering a truck stop in the middle of nowhere wearing a caftan.

"Well, whatever it is, it sucks," Rock said. "My balls are

going to chafe. Besides, you said we were trying not to draw attention to ourselves. Somehow I don't think any of this is going to help in that department."

He had a point. Oscar was the least obtrusive of us in black sweats and a black T-shirt with an image of a semitruck and the words *Sit Down and Let Daddy Drive*, but Neo had ended up with plaid Bermuda shorts and a flowery oversized Hawaiian-print shirt.

Add that to Rock's caftan and they were definitely a motley crew.

Neo shifted inside the boxy Hawaiian shirt. "This thing looks like a kindergartner cut it out with safety scissors."

"Stop complaining," Oscar said. "You had to make a big deal about wearing an extra-large. This is what they had in the extra-large section."

"I think you all look amazing," I tried to say with a straight face. I took Rock's hand. "And dresses are very fashionable for men now."

He looked down at me. "One, it's not a dress, it's a caftan. Two, you're just trying to make me feel better. Three, that's easy for you to say. You look cute as fuck."

He was probably just being nice, but I hadn't made out too badly. Oscar had chosen a pair of pink track pants and a too-small pink T-shirt with a picture of a bulldog inexplicably wearing a sparkly beret.

I'd given him shit about the size of the shirt, reminding

him that he'd claimed to know my size, at which point he'd glanced suggestively at my tits, on full display in the tiny T-shirt, and said, "I do."

Fucker.

He'd also grabbed me a pair of red sunglasses with heart-shaped frames just because they were cute. I was wearing them into the truck stop even though it was after midnight because he was right — they were cute.

We'd been hoping to fly under the radar now that we were wearing clothes, but that's... not what happened.

Oscar reached for the door and held it open. Neo swaggered in first, his trademark cockiness on full display despite his less than fashionable attire. I was right behind him, the florescent lights of the truck stop mini-mart dimmed by my new sunglasses.

Which didn't stop me from seeing the people who turned to stare.

I couldn't really blame them, especially when Rock stepped through the door in his caftan. I looked back to make sure he and Oscar were with us and had to hand it to Rock. He held his head high despite the fact that only one arm was protruding from the caftan, the other one still strapped to his side under the fabric the way Oscar had planned it.

I could only imagine what everyone thought as we sailed past them and made our way deeper into the mini-mart.

Fresh from a costume party?

Rave refugees?

Or just a ragtag bunch of twenty-somethings with the late-night munchies?

Oscar had found flip-flops for him and Neo, so at least they weren't barefoot on top of everything else. I was sure their feet were freezing in the late-December cold, but flip-flops were better than nothing.

"Meet back at the cash register in twenty minutes," Neo said.

"Twenty minutes?" I asked. It wasn't much time to think about the supplies we would need for the next few days.

He turned to look at me. "In case you haven't noticed, Jezebel, we're the star attraction in this place right now. We still need to get out of here ASAP."

He and Oscar headed toward the nonfood items.

"Come on, kitten," Rock said. "Let's see what kind of sustenance we can find in this place."

We passed the racks of candy bars and other snacks near the front of the register and headed toward what looked like a small grocery section in the middle of the store.

Rock stopped in front of a shelf stacked with canned goods, reached for a can of black beans, and looked down at the caftan where his missing arm was nestled inside. "I think we're going to need a cart or something."

I looked around. "I don't think they have grocery carts in places like this." I wasn't exactly an expert in the minimart department. "Let me go see if they have baskets or something."

I hurried toward the front of the store and scanned the area around the cash register and main entrance but I didn't see anything resembling a basket.

This was a problem I hadn't even considered. Most people didn't do major grocery shopping at a truck stop.

My gaze landed on a small section of clothing — probably the same section where Oscar had found our clothes — and a row of tote bags emblazoned with pithy tourist sayings.

I grabbed six of them and hurried back to Rock, glaring at an older man with a weathered face who was staring at Rock with narrowed eyes.

Great. Just what we needed. Some bigoted boomer looking to start trouble because of the way Rock was dressed.

I slid my hand into his. "This was the best I could do," I said, holding up the tote bags.

"Good thinking." Rock glanced nervously down at me. "Let's hurry and get out of here. I'm in no condition for a fight and I have a feeling that asshole over there might be looking for one."

"I'll hold the bags," I said. "You tell me what to get."

The next twenty minutes passed in a blur of

instructions from Rock as he scanned the shelves and told me what to put in the bags. I could almost hear his mind working, trying to conjure meals out of the sparse selection in the mini-mart and without any information about where we would be next.

We grabbed canned beans and canned tomatoes, tuna and soup, crackers and wheat bread, plus a plethora of snacks even though Rock protested that they were nutritionally bankrupt. Then we went to the refrigerator case for milk, eggs, cold cuts, cheese, and butter.

"We need a cooler," Rock said. "And some ice."

I set the bulging bags on the floor near his feet. "Wait here."

I walked quickly through the mini-mart and spotted Neo grabbing stuff off one of the shelves. Oscar was nowhere in sight, but I eventually found a section of camping supplies and grabbed a large cooler with wheels and a handy towing handle.

I dragged it over to Rock. "Is this big enough?"

"It'll do for now," Rock said.

We piled bags of ice inside the cooler and Rock dragged it with his good arm to the cash register while I threaded the tote bags onto both my arms.

They were heavy and by the time we reached the front of the store my arms ached from the effort. I wasn't as injured as the Kings, but my body still felt battered. I was ready to be back in the car where I could stretch out and maybe even catch a nap.

"Where's Drago?" Neo asked, joining us by the cash register.

"Not here yet." I eyed the supplies in his arms. "Please tell me you have some Tylenol or something in there."

His eyes darkened. "Are you okay?"

It was as close as Neo would come to showing concern for me unless he was beating the shit out of someone for looking at me the wrong way or pulling me away from a team of killers as he tried to save my life.

"I'm fine," I said. "Just achy."

Oscar joined us a minute later, dragging another cooler behind him.

He looked at the one next to Rock. "Great minds think alike."

"It was Willa's idea," Rock said. "We got ice too."

"Good," Oscar said, "because mine's filled with toilet paper and shampoo and shit. Plus burner phones and gift cards to pay for time."

Neo glanced at a young bearded guy wearing a *Truckers Do It on the Road* cap. He was staring at us as he got in line for the cashier and I shifted on my feet and moved closer to Oscar.

"Let's get out of here," Neo said.

We nudged our stuff forward a little at a time until it was our turn to pay and I grabbed handfuls of chocolate bars and bags of candy and tossed them on the pile of stuff being rung up by a tired-looking girl with pink hair.

"I'm not even going to bother telling you how bad that shit is for you," Rock said with a sigh.

"Good," I said, "because I'm crashing hard and need something I can shove in my mouth fast."

Neo smirked. "I'm sure any one of us would be more than happy to help you with that, Jezebel."

"Haha, you're hilarious," I said with a straight face.

I wasn't at all offended. Nothing said normalcy like Neo giving me shit.

Oscar inserted the credit card into the reader and a couple minutes later we were on our way back to the car, Oscar and Rock pulling the coolers behind them while Neo insisted on taking most of the tote bags filled with food in addition to the first aid supplies.

We stowed everything but the phones and a bag full of snacks and drinks — plus the Tylenol — in the Impala's trunk and piled back into the car.

This time Neo took the wheel and Oscar took shotgun. I was more than happy to be in the back with Rock where I could stretch out, and I opened the bottle of Tylenol and shook two into my hand, then passed the bottle to Rock.

I washed the pills down with a swig of Gatorade and tore off the wrapper on a Snickers bar.

"Now what?" I asked around my first bite.

"Now we find a less crowded place to switch cars,"

Oscar said. "Then we find a place to lay low." He looked at Neo and Rock. "Thoughts?"

"Someplace close to campus," Rock said.

"Why close to campus?" I asked before taking another bite of the candy bar. I was suddenly ravenous and I could already feel the sugar working its way into my bloodstream.

I figured I had about ten minutes before I completely crashed.

"We're going to need help," Rock said. "We're owed favors in Blackwell Falls. Plus, we have allies in the other houses at Aventine."

"So we need a place close to campus that's also hidden from Roberto?" I asked.

"Exactly," Rock said.

"Not sure if it's doable," Neo said, "but I'm having a thought..."

"I might be having the same thought," Oscar said.

Neo looked at him across the front seat. "Daisy?"

Oscar nodded. "Daisy."

Neo started the car. "Activate one of the phones."

Chapter 9

Willa

I was surprised to feel the sun on my face when I woke up with my head in Rock's lap. It had been dark when I'd fallen asleep, the muffled quiet of the car and darkness all around combining with the sugar and adrenaline crash finally hitting me all at once.

We'd stopped once at a roadside bar to switch cars — swapping the plates with another car in the lot to prevent being pulled over in a car reported as stolen — but I barely remembered making the switch.

I'd waited groggily in the Impala while the Kings did their thing, then piled into the backseat of our new ride — a shit-brown Buick — with Rock where I promptly fell back asleep.

Now I blinked against the sunlight in my eyes and tried to place the sound of snow crunching under the car's tires.

"Morning, kitten," Rock said. He smoothed my hair back from my forehead. It was so soothing I was tempted to try and go back to sleep, pretend everything that had happened in the last couple of days hadn't actually happened.

"We're here."

"Where's here?" I asked.

"At our new digs," he said.

I sat up with a groan. My body hurt all over, the Tylenol I'd taken when we left the truck stop long since out of my system.

Oscar twisted around in the passenger seat to look at me and the ruby in his ring glinted like a warning. "Feel better now that you got some sleep?"

"Define better." I tried to get my bearings by taking in our surroundings. We were cutting through the woods on an overgrown path. "Did I miss something? Are we camping?"

"Not exactly," Neo said from the driver's seat.

"What's that supposed to mean?" I asked. This wasn't at all what I'd expected when they said we needed a place to hide.

"Conditions might be a little... rough," Neo said. "But we'll have shelter, and most importantly, no one will ever think to look for us here."

"Okay, you're all being a little cryptic and it's freaking me out," I said.

"Nothing to be freaked out about, tiger," Oscar said. "I wouldn't call this roughing it, would you?"

I looked through the windshield and was surprised to see a giant old house rising up out of the woods. It had the kind of multi-peaked roofline that made me think of murder mysteries and Gothic novels.

I spotted three chimneys and more windows than I could count, but as we got closer to the front of the house I saw that its grandeur was something of an illusion.

The place looked utterly abandoned.

The paint was peeling and two of the windows on the second floor were broken, exposing the house to the elements.

It was beautiful in the way of a lot of abandoned buildings, but also a little spooky, especially in the middle of nowhere.

"What is this place?" I asked.

Neo pulled up in front of the house and put the car in park. "This is where we're going to stay for a while."

"Okay, but what is *this* exactly?" I asked.

"It's Daisy's house," Rock said, as if that should mean something to me.

"Who's Daisy?"

Rock opened his mouth to answer and was interrupted by the crunch of snow behind us. I turned around to see an older-model red car approaching from the woods along the same path we'd driven.

"That would be Daisy," Rock said.

Okay, not exactly helpful, but I didn't get a chance to ask for clarification because a second later everyone was getting out of the car.

I followed suit, groaning inwardly as I unfolded my aching body. I hadn't had a chance to ask the Kings how they were feeling, and I was anxious to get a better look at their wounds and make sure they weren't infected.

I walked around the car with Oscar to join Neo and Rock and we waited as Daisy, whoever she was, cut the engine on the old car. It had been meticulously restored, and while I didn't know much about old cars, I was willing to bet it was worth a fortune.

A few seconds later a petite brunette stepped from the driver's side and out into the cold December sunshine.

She came toward us with a smile and I saw that while she was short in stature, her curves were banging. She had an impressive rack coupled with the kind of tapered waist and full hips that were the stuff of middle school fantasies.

But it was her face that was truly striking. With a smattering of freckles across her nose and big eyes that were an interesting shade of blue bordering on violet, I found myself staring, trying to unlock the puzzle of her unusual beauty.

Then she smiled, and it was so warm that it almost felt like the temperature had risen by ten degrees.

"You made it," she said, looking at the three Kings. Her gaze landed on me. "You must be Willa."

I returned her smile. "That would be me."

I was surprised when she wrapped me in a honeysuckle-scented hug. "It's nice to meet you. I'm Daisy. You must be exhausted."

"I am." Neo must have filled her in when he'd called her from the car. I'd only been privy to the first part of their conversation, owing to my hard-core crash on Rock's lap shortly after finishing the Snickers bar.

"Well, I'll take you into the house and get you guys settled." She released me from the hug and looked at the Kings. "I brought some blankets and other supplies. It sounds like you might need them. Like I said, no one's lived here for years and the house is in rough shape, but I doubt anyone will think to look for you here."

"We appreciate it," Oscar said. "We'll try to come up with a long-term solution so we can get out of your hair."

"No rush on my end," Daisy said. "I won't need the house for another six months. I'm sure you'll have all this sorted by then."

"It'll be sorted," Neo said firmly. "One way or another."

I didn't exactly like the sound of it but he was right: we needed an exit plan and we needed one fast.

I could feel the mystery of Emma's disappearance — the disappearance of all the Bellepoint girls — barreling toward some kind of end. We didn't have all the pieces yet, but they were out there, waiting to be pressed into place.

"Let me show you around, then we can bring everything in from the car," Daisy said.

She fished an old key out of the pocket of her jeans as she led us toward the house. "I had the electricity turned on for you, but I would try not to use it after dark. You know how the locals are about the falls, especially at night."

"The falls?" I asked. We trudged our way through a foot of snow on what appeared to be a winding walkway toward a wide porch that wrapped around the old mansion.

"It's right behind the house," Daisy said. "It's not running as fast as in the spring when all the snow melts, but when it's quiet you'll still be able to hear it. The locals like to swim under it in the summer. There's a lot less partying in the winter obviously, but I'd still be careful with the electricity."

We climbed the snow-covered steps of the front porch and huddled around the front door while Daisy inserted the key. The cold had woken me up and I was eager to see where we would be staying.

She shimmied the key in the lock and the door swung open. "There are snow shovels and other tools in the back shed," she said. "But I don't know if you want to shovel the walk and make it obvious that someone's living here. Might be better to let it be even though it'll be a pain to come and go."

"We won't be doing a lot of coming and going," Rock said.

We followed her inside, me first with the Kings at my back, and I let my gaze travel up a long winding staircase, over the old plaster walls, and up to the triple-height ceiling, a dusty chandelier hanging from an ornate plaster medallion.

The floors were black-and-white checkered marble and the grand foyer was flanked on either side by shadowed cavernous rooms.

"Wow," I said. "This place is amazing."

"It belonged to my mother's family," Daisy said. There was something wistful in her voice and I turned to see her gazing at our surroundings with an unreadable expression.

"It's beautiful," I said. "When was it built?"

"In the late 1800s," Daisy said, setting the key on some kind of table that was covered with a sheet. "My great-grandfather was one of the early settlers of Blackwell Falls."

"Wow," I said.

"You're welcome to use the whole house of course," Daisy said. "But I was thinking on the drive up here that you might want to stick to the third floor. It was originally built as servants' quarters so there's a small kitchen up there, plus bathrooms and bedrooms. It's not as fancy as the first two floors but you'll have some warning if someone discovers you here. Also, my grandfather had fire escapes installed at the back of the house when regulations changed in the early 1900s, so that gives you another way out."

"Sounds perfect," Neo said.

"Let's start there then," Daisy said, heading for the stairs.

She led us up the winding staircase and I trailed my hand along the dusty mahogany banister. We passed the second floor without stopping and continued to the third.

Daisy was right: it wasn't as fancy as the first two floors, but as an emergency refuge went, we could have done a lot worse.

The house was huge and the third floor alone had eight bedrooms and three bathrooms Daisy said had been added in the early 1900s. The kitchen was small but serviceable, complete with an old refrigerator that was half the size of the refrigerator in the Kings' house.

I was glad we'd bought the coolers as backup storage but at least there was a refrigerator.

The old furniture was covered with dust cloths but Daisy said it would all be usable, if a little worn. She was warm and thoughtful and had even brought sheets, towels, and a few things for the kitchen.

I had no idea why she was helping us but I had a feeling the story was an interesting one.

After Daisy had shown us around the third floor we went outside to unload the cars. Daisy and I carried the sheets and towels while the Kings took the heavier stuff, including the coolers full of ice and food, which Neo and Rock carried up three flights of stairs as if they were nothing.

"Is there anything else I can do for you before I go?" Daisy asked.

"I don't think so," Neo said. "We really appreciate this, Daisy."

"It's the least I can do," she said. "I hope you're all comfortable here for as long as you need it. I'll come back and check on you in a few days but you can also call if you need anything."

"We owe you big," Oscar said.

She shook her head. "I'd say we're about even." She looked at me. "It was nice to meet you, Willa."

I was dying to know what kind of exchange made Daisy feel like she owed the Kings such a big favor, but it seemed rude to ask.

"It was nice to meet you too." I meant it. I had a feeling that if we'd had the time to get to know each other we would have become fast friends.

She turned to go, then seemed to remember something.

"Don't forget what I said about the electricity. There's

nothing for miles out here," she said. "If you light the house at night, there's a good chance someone will notice. And don't forget about the falls. You're at the top of it and the cliff comes up fast, so be careful outside, especially at night."

Chapter 10

Willa

After Daisy left we spent a couple of hours getting settled. Oscar and I made the beds with the sheets and blankets Daisy had brought while Rock situated the food in the small kitchen.

Neo investigated the boiler room in the basement and got the lay of the land outside, warning us that Daisy had been right about the cliffs: the river that fed the falls ran behind the house and the edge of the cliff came up suddenly beyond what must once have been a lawn at the back of the house.

"I need a shower," I said when everything had been unpacked.

Rock grinned. "I'm down for a shower."

I narrowed my eyes. "I can already tell you have more in mind than a shower."

"Can you blame me?" Rock asked. "It's been days!"

I rolled my eyes. "Days where we've been shot at, run off the road, taken to the hospital, and fled for our lives."

"Minor annoyances until they keep you from our bed," Rock said.

"I'm with Rock," Oscar said. "Let's get wet and naked."

"I'm down for wet and naked," Neo said, his eyes darkening with familiar lust.

"We can take a shower together," I said, "but that's all we're doing. And only because Rock probably needs help keeping that cast dry. No fooling around until I check out those gunshot wounds and make sure they're not infected."

"Fine," Rock said. "If that's what it takes to get you naked, I reluctantly agree."

We chose the bathroom with the biggest shower, one that I guessed had been modernized sometime in the 1980s based on the tacky tile and brass fixtures.

I turned the hot water all the way on, guessing it might take a while to reach the third floor from the hot water tanks that were probably in the basement with the boiler. Then I helped Rock get his shirt off and started stripping my own clothes while the Kings did the same.

They eyed me hungrily as I pulled off the underwear Oscar had chosen for me from the truck stop, a pink bikini with the word *Monday* written across the ass. It had come in a pack with six others, all in different colors and labeled with different days of the week.

And the Kings weren't the only ones who were hungry.

I'd been full of big talk about abstaining from vigorous activity when the Kings had been clothed, but I felt my resolve fizzle as I took in their strong naked bodies.

Neo's shoulders looked broader than ever in the relatively small bathroom, the blood-soaked bandage over his chest only making his angel tattoo — the tattoo of me — look more dangerous and enigmatic.

I wasn't surprised to see his massive dick was hard as granite, jutting between his thighs like an eager warrior, because despite my earlier protestations, I was wet for them, my cunt slick with desire.

What the fuck was wrong with me? We were running for our lives, hungry and exhausted, and all my body wanted was the Kings buried inside me.

The bathroom was filling with steam and I hurried to the faucet to add some cold water, hoping it would cool the fire in my blood. It was a lot to ask my body to stand down when confronted with three gorgeous naked Kings, but I meant what I'd said earlier: no fooling around until I knew they were okay.

I turned around just as Oscar's hands slid between my thighs from behind, his fingers stroking through my wet pussy.

I slapped his hand away and opened the shower door. "Be a good boy and get in the shower."

Fuck me.

Even with a trickle of blood oozing down his thigh

from the gunshot wound, he was hot as hell. His lean physique highlighted every cut muscle of his biceps, his chest as chiseled as a statue.

His abs were as ripped as a washboard and my gaze traveled unwillingly down the trail of dark hair that led to his rigid pierced cock.

When my gaze finally made it back to his face, he was staring at me with a knowing grin. "If you say so, tiger."

He got in the shower, followed by Neo.

I looked at Rock and ordered my hungry pussy to calm down at the site of his sculpted chest, engorged dick, and massive thighs.

"Don't even think about it," I said with a scowl.

He stopped on his way into the shower and bent his head to kiss me, his tongue stroking the seam of my mouth, then tangling with my tongue in a languid dance.

For a second, I forgot the order I'd given him and let myself sink into the kiss. Then his hand closed around my tit, his thumb stroking my nipple, and I jerked to my senses.

"Nice try," I said, breaking our kiss. I looked up at him. "You almost had me. Now get in the shower."

He grinned like a cat that had eaten a canary. "Whatever you say, kitten."

I got into the shower after them and Rock grabbed my hips to move me under the spray of the hot water. It was definitely crowded but I could hardly complain being surrounded by naked Kings as I tipped my head back into the hot water.

I moaned with pleasure as it soaked my hair and streamed over my bruised body. "Oh my god, that feels so good."

When I opened my eyes, all three of the Kings were staring at me like lions preparing to take down a gazelle.

"Keep moaning like that and I won't be able to be a good boy," Oscar said.

"Yeah, well if you ever feel the urge to be anything but good, just take a look at the water swirling around our feet," I said.

They looked at the blood mingling with the water as it made its way toward the drain, but apparently they weren't nearly as freaked out by the sight as I was because Rock just shrugged.

"It's just a little blood," Rock said. "And it's not even coming from me so I don't see why I'm being punished along with these two assholes."

"In case you haven't noticed, you're down an arm," I said.

He grinned. "I don't need this arm for what I want to do to you."

The words sent a wave of heat through my body and I forced myself to pick up the shampoo instead of wrapping my hands around something else.

I shimmied past them to the back of the shower, trying

not to touch their bodies on my way there. It was insane that after all we'd been through what I wanted more than anything else was a good solid fuck with the three guys I once despised, but there was no point lying to myself.

"I'll wash my hair while you soap up," I said. "Except for you, Rock. You need to keep that cast dry. Give me a second and I'll help you out."

He looked triumphantly at Neo and Oscar. "Hear that? She's going to help me out."

"Fuck you," Neo said, moving under the spray of the shower.

Twenty minutes and countless similar exchanges later, we climbed from the shower and grabbed the towels Daisy had brought for us.

I was exhausted from the effort of keeping the Kings in line, slapping their roaming hands away from my body when all I really wanted to do was give in to the pleasure I knew they could deliver.

In all the trauma from the car accident and shooting — not to mention the harrowing escape from Roberto's men in the hospital — I'd forgotten about the hot night the Kings and I had spent together on Christmas.

Now it all came rushing back, and I remembered how it felt to be sprawled out in front of the fire, Oscar's dick in my mouth while Rock filled my ass and Neo pounded into my pussy.

In spite of our precarious situation, I wanted more.

A lot more.

I hadn't had time to figure out what that meant in terms of my feelings for the Kings — especially Neo — but my body didn't give two fucks about my feelings.

I inspected the Kings one by one. Neo's and Oscar's wounds were inflamed from all the running around they'd been doing, but they didn't appear infected. I covered them with the antibacterial ointment in the first aid kit Neo had bought at the truck stop and re-bandaged them with fresh gauze.

Outwardly, Rock was just a little beat up, the same kind of cuts and bruises that covered my body covering his. But I was still worried about his head injury. No matter how much he tried to make light of it, running around and exerting himself the way he had over the past twenty-four hours was the last thing he needed.

Luckily, Daisy had brought a wireless hotspot along with the other supplies and I made a mental note to check the internet for warning signs of a complication. We would have to keep our eyes on Rock until we were sure he was out of danger.

Clean and freshly bandaged, we put on the clothes we'd been wearing before because we didn't have a choice. I wondered how long it would be before we could pick up some of our things from the Kings' house, or at the very least, make a real shopping trip to buy some new clothes. I only had six more days of clean underwear and the heart-shaped sunglasses and too-small pink T-shirt were only going to get me so far.

We filed into the small kitchen and sat around a worn wooden table while Rock cooked up grilled cheese. It wasn't the gourmet variety he'd made when I'd first arrived at the Kings' house in September, but with some of the canned fruit cocktail from the truck stop I thought it might be the most delicious meal I'd ever eaten.

We were all starving and I wolfed two of the gooey grilled cheese sandwiches and half a bowl of the fruit while I researched head injury care on my burner. The Kings put down three of the sandwiches in less time than it took me to eat one and by the time we were all finished, we'd grown quiet. I couldn't speak for them, but I was exhausted, the food and shower leading me toward an inevitable crash.

"We should talk about what's next," Neo said.

I stood. "You'll have to do it without me," I said. "I can't even think straight. I'm going to bed."

"She's not the only one," Rock said. "I need to crash."

Oscar stood to join us. "They're right. We're all exhausted. We're not going to be firing on all cylinders until we sleep."

"Someone needs to watch Rock and wake him up every hour or two," I said, reciting my findings from the internet.

"I'll do it," Neo said. "I'm too wired to sleep right now anyway."

How anybody could be wired after all we'd been through followed by the hot shower and carb bombs we'd just consumed was beyond me, but I was glad someone would be able to stay awake and keep an eye on Rock.

"We can take it in shifts," Oscar said. "Wake me up when you're ready to sleep and I'll take over."

"I'll take the bedroom at the end of the hall," I said.

"The fuck you will," Neo said.

I looked at him. "If it means that much to you I'll just take another one."

Oscar draped an arm around my shoulders. "I think what he means, tiger, is no way in hell are you sleeping alone."

"I know I said I needed to check you guys out before we did any fooling around, but I really am exhausted," I said.

"No one is talking about fooling around," Rock said. "Although I'm more than open to the discussion. I think what we're saying is, we don't want you out of our sight."

Now I understood. They were worried about me. That was what this is about.

"Okay, so who's the lucky fellow?" I asked.

"All of us," Neo said.

"Agreed," Oscar said. "We'll sleep in the same room, for now at least."

"The beds will be too small," I said.

Neo folded his massive arms over his equally massive

chest. "Then we'll push two of them together. We're not letting you out of our sight, Jezebel."

In any other situation their protectiveness would have been as annoying af, but right now it felt good to know they were looking out for me.

For better or worse, we were in this together. The fact that I was glad raised a whole lot of problematic questions and exactly zero answers.

Chapter 11

Willa

It was dark when I woke up, groggy and disoriented, my cunt throbbing with need. It took me a few seconds to place the source of my sexual hunger: namely, the big dick nestled between my thighs from behind.

Right, the Kings and I had piled into one of the bedrooms after Oscar and Neo pushed two of the double beds together. Neo had taken the chair against the wall and I'd fallen asleep between Oscar and Rock with Neo's steely gaze on my face.

Just a few weeks before I'd been unsettled by the way he watched me in my sleep. Now, I felt comforted. Enemies were all around us — deadly ones — but I'd never felt safer than under Neo's watchful eyes.

I turned my head to see whose dick was between my thighs and caught the flash of Oscar's smile in the dark.

"You can't really blame me now can you, tiger?" he asked softly. "How was I supposed to stay asleep with that luscious ass of yours only inches away?"

I didn't bother protesting. After two days of fighting for my life, I just wanted to escape reality for a while.

I wiggled against him and felt the cool steel of the piercing on the head of his cock.

He slid an arm around my waist and his hand traveled down my stomach and between my thighs.

I moaned as he stroked through my wet folds.

"I think Jezebel's ready for a little late-night party."

I followed the sound of the voice and came face-to-face with Neo, completing the sexy bookend where Rock had been when I'd fallen asleep. Apparently, they'd played musical positions while I'd slept, and I was now the filling in an Oscar and Neo sandwich.

Neo reached out to touch my cheek, then stroked his thumb over my lips before shoving it into my mouth.

The invasion sent a rush of fresh heat to my cunt and I moaned around his thumb as his other hand closed around my neck.

He inched closer, his hand sliding from my neck to one of my tits. He squeezed, pinching my nipple between his fingers while I sucked on his thumb, and I felt my temperature rise a few more degrees.

Behind me Oscar pushed his dick through my thighs and back again, making me more than ready to feel him inside me, his piercings an erotic counterpoint to the warmth of his flesh.

Neo bent his head to my tit and sucked my nipple into his mouth, and I gasped, threading my fingers in his hair and spreading my thighs for Oscar to let him know what I wanted.

"It's dark as fuck in here," Rock said from the chair against the wall. "But it kind of sounds like you're having a party and I wasn't invited."

I followed the sound of his voice. My eyes had adjusted to the dark room and I could just make him out, naked in the chair because he hadn't wanted to sleep in the caftan, his blue eyes reflecting his lust.

"You're not allowed to play," I said as Neo scraped my nipple with his teeth. Oscar's fingers were working magic on my clit, rubbing rhythmic circles that threatened to push me over the edge. "You have a head injury."

"I don't need my head to play," Rock said. "Not that one anyway."

"No, but we need your thinking head for other things," I said, my voice breathy. "You'll just have to watch."

"The next best thing," he said, taking his dick in his hand.

I moved my hips, working with the rhythm of Oscar's fingers as an orgasm blossomed at my center.

"Goddamn," Oscar murmured against my neck. "I think our tiger is about to come."

Neo lifted his head from my tit and nipped his way up to my throat. "That right, Jezebel? You going to come already?"

"Yes," I gasped.

"I hope you plan on looking at me while you do it," Rock said. "It's the least you can do."

I couldn't have taken my eyes off him if I'd tried. The sight of him stroking his hard cock while he watched Oscar and Neo get me off was too much of a turn-on to ignore. It only added fuel to the fire burning in my body as Neo fondled my tits and sucked at my neck while Oscar worked my clit, his dick sliding between my thighs from behind.

Neo drew one of my nipples into his mouth and sucked hard enough to make me moan just as Oscar slipped his fingers inside me. He rubbed my clit with the heel of his palm and I tumbled over the edge, crying out into the room as I shuddered against them, Neo's sculpted body in front, his giant dick pressed against my stomach, Oscar behind me with his pierced cock pressed against my pussy.

"Fuck yes," Oscar breathed into my neck. "Come for us, tiger."

I was all too willing to obey and I felt myself grow tighter around his fingers as he plunged them in and out of me, never letting up on my clit.

Through the dark, Rock held my gaze while he stroked his dick.

"Jesus," he said. "I hope you lucky bastards plan to fuck her soon. I can't take much more of this."

I went limp between Neo and Oscar, my body wrung out from the intense orgasm. But they weren't done with me yet and I wasn't about to complain when Oscar rose to his knees, maneuvered between my thighs, and spread me wide.

"I can't fucking wait to be buried inside your sweet little pussy," he said.

Neo had risen to his knees next to my head, his gloriously perfect dick near my face making his intentions clear.

"Drago, hand me those extra pillows," Neo said.

Oscar leaned over my body and I felt the pierced head of his cock push the tiniest bit into my wet cunt.

I squirmed, trying to get more, and he laughed wickedly in the dark. "I think our tiger here is ready for some dick," he said, handing a stack of pillows to Neo.

"Good because I'm ready to feel her mouth wrapped around mine," Neo said. "Lift your head, Jezebel."

I obeyed, because that was all I ever fucking did when they ordered me around in bed. But who could blame me? The combination of Neo's cock close to my face and Oscar's pierced dick pushing against my entrance had me delirious with need.

Neo stacked the pillows behind me so that when I laid back my head was slightly elevated. I might have been surprised by the thoughtfulness of the gesture, but I'd caught him being considerate more than once when he thought no one was paying attention.

Don't get me wrong, he was still a monumental dick most of the time, but every now and then he did something nice, even if he did try to make sure no one noticed.

Now my head was more level with his cock and he inched closer, touching his swollen crown to my lips.

"Fuck, your lips are so soft," he breathed.

I darted my tongue out to lick the semen that had gathered at his tip while Oscar hooked my knees over his shoulders.

Neo slid his hands into my hair and tightened his grip, pulling on the strands just enough to make me wetter.

"That's right," he said. "Take a taste, Jezebel. Take a taste before you take it all."

Between my thighs, Oscar ran the head of his dick through my folds and circled my clit. The warmth of his skin combined with the smooth steel of his piercing sent a shudder through my body.

"You're so fucking beautiful, tiger." His cock was back at my entrance, stretching the opening. "I can't wait to watch your face while you come for us."

Neo pressed the head of his cock against my lips. "Open up and take it, Jezebel."

He didn't have to ask me twice. I was fucking

desperate to have him in my mouth while Oscar fucked me.

He slid it between my lips and a long low moan was torn from my throat as Oscar pushed all the way inside me.

"Fuuuuuckkk..." he groaned.

I wrapped my hand around the base of Neo's cock while he dragged out of my mouth and pushed back in again. He was enormous, pushing all the way to the back of my throat with enough room to spare for my hand at his base.

I relaxed my jaw, encouraging him to push even farther into my mouth, and he sank deeper as I removed my hand from his shaft so I could take every inch of him.

"That's right, Jezebel," he coaxed. "I always knew you could take that dick like a good girl."

Oscar used his shoulders to push my thighs closer to my torso and he sank deeper too. I was filled by them, the piercing at Oscar's base teasing my clit while Neo fucked my mouth.

"Fuck, you feel so sweet," Oscar said.

He bent his head to one of my tits and sucked while he stroked into me, the barbell at the tip of his cock rubbing against the walls of my cunt on the way in, the piercing at his base stimulating my clit.

Neo had grown even harder and bigger in my mouth, his hand still fisted in my hair. He was relentless in his push into my mouth but it only made me hotter, my pussy soaking wet as Oscar stroked into me and sucked my tit.

Neo groaned. "Your mouth was made for me, Jezebel. Take that dick like you know it."

His words were a hot wind on the fire burning in my body and I moaned as Oscar's piercing rubbed against my clit, another orgasm on the verge of detonating at my core.

Oscar lifted his head from my tit. "Keep talking," he said to Neo. "She just keeps getting wetter."

"That's because our sweet little rule-follower is actually a dirty dirty girl," Neo said. "Isn't that right, Jezebel? You love to take our dicks like a good girl."

I moaned around his cock. I mean, it wasn't like he was wrong. He was driving his giant dick all the way to the back of my throat while Oscar pounded me into oblivion and I'd never been happier.

My orgasm was building and I moved my hips with Oscar's rhythm, holding on to Neo's muscular thigh for leverage.

I could no longer see Rock but I could hear his heavy breathing as he jacked off to the rest of us fucking, and I had to say, it was a monumental turn-on knowing he was watching while Oscar and Neo fucked me senseless.

They were both moving faster now, lost in the climb to their own release and I sank deeper into my own pleasure. The thrust of Oscar's dick, the smooth piercing teasing my clit with every stroke, and Neo's cock pushing between my lips again and again accelerating my climax.

I hovered at the edge of the precipice, in such ecstasy that I didn't want it to end.

"Fuck, I'm close," Neo panted. "Are you going to swallow my come, Jezebel?"

His words sent me over the edge and I cried out around his dick in my mouth, the orgasm hitting me like an atomic bomb.

"Fuck yes," Oscar said. "She's fucking coming."

He groaned as he joined me, driving into me in frenzied movements that extended my orgasm, shudders wracking my body as Neo came with a growl.

His warm come exploded in my throat, and he let loose a string of unintelligible curse words, his fingers tightening in my hair, sending lightning bolts through my body, already on pleasure overload.

I swallowed him down eagerly as my orgasm rolled through me like a tsunami, grinding my hips into Oscar's, trying to wrench every ounce of pleasure from my climax.

He finished with a long groan and Neo slowly withdrew his dick from my mouth.

We were still gasping for air when they stretched out on either side of me, Oscar pulling me against his body while Neo flung his giant thigh possessively over my hips.

"I was an observer to the party," Rock said, standing

over the bed naked. "But you're not keeping me out of this part. I fucking love to cuddle."

"Fine," Neo said. "But keep your fucking dick off me."

Rock wedged himself between Neo and me. "My dick only wants one person right now and it's definitely not you."

He snuggled up next to me and I nestled between him and Oscar, wishing there was a way to split myself into thirds so Neo could be next to me too.

But it didn't really matter because my eyelids were heavy, my body loose and limp from the orgasms. For the first time in days, I felt safe.

Deep down I knew it wasn't true. We were about as far from safe as you could get.

But we were together, and that felt like the only thing that mattered.

I didn't have time to think about what that meant for us long term. I was too sleepy, too comfortable, and the last thing I remembered was Oscar's lips pressed against my forehead as I fell into sleep.

Chapter 12

Willa

The Kings were already awake and sitting around the kitchen table when I got there the next morning. I'd slept like the dead after our fun in the middle of the night and hadn't even heard them leave the bedroom.

The old microwave said it was just after 9 AM but it looked like the Kings had been up for hours.

Rock jumped to his feet when he saw me and came over to give me a quick kiss on the lips.

"Morning, kitten," he said. "You must be hungry after all that, uh, *exercise* last night."

"Haha," I said. But he wasn't wrong. I was starving.

"I'll take that as a sheepish yes," Rock said, moving toward the stove. "Lucky for you, I kept your French toast warm."

He opened the oven door and withdrew one of the

plates Daisy had brought with all the other supplies. Three thick slices of French toast were stacked on its surface.

He set it down, opened the little fridge, and withdrew a bowl of the canned fruit cocktail.

"It's not fresh strawberries, but it'll have to do until we get some real groceries, which I hope will be soon, because I don't have much to work with here," he said, spooning some of the fruit onto my plate next to the French toast.

He set it down in front of one of the two empty chairs at the table and I slid onto it and bent my head to smell the French toast. It smelled delicious even though I knew Rock was working with a limited assortment of supplies.

"It smells good," I said. "Is there coffee?"

"Is there coffee?" Rock scoffed. He walked to the old drip coffee maker and poured me a cup, then set it down in front of me.

I picked it up and inhaled the scent. "Thank god. And thank you."

"I aim to please," he said with a grin, returning to the table.

I took a careful drink of the coffee, then another, closing my eyes with a sigh. It was probably just the placebo effect but I felt better already.

I looked at Neo and Oscar, their large frames making the diminutive kitchen table seem even smaller. "Good morning."

Oscar flashed me a knowing smile. "Indeed."

I rolled my eyes and doused the French toast with syrup. It wasn't the all-natural organic kind Rock preferred but it would definitely do. "Don't be smarmy just because Neo's dick was in my mouth while you fucked me last night."

"She's right," Neo said. "If anybody should be smarmy, it should be me."

"You're always smarmy," I said before taking a giant bite of French toast.

"One of my many charms," Neo said.

And fuck me if I wasn't starting to agree.

He looked hot in spite of the fact that he was still wearing the Bermuda shorts from the truck stop, probably because his chest was bare, every stupid perfect muscle on display.

The French toast hit my tongue in a flavorful burst of buttery dough, cinnamon, and maple syrup. "This is delicious," I told Rock.

"Store-bought bread and fake syrup," he said sadly.

"Tastes good to me," I said.

"That's because you're a brown noser," Neo said from across the table.

"Being nice doesn't mean you're a brown noser," I said.

"I hate to break up this important debate about what constitutes a brown noser," Oscar said, "but we have more important things to talk about."

He looked at least as delicious as the French toast, his

defined chest and corded abs bare over his black sweats.

What was it with guys walking around with their shirts off? And how could we make them do it more often?

"I agree," Rock said. "Like when will I have something to wear that doesn't chafe my balls?"

"If I'd known how much I was going to have to hear about your balls I never would've bought you a caftan," Oscar said.

"Karma's a bitch," Rock said, pouring himself another cup of coffee and sitting down at the table.

"Apparently," Oscar said. "And as sick as I am of listening to you bitch about your balls, it does bring up an important point. We're going to need more supplies. At least one computer, more clothes, cash and credit cards, among other things."

"Guns," Neo said firmly.

There was a violent light in his eyes that would have scared me if it hadn't been directed at Roberto and his men.

Oscar nodded. "Guns."

"Better food," Rock said.

"This all makes it sound like we're going to be here a while," I said.

"I think that's safe to say," Oscar said.

"We can't go back to the house as long as my dad is trying to kill us," Neo said.

"Agreed," Rock said. "And as much as I'd like to hole up

in a five-star hotel, we need to stay under the radar."

I looked around the tiny kitchen. "Well, it doesn't get much more under the radar than this."

"I can take care of the guns," Neo said.

"We can't use Rock's credit card again," Oscar said. "Someone needs to get to a bank and withdraw enough cash from the offshore account to get us by until we figure out what's next."

"What about our things?" I asked. "I'm not quite as desperate as Rock, but I can't live in this one outfit forever."

"I wouldn't mind getting our computers back," Rock said. "We have a lot of... data I wouldn't want in Roberto's hands."

"Then we wouldn't need new computers," Oscar said. "We can use a VPN to hide our activity."

"Except we can't just go home and pack up," I said. "Roberto will have someone watching the house."

The room grew silent as we considered our options. I thought about Claire. She would go to the house for us and get our things. Even Mara, as far away as she was, would come if I needed her.

But it would draw attention to them, especially if they were seen entering the house and exiting an hour later with a bunch of stuff. Someone might follow them. It was too dangerous, for them and for us.

Oscar hesitated. "What about Reva?"

"What about her?" I asked.

Oscar shrugged. "We can ask her to bring us some things. She's at the house at least twice a week."

"No way," I said. We didn't need any more proof that Roberto was dangerous than the four of us sitting around the table with two bullet holes, a broken arm, and more bruises and scratches than I could count between us.

I wasn't risking anyone else's life, especially not Reva's.

"It's not a terrible idea," Rock said. "She could bring stuff in trash bags. No one would ever know."

"It's a hard no from me." The thought of someone being hurt because of my search for Emma made me feel sick.

I half expected Neo to fight me and I was surprised when he nodded. "Then we'll find another way."

Huh. That was new.

"What about Emma?" I asked. "We can't just go into hiding now that we know your dad is involved in her disappearance and the disappearance of the other girls."

Neo's expression grew cold. "We're not hiding. We're regrouping. There's a difference."

"Call it what you want," I said, "but we aren't getting any closer to finding out what happened to Emma while you're running around trying to get guns. I think I should go talk to Mrs. Giordana again."

"The fuck you say," Neo said.

"She's just a woman," I said. "A widow. She's completely harmless."

"Famous last words," Rock said. "It's all fun and games

until the crazy widow catches you snooping and chains you up in her basement."

"She's not going to catch me snooping because I'm not going to snoop," I said.

"I'm starting to feel like I'm the one with the head injury," Neo said.

"I'll tell her the truth," I said. "I'll tell her that Dean Giordana tried to kill me at the cabin and that he was involved in something bad. I'll just... tell her everything and ask her to let me see those binders again."

I'd taken pictures with my phone, but that was long gone, lost in the car crash and shooting after we'd left the island.

"Now I'm starting to think you're the one with the head injury," Neo said.

Oscar got to his feet to pace the kitchen. "It's actually not a bad idea."

"Maybe we all have head injuries," Rock said.

"Think about it," Oscar said. "Whatever was going on with the girls, including Emma, was big. Someone had to take the girls, hurt them or kill them, hide the bodies."

My stomach turned, the French toast and coffee turning sour with Oscar's words.

Because they weren't just words. He was talking about real people.

About Emma and the other girls.

My feelings must've shown on my face because Oscar

stopped pacing and crouched next to me at the table.

He took my head in his hands. "I'm sorry."

The truth of it was written in his dark eyes.

"It's not your fault," I said. "I know something bad happened." I drew in a long shuddering breath, forcing myself to say the next words. "I know she's probably dead."

The last sentence came out in a whisper. I was surprised it came out at all. It was the first time I'd ever said it out loud even though the thought had haunted me for nearly two years.

"Whatever happened, to Emma and the others, we're going to find out who's responsible and make them pay," Neo said.

His voice was icy and I knew this was Neo's way of looking out for me. He might not have Rock's soft words or Oscar's gentle touch, but he cared, and he would show he cared by unleashing his rage on anyone who hurt me.

I was beginning to understand him. My own sadness, fear, and frustration had slowly morphed into anger. Neo wanted to make whoever had hurt Emma pay and I was right there with him.

I fingered the choker around my neck.

Sic temper tyrannis.

Death to tyrants.

"Someone can only pay if we find out who they are," Rock said. "And Dean Giordana's widow is as good a place to start as any."

Chapter 13

Neo

I drove away from the house with my fucking heart in my throat. After what had happened when we'd left the island, I was tempted to handcuff Willa to my side.

It wasn't so much that I didn't trust Drago and Rock with her safety.

I knew they would protect her with their lives.

But it had started to seem like nowhere was safe. I hadn't even wanted to close my eyes the night before out of fear that something would happen to Willa while I slept.

Unfortunately the choice to leave had been made for me. The Blades had dealt with all of us at one time or another, but I was asking for something big and the request had a better shot of being granted if it came from me.

It took me forever to get to the giant mall that was our designated meeting spot. I didn't like being so far away from Willa — if something happened to her again it would take me a while to get back to her — but I needed to stay hidden and nobody was going to look for me in a homogenous suburban mall two hours west of Blackwell Falls.

I'd stopped at a local bank along the way and withdrawn a large amount of cash from the offshore transfer Rock had initiated. It would see us through until we figured out where to go from here.

I parked in one of the crowded lots and stashed half of the cash under the seat in the Buick. Then I made my way into the mall, wondering how things were going for Willa, Drago, and Rock. We'd only realized after we made our plan for the day that we only had one ride. Lucky for us, Daisy had come through again, loaning us a car so they could go to the Giordana house while I was at the mall.

Not Daisy's hot rod of course. I had no idea where she'd gotten the old car or who had fixed it up, but I knew from the way she drove it that it was her prized possession and there was no way in hell she was letting anyone else drive it.

I would have loved to take it for a spin, but I was grateful for the loaner, a Mercedes she'd left parked in a grocery store parking lot outside of Blackwell Falls. I'd dropped off Willa, Rock, and Drago on my way out of town and they'd taken it to Mrs. Giordana's house.

It was the Saturday between Christmas and New

Year's and the mall was packed with people trying to cash in on after-Christmas sales. It was exactly what I'd hoped for, and I weaved my way through the milling crowd feeling as close to invisible as was possible with my psycho dad determined to kill me.

It wasn't like I was surprised. I'd never bought the story that my mom had bailed. Sure, I was only a kid when she'd disappeared. I hadn't known her the way you knew someone when you were adult enough to see through the mask they wore for the world.

But she was my mom. I knew in my bones that she wouldn't have left me and no one would ever convince me that knowing was some kind of fucking fantasy.

Roberto had killed her. I knew it like I knew Willa belonged to me.

To us.

He'd tried to kill Willa to keep her quiet just like he'd killed my mom to keep her from telling everyone what he really was. To him, they were like ants at a picnic. An annoyance to be eliminated.

He wouldn't think twice before trying again. I knew that too.

I looked at one of the directories and followed the map to the food court. It was one of those times when I was glad to be taller than everyone else, and I peered over the crowd standing in lines and carrying trays of food to the grimy tables littering the area.

I spotted the person I was looking for standing in line for pizza at the far end of the food court. He was taller than everybody else too, and I made my way through the crowd toward him, his shaggy blond hair and leather MC cut standing out amid everyone else's suburban attire.

He glanced at me disinterestedly as I joined him in line. "Pizza?"

"Always," I said. We didn't speak again until we'd both ordered, carrying our plates and drinks to a semi-isolated section of the food court.

"What kind of shit have you gotten yourself into?" Hawk asked, tearing the wrapper from his straw.

"What makes you think I've gotten myself into any shit?" I asked before taking a bite of my pizza.

It was delicious, hot and cheesy with the sharp tang of tomato sauce, and I suddenly wished Willa was with me.

Willa loved pizza.

"You asked me to meet you in the middle of this fucking mall two hours from Blackwell," Hawk said. "Also, word on the street is you've been cast out."

I wiped the grease from my lips with one of the thin paper napkins I'd grabbed after paying for my food. "Can't cast me out of something I built."

"Not talking about the thing you built," Hawk said. "I'm talking about the thing your dear old dad built."

I shook my head. "My dad didn't build shit. He's just sitting on the throne of an empire built long before him.

The empire will still be there when he's gone. And he *will* be gone."

Hawk sighed. "I'm not looking to get caught up in some kind of turf war between you and daddy dearest."

"I'm not interested in Roberto's turf," I said. "When I'm done with him it won't belong to him anyway."

"Still sounds like a pile of shit I don't want to put my boot into."

"What if I told you Roberto had something to do with the missing girls? Not just Emma Russo but all of them?" I asked.

Hawk put down his pizza and wiped his fingers on one of the napkins. His gaze bore into mine, and I wondered if he was thinking about his little sister. I didn't know much about her, but I knew she attended the local community college.

I also knew he protected her like a fucking Rottweiler.

"Then I might be a little more inclined to scrape my boots," he said.

"It's not just Roberto. It's too complicated for one person. But he's at the top, or close to it."

"You got proof?"

"Does the bullet hole in my chest count?" I asked.

He leaned forward, bracing his elbows on the small Formica table. "Tell me what you know."

I filled him in, pausing to answer his questions along the way. His expression remained impassive until I got to the part about the ownership of the cabin. He obviously didn't think it was a coincidence either.

By the time I'd caught him up, our plates and cups were empty.

"Where are you holed up?" he asked.

"Not important." Daisy had a complicated history with Blackwell Falls and its residence. The last thing she needed was to be dragged into our mess.

"How many guns do you need?" Hawk asked.

"A lot," I said.

He turned to look out the food court's wall of glass. "Things move slow this time of year."

I followed his gaze out the window and saw that it had started to snow. "How slow?"

He shrugged. "Could be... a week, maybe two, for a significant order."

"I'll pay a premium if you make it a week," I said.

"You'll pay a premium anyway," he said.

I nodded. I couldn't blame him for taking advantage of the situation. Business was business.

"Need cars?" he asked.

I shook my head. I'd planned to ask him for a couple of cars but had decided against it. I hadn't been thrilled by Willa's insistence that we not involve Reva, but she was right.

Reva was like a mother to us. It was too dangerous.

And if we couldn't find a way to supply ourselves, we'd

have to go back to the house. On the plus side, our place could be defended — assuming Rafe could get us the manpower to defend it and Hawk could get me the guns — and I would be able to use the wireless network to access our data in the cloud.

Having access to our cars and bikes was a bonus.

"I'll see what I can do," Hawk said, throwing his used napkins on his empty paper plate. "Anything else?"

I shook my head and we stood to shake hands. Life really had turned upside down if I was shaking hands with the fucking VP of the Blackwell Blades.

"Don't get yourself killed out there," Hawk said.

"Not planning on it," I said.

He turned away and I watched him make his way through the crowd, one thought echoing in my mind.

It's not me I'm worried about.

Chapter 14

Willa

My chest tightened with nervousness as we made our way down the tree-lined drive to the stately house in the distance.

The last time I'd been here, I'd been alone and nervous for another reason: I'd known my plan to gain access to Dean Giordana's library hinged on the delivery I'd scheduled to arrive at exactly the right time.

It had also depended on Dean Giordana's widow reacting to the delivery in the way I'd expected.

Luckily, my plan had worked, but now I was back to square one because of my lost phone.

This time I wasn't nervous about being caught. I was nervous Dean Giordana's widow would take one look at me and slam the door in my face — she'd already been exasperated (suspicious?) when she'd finally kicked me out of the house on my last visit — or worse, that she wouldn't care what I had to say about the missing girls.

About Emma.

"I still think it's smarter for one of us to go with you," Oscar said from the driver's seat of the Mercedes Daisy had loaned us.

I still hadn't had a chance to ask about her story, but with every favor, I was more curious. She'd left a car for us — not the beautiful red car that looked like it was literally built for her but a luxurious black Mercedes — at a hiking turnout at the top of one of Blackwell Falls's trailheads. Neo had taken us to pick it up on his way to wherever he was meeting Hawk.

"I agree," Rock said. "Even if she doesn't chain you up in her basement, she might try to poison your tea or something."

"She's not going to poison my tea," I said. "She doesn't even know I'm coming. Besides, how would it help me if you were there? She'd just poison your tea too."

"That's where you're wrong," Rock said. "I don't even like tea."

"You're not coming." I looked from Rock to Oscar as he pulled to a stop next to a BMW in front of the house. "Either of you. She won't talk to me if you're there."

I didn't bother saying she might not talk to me at all. It was a risk we knew we were taking. If Mrs. Giordana had been aware of what her husband was up to, my visit might just make things worse.

She would know we knew.

She might even alert Roberto to our presence, giving him a heads-up that we were back in Blackwell Falls.

In the end, I still thought it was worth the risk. Roberto probably knew we would end up back at Blackwell Falls anyway, and if Mrs. Giordana preferred to live in denial about her husband's activities, we'd be no worse off than we already were.

"Then we're setting a time limit," Oscar said. He glanced at the dash on the Mercedes. "It's just after noon. If you're not out by one, we're coming in."

I sighed. "Fine."

I didn't love the constraint — I had no idea how long it would take to get Mrs. Giordana to listen — but I knew they were just looking out for me.

"And don't drink the tea!" Rock said as I got out of the car.

I laughed in spite of the seriousness of the situation. He was still wearing his caftan, the absurdity of him crammed into the backseat in the billowy garment and shouting at me about tea temporarily overriding my nervousness.

I looked up at the stately mansion as I walked to the front door. It really was a beautiful home, old-fashioned and grand and tucked away on a private wooded lot, thanks to Mrs. Giordana's family money.

I wondered again what had prompted Dean Giordana to risk it all. He'd clearly struck gold with his wife. It had been clear in my last visit that she'd loved her husband despite their obvious differences in social standing.

He'd lived in this beautiful house with a woman who loved him and without a financial worry in the world.

It didn't make sense. Did Roberto have something on him? Something he'd been holding over Dean Giordana's head? Or had Dean Giordana, like so many people, harbored a dark side that prompted him to hurt others and risk everything that mattered to him?

I didn't have the answers. I wasn't even sure Mrs. Giordana had the answers, but Dean Giordana was the only connection I had to what Roberto had been up to and he was dead.

That meant Mrs. Giordana was our last resort.

I approached the carved door set into the house's aged stone facade and rang the bell.

The last time I'd been here, I'd been clutching a notebook, a prop that had felt like a security blanket at the time. I'd been posing as a journalist from the school newspaper, had been able to hide behind a fictional purpose and identity.

Now I felt exposed. There was nothing to do but tell

the truth at a time when the truth was feeling more and more dangerous.

I was lifting my hand to ring the bell a second time when the door opened.

At first I thought maybe it was Mrs. Giordana's housekeeper. The woman standing in the doorway was disheveled, her graying hair loose around her shoulders in a tangle of waves. Her face was devoid of makeup, her lips pale and thin under brown eyes shadowed with grief.

It was only when she straightened the baggy beige cardigan that hung on her thin frame, lifting her chin imperiously, that I realized it was Mrs. Giordana.

She'd aged ten years in the two months since I'd seen her last, but the light of recognition in her eyes made it clear she had no difficulty remembering me.

She started to close the door in my face with a simple word. "No."

I stopped her with the only thing I could think of: the truth.

"I lied to you the last time I was here," I said hurriedly.

She stopped, eying me sharply, her resignation turned into something like bitterness. "Unless you're here to tell me something I don't already know, you can leave."

"I..." I searched for the right combination of words that would make her trust me, or at the very least, let me in. "I want to tell you why I lied."

"Why should I care?" she asked.

"Because I don't think you're a bad person," I said. "And..."

She lifted her eyebrows. "And?"

"And I'm not entirely sure your husband was a bad person either." I had to force the lie from my mouth. Whatever Dean Giordana's motive, no one good planned to kill someone and bury them in an unmarked grave in the woods.

There was a long moment when I wondered if she would slam the door in my face anyway. Then, she opened it wider and stepped back into the elaborate but tasteful foyer.

"Don't expect me to leave you alone this time," she said. "Your little delivery was smart — but not that smart."

Chapter 15

Neo

I made my way back through the mall, intending to head straight for the car and get back to the house as soon as possible. In my head I knew Willa was safe with Rock and Drago, but I wouldn't rest easy until I could see her with my own eyes.

I stared blankly at the storefronts as I passed — right up until I came to a store with suggestively posed mannequins dressed in a variety of lingerie.

I stepped into the store. Willa deserved to have nice things, even while we were in hiding, and it would feel good to buy her something.

Like she was really mine.

One stop turned into several, because if I couldn't have Willa wearing cheap truck stop underwear, then I couldn't have her wearing cheap truck stop clothes either, even though she did look cute as fuck in the tiny T-shirt (thank you, Drago) and heart-shaped sunglasses with nothing else but her Tuesday panties.

Then — fuck me — I felt bad about Rock and his chafing balls so I stopped to pick up some things for him, and because I didn't want to be a total dick (why didn't I want to be a total dick again?), I bought a few things for Drago too.

I was on my way out of the mall, my wallet significantly lighter than when I'd entered it, when I spotted an array of blinding diamonds shimmering from a jeweler's window.

I stopped without thinking, drawn to the glittering display of earrings, necklaces, and bracelets before my gaze landed on the rings.

I walked into the store feeling like an alien who'd just landed on a new planet. My mother had been gone since I was a kid and buying jewelry for a girl I was dating would have sent all the wrong messages.

Basically, I'd never been in a jewelry store in my life. Now I was here and feeling weirdly nervous.

What the actual fuck?

An older man in a suit approached me, his thick silver hair nearly white under the bright fluorescent lights.

"Good afternoon," he said. "Looking for something special today?"

I shifted nervously on my feet, then stared him down because I didn't usually do nervous and I wasn't going to start now.

"Where are your rings?"

Chapter 16

Willa

"Y ou really didn't have to go to the trouble," I said as Mrs. Giordana set down a silver tray with a small teapot and two teacups.

"I know," she said, "and to be honest I'm not sure why I have."

"Manners probably," I said.

She met my gaze. "Probably."

She sounded resigned, like good manners were a cross to bear.

I couldn't really blame her. Good manners were what had gotten her into this mess. If she hadn't let me in the first time, I wouldn't be here now.

She poured tea into the two cups, then took a seat in one of the chairs across from the sofa where I was sitting.

"Now that I've dazzled you with my good manners, why don't you say what you came to say," she said.

I was surprised to hear a note of humor in her voice and I understood how Dean Giordana must've fallen in love with her. She was beautiful and elegant even in her disheveled state and she clearly had a sense of humor under all those good manners.

"My real name is Willa Russo," I said. "My sister Emma was a Bellepoint student who went missing two years ago. She was last seen at Aventine."

Something shifted in her expression. It was subtle but I was sure I wasn't imagining it. A kind of recognition, like she wasn't completely surprised by what I'd said.

"What does that have to do with me? With my husband?" she asked.

"I came to Aventine this year to look for her. I didn't have any leads or anything, I just had a feeling that something had happened to her on campus. But when I started asking questions, I started to get threats."

She swallowed nervously and took a drink of her tea. "What kind of threats?"

"Pictures taken of me around campus that made it clear someone had been following me," I said. "Threatening letters and... an earring I'd dropped in your husband's office."

"What were you doing in his office?" she asked.

"Snooping." I wasn't going to apologize for snooping in her husband's office when he'd later tried to kill me.

"Looking for some kind of clue about what happened to my sister."

"And did you find anything?" she asked.

"No," I said, "but I knew whoever had sent me the earring must have found it in Dean Giordana's office. "And then later, I got another note telling me to come to a cabin in the woods around Aventine, that whoever was sending me the letter would be there with answers about Emma."

"Why didn't you call the police?"

"I don't know," I said. "I probably should have. At the time I didn't know who I could trust. I just wanted to know what happened to my sister."

"So what did you do?" she asked.

"I went to the cabin alone, like the letter said. And when I got there, Dean Giordana, your husband, was there with another man." I hurried to continue, just wanting to get the next part over with because even though Mrs. Giordana was technically on the side of the bad guys, I felt a little sick at the thought of having to tell her the truth. "They grabbed me in the woods and took me into the cabin, and then your husband told the other man to start digging a hole for my grave."

My heart was pounding in my chest, the memory triggering a shit-ton of physiological responses in my body that made me want to run.

I expected her to deny it, to protest. To kick me out. Anything but what she did, which was stare at me across the tea service like I was a debt collector she'd been expecting for a long time.

"That's why I lied to you," I said. "I didn't think you'd believe me."

"And you think that gives you the right to violate my private space?" she asked.

"Was I wrong?" I asked. "If I'd knocked on your door and told you everything I knew, everything that had happened to me at the cabin, would you have believed me? Would you have wanted to help?"

She reached for her teacup and brought it to her lips with shaking hands.

I resisted the urge to fill the silence with more words. She hadn't kicked me out yet and I had the sense that she was actually considering what I'd said.

I'd almost broken through. I could feel it.

She set her cup down with a sigh. "I loved my husband, even with all the flaws one discovers after twenty-five years of marriage, but he was no mastermind."

I hesitated over my next question. Dean Giordana had died in the cabin fire. Whatever else he'd done, he was this woman's husband and his death had obviously leveled her.

"The cabin that burned down," I started, trying to be sensitive to the fact that it had been the site of her husband's death, "it was owned by Roberto Alinari. I only know that because of the binders in Dean Giordana's study."

She furrowed her brow. "That cabin isn't campus property. I don't know why my husband would have had information on it."

"I don't know either," I said. "But when I was there with him and the other man, I got the feeling that they weren't working alone. That they were taking orders from someone else. Then I found out the cabin was owned by Roberto, and I started to wonder who else might be involved."

"How do you know all of this is tied to the disappearance of your sister?" she asked.

"I don't. Not for sure. I'm just putting pieces together and seeing what makes sense. I started digging for information about my sister and then I got threatening letters telling me to stop looking. Next thing you know, I'm about to be buried alive." I leaned forward. "And the thing is, Emma wasn't the only girl to go missing from Bellepoint."

She was either an excellent actress or she was truly surprised. "I haven't heard of any missing girls from Bellepoint except your sister."

"No one has," I said. "It was made to look like they'd all left voluntarily. Plus, they were girls of color."

She nodded her understanding. "I see."

"I could always be wrong, but it all feels connected. I don't know how but..." I looked down at my hands and drew in a breath, feeling the ache of Emma's absence from my life all over again. "I have to figure it out. My sister was here and then she wasn't and no one has any idea what happened to her. It's... well, it's torture actually."

"I'm sorry." She sounded like she meant it. "I just don't know how I can help. Stephen was... eager to impress his old classmates from Aventine. He'd attended on a scholarship and had never quite fit in. His need to be accepted by men who were half as smart and morally bankrupt besides was one of his flaws. It was a point of contention between us. We avoided the topic as much as possible."

A picture of Dean Giordana was crystallizing in my mind: the poor kid at a school filled with rich ones. Maybe his father had been a minor criminal with big dreams for his son and had pushed him to attend Aventine. Maybe Stephen Giordana had his own big dreams.

Whatever the circumstances that had led him to the school, he'd ended up an outcast, something Roberto could have used to cultivate a groupie.

Maybe Roberto had accumulated dirt on Dean Giordana at some point in their friendship. Maybe Dean Giordana didn't need that kind of blackmail to try and make a place for himself as Roberto's friend and ally.

Either way, he'd wound up doing Roberto's bidding.

But Mrs. Giordana had been right when she said her husband was no mastermind, and I still had a feeling there was more to the picture than just Roberto.

"The only reason I know Roberto Alinari owned that

cabin is because of the binders I found on the shelf in your husband's study," I repeated, circling back to the information I hoped to find.

"You think there might be more information there," she said.

"I don't know, but it's the only place I can think of to look," I said.

She got to her feet and looked down at me. "You asked me if I would have believed you when you came to the house before. The truth is, I don't know." Her dark eyes, weary and resigned just an hour before, now held a spark of conviction. "But I believe you now."

Chapter 17

Oscar

I opened my phone as a reflex, planning to check my text messages, before I remembered it was a burner.

No one had the number so I closed it again and slid it into the Mercedes's console.

I glanced at Dean Giordana's house, wondering how things were going with his widow and Willa, then shifted my attention to Rock, still in the backseat.

It was obvious something was eating him. It didn't matter that he'd been trying to keep up his usual cheerful personality. He was my brother, had been ever since we'd faced the boogeyman that was Roberto together with Neo.

"You going to tell me what's eating you?" I asked.

He almost tried to bullshit me. I saw it in the way he grinned and opened his mouth to issue some dumbass retort that would make light of the situation.

But a second later the mask dropped from his face. "I don't see the point."

"The point is, until you get it off your chest you're going to walk around like the Grim Reaper with one of those big red clown noses."

"What the fuck are you talking about?" he asked.

"It's obvious something's on your mind. You can try to cover it with your cooking and a stupid smile, but anyone who knows you can see right through it. And we all know you, even Willa."

I wasn't sure I'd realized how true it was until I said it. Willa had only been living with us for four months and it felt like she knew us as well as we knew each other. She might not have called Rock out on his weird mood, but I had no doubt she knew something was up too.

"I fucked up," Rock said. "There's no point talking about it because it's done."

"Are we talking about a fuckup I don't know about or a fuckup we've talked about before?" I asked.

"We're talking about the fuckup where I almost got Willa killed," he said.

"Still don't know what you're talking about." Normally I'd be annoyed by the cryptic conversation, but with Willa talking to Mrs. Giordana, I was almost grateful for the distraction.

Rock looked out the window. "She was with me when

those assholes drove us off the road. She had to shoot while I drove for fuck's sake."

"She shot at them?" I remembered game number two, the way she'd had every reason to hurt Connor, the fucking traitor who'd worked with Zachary Walsh to stalk her, and still hadn't been able to do it.

"She didn't have much of a choice with me driving," Rock said. "The point is, she shouldn't have had to shoot at all. If I'd protected her, we wouldn't have been in that situation and she would never have ended up in the hospital." He paused, but I sensed there was something else he wanted to say, and a few seconds later he said it, so low that I almost couldn't hear it. "She could have died."

I understood how hard it was to say the words, to even think them.

Fuck, I wanted to go on a rampage just hearing Rock say them.

None of us wanted to think about the possibility that Willa could be taken from us.

Because a world without Willa Russo's sparkling green eyes, wry smile, and smart-ass sense of humor wasn't a world worth living in.

We all knew she'd leave when we found out what had happened to Emma, but we wanted her out there, living her life, lighting up the world the way she'd lit up ours.

"All of that's true but I don't see how any of it's your fault," I said.

"She was under my care, my protection. I know I don't have Neo's big dick energy or that whole brooding bad boy thing you have going on, but I'd always believed when it came right down to it, I'd be able to protect her," he said. "I was fucking wrong."

"By that logic, we've all fucked up." It was hard to say because it was true. The fact of it haunted my dreams. "Willa almost died at the cabin, then those assholes broke into the house and were literally seconds away from getting their hands on her."

"Exactly," he said. "We all suck at taking care of her, but I'm the only one who actually got her sent to the hospital."

"That's why you've been sulking for the past two days?" I asked.

He looked offended. "I wouldn't call it sulking."

"What would you call it?"

He took long enough to answer that I knew I'd hit the nail on the head. "Brooding? In an attractive way?"

"If that makes you feel better," I said. "It doesn't really matter what you call it. The point is, the only person at fault here is Roberto. That's what we told Willa when she felt guilty about the lighthouse because it was true. We've kept Willa alive so far, close calls aside, and as insane as it makes me to say it out loud, I'm not sure that would be true if she'd been with anyone but us."

"You're right about that part," Rock said.

"Good," I said. "So stop *brooding*. And next time you're feeling some kind of way about something, just speak up for fuck's sake. No reason to carry this shit alone when you have us."

He nodded. "You're right. I don't know why I was being such a dumbass, like I had something to prove. I think this fucking dress is making me toxically male."

I put a hand on his shoulder and looked deeply into his eyes. "It's not a dress, remember? It's a— "

He held up a hand to stop me. "Don't you fucking dare."

Chapter 18

Willa

I was still clutching the binders on my lap when we pulled down the long road leading to Daisy's house.

I was still in shock. I'd hoped Mrs. Giordana would let me look at the binders again, but I'd never dreamed she'd let me take them.

"And you're sure she showed you everything in the study?" Rock asked from the backseat.

"As far as I could tell," I said. "It definitely didn't seem like she was hiding anything."

The whole visit had been one surprise after the other. In spite of the strange circumstances, Mrs. Giordana had been more helpful than I'd expected, letting me stand by in the dean's study while she searched his desk for clues and even asking me to search the bookshelves for something other than the binders that might be a hint about what her husband had been up to and with whom.

"Well, it doesn't seem like she spiked your tea at least," Rock said as Oscar pulled up in front of the house.

The Buick was gone which meant Neo still wasn't home.

"We're definitely safe in that department," I said.

Oscar looked at me across the front seat of the Mercedes. "I still can't believe she didn't even want to look inside the binders."

"I was surprised too," I said. "But I think I get it now."

"Get what?" Oscar asked.

I thought about my mom, how crushed I felt at the hospital when she'd dismissed everything I told her about Roberto, choosing to believe in him against all evidence to the contrary because she was too scared to see what life would look like on her own.

"Sometimes it's hard to see the truth about the people we love," I said.

We sat in the car, the cooling engine a soft tick in the quiet late winter afternoon. I wondered if they were thinking about their own families, about all the ways people could disappoint you.

"Well, that's depressing as fuck," Rock said.

"Yeah, sorry." I hadn't meant to get all philosophical just because I'd spent a couple of hours with Dean Giordana's widow.

I reached for the door. "My body hurts. I need a hot shower and my Wednesday panties."

I was beyond tired of being in the same clothes and really looking forward to getting some other ones, whenever that would be.

Oscar reach across the front seat and rested his hand on the back of my neck. He stroked my skin with his fingertips and a shiver traveled down my spine.

"Is this an I-want-to-be-alone shower? Or an I'm-up-for-company shower?" he asked.

I pretended to think about it just to keep him and Rock on their toes because there was no universe in which Rock was planning to let me shower alone with Oscar.

It wasn't like I minded. Going to Dean Giordana's house and telling his wife the truth about lying to her had been stressful. I wasn't above a little sexy R&R to unwind.

"I might be persuaded to entertain company," I said.

"Thank fuck," Rock said, opening the door of the backseat. "I can't speak for Oscar but I felt like my whole fucking life was hanging in the balance there for a minute. What are you waiting for? Let's fucking go."

He was almost to the door of the house by the time I got out of the car.

Chapter 19

Willa

I didn't mention the bottle of lube Rock placed next to the shower while we pulled off our clothes in the bathroom as it filled with steam.

It was one of the things Oscar had bought at the truck stop along with toilet paper, toothpaste, shampoo, and an assortment of other toiletries.

I hadn't said anything at the time. I'd been too exhausted and stressed to think about it, but clearly they had priorities.

Now the sight of it sitting on the shower ledge soaked my cunt. I didn't have the logistics of Rock's broken arm figured out but there wasn't a doubt in my mind that he and Oscar would come up with a plan.

"Good job on the panties by the way," Rock said to Oscar as he eyed my tiny Tuesday bikini underwear.

I was pretty sure it was Saturday but my days of the week were all mixed up.

"Thanks," Oscar said, taking off the black sweatpants he'd been wearing for three days.

"I don't know why," Rock said, "but they're sexy as fuck."

He pulled off the caftan with one arm, and I'm not sure any man had ever looked as hot wearing nothing but a cast and a smile.

His broad shoulders extended to cut biceps that were usually on display in a tight white T-shirt but that had been hidden in his caftan since the truck stop.

It was easy to forget that behind his affable demeanor was a smoking-hot specimen of manhood, but there was no forgetting it now. My gaze traveled over his sculpted pecs, down his defined abs to the perfect dick jutting between his thighs.

My pussy throbbed with anticipation.

When I finally made my way back up to his face, he was wearing a shit-eating grin like he knew exactly what I'd been thinking.

"See something you like, kitten?"

"Don't let it go to your head," I said.

His grin grew wider. "Too late."

"Too much talking, not enough fucking," Oscar said, taking my hand and pulling me into the shower.

I didn't even try to resist. I was more than ready to be wet and naked with them both.

Oscar positioned me under the stream of water first, letting it soak my hair and body, warming me before he rotated under it himself so that I was between him and Rock.

He pulled me against his wet body and I felt the rigid shaft of his cock against my stomach, the silver piercing on his head stroking the skin above my navel.

Rock moved into position behind me, pressing his muscled body against my back as Oscar took my face in his hands and captured my mouth in a searing kiss.

I sank into it, moaning as he teased open my mouth, his tongue tingling with mine.

Rock's arm slid around my waist, his big hand cupping my tits. He teased my erect nipple with his fingers as Oscar took our kiss deeper, and a bolt of desire shot straight to my cunt.

I moaned and Oscar broke our kiss with a deep chuckle.

"The water isn't the only thing that's hot," Oscar said to Rock over my shoulder. "I think our tiger's ready for us."

"I like the sound of that," Rock said, his breath a whisper against my neck that made my nipples even harder. "Maybe I should check it out."

His hand grazed my stomach and slid between my thighs.

I gasped as he teased my swollen folds, brushing against my clit before sliding two fingers inside me.

"Damn," Rock murmured against my shoulder. "You weren't kidding. She's ready."

"That right, tiger?" Oscar asked. "Do you want to come?"

"Yes." I barely managed to say the word. Rock was finger-fucking me, his dick pressed up against my ass. Between that and Oscar pressed against the front of my body, his pierced dick inches from my needy cunt, I was already on the edge.

"Tell us," Oscar said. "Tell us you want to come."

Rock was making circles around my swollen clit while his fingers plunged into my pussy, the pleasure so intense I almost couldn't speak.

"I want to come," I gasped, the promise of release blooming at my core.

Oscar stared down at me, his brown eyes liquid with hunger. He ran his thumb over my lips. "Why didn't you say so?"

Rock withdrew his fingers and pulled me back a few steps in the shower, executing some kind of instinctual dance that allowed Oscar enough room to kneel at my feet.

The new configuration allowed more of the water to splash on the front of my body and I remembered Rock's broken arm.

"Keep that cast dry," I ordered as Oscar pulled open my thighs.

Rock chuckled behind me. "Better step up your game, Drago. She's thinking about my cast."

"Can't have that," Oscar said, running his thumb over my pussy. "I don't want you thinking about anything but coming."

He ran his tongue through my slit and I threaded my fingers through his dark hair, wet from the shower, making it clear I wanted more of *that*.

Rock kissed his way across my shoulder and up my neck. He sucked my sensitive skin and pinched one of my nipples between his fingers, grinding his cock against my ass while Oscar buried his face in my cunt, his tongue slipping through my pussy and lapping at my clit like a thirsty animal that had just found an oasis.

A monster orgasm gathered at my center, accelerated by the press of Rock's dick against my ass and the promise of what was still to come.

Emphasis on the word *come*.

Oscar seemed to feel it. He picked up his pace and slid two fingers inside me, doubling down on my clit with his mouth.

"Fuck yes," Rock murmured behind me.

I was grinding against Oscar's face, out of my mind with need, the rhythm of my hips stroking Rock's dick.

The peak of release was close enough to touch, and I closed my eyes and ran for the edge.

"You make me so fucking hard, kitten," Rock said against my ear. "I can't wait to be buried in your luscious ass. I'm going to fuck it so hard while Drago fucks your sweet little pussy."

His words, murmured against my ear while his cock slid between my ass cheeks, Oscar's mouth working its magic on my cunt, pushed me over the edge.

I came hard, my cries echoing off the tiled walls, my body shuddering as the orgasm washed over me.

"That's right," Rock coaxed. "Come on his face, kitten."

Oscar didn't stop licking and lapping until my body stilled.

I was still gasping, trying to catch my breath, when he got to his feet.

He looked down at me with naked adoration. "Nothing is hotter than making you come with my mouth. I fucking love it."

He kissed me long and slow, every stroke of his tongue stoking the embers still burning at my center.

He grabbed my hips and lifted me off the shower floor and I wrapped my legs around his hips to straddle him. The tip of his cock pressed against the entrance to my cunt as his tongue swept my mouth.

Behind me Rock pressed closer, the thick head of his cock poised against my ass.

I broke the kiss with Oscar. "Lube?"

"Done," Rock said, his good arm guiding his cock gently inside. "Don't you know by now that we'd never hurt you, kitten?"

"We only want to make you feel good," Oscar said. His hands were occupied supporting my body weight, but that didn't stop him from pushing his pierced dick inside me. "Like this."

I moaned as the piercing at his base came into contact with my clit and Rock slid deeper into my ass.

"Does that feel good, tiger?" Oscar coaxed, pulling out of me and driving back inside. "You like the feel of us fucking you at the same time?"

"Yes," I said, my arms wrapped around Oscar's neck, using it as leverage to move with them.

"You're so fucking beautiful," Oscar murmured, bending his head to kiss me again.

"Give me some of that sugar," Rock said, kissing my neck.

I broke the kiss with Oscar and turned my head, meeting Rock's mouth at an angle that might have been awkward if not for the inferno raging in my body.

His tongue collided with mine as he pushed all the way into my ass.

I moaned into his mouth, sinking all the way onto their cocks, filling me up every which way, Oscar's piercing massaging my clit.

"Fuck yes," Oscar said. "She just got wetter. She likes the way you fuck her ass."

"Or maybe she just likes the way you fuck our pussy," Rock said to Oscar before speaking against my neck. "Because it is our pussy, isn't it kitten? It belongs to us now."

"Yes!" I gasped, bouncing on their dicks, my body lost in its demand for release.

It unfurled at my center, slowly at first and then all at once, an explosion at the core of my body that discharged like a stick of dynamite.

Light exploded behind my eyes, a litany of dirty words spilling from my mouth as I rocked against Oscar's dick in my cunt.

They were right behind me.

"Fuuuuuckkk," Oscar said.

"So fucking good," Rock said, filling my ass again and again, coming with a long groan.

When it was over, I was draped over Oscar's body, dead weight in his arms as Rock kissed his way across my shoulders from behind.

"I like that you know you're ours," Rock murmured.

Oscar's gaze burned into mine. "And we're yours. Always."

I had no idea what the future held, but that much felt true.

Chapter 20

Willa

I was at the table in the kitchen poring over one of the binders while Oscar flipped through one of the other ones, Rock stirring spaghetti into boiling water on the stove, when Neo stomped up the staircase.

He entered the kitchen carrying several shopping bags and dropped them on the floor.

His gaze found mine like a homing beacon and I wondered if I was imagining the relief in his eyes.

"How'd it go?" he asked.

"Better than I had a right to expect," I said. "She gave me the binders."

I was almost proud of the surprise on his face. Surprising Neo was hella hard.

"She just gave them to you?" he asked.

"Yep," I said. "She even looked around his study for more evidence."

He dropped into one of the chairs at the kitchen table. "Damn. I didn't expect that."

"Same," I said.

"How'd you make out with Hawk?" Oscar asked.

"He seemed agreeable enough," Neo said. "But I guess time will tell."

He looked tired, another unexpected emotion from Neo, but I knew better than to mention it. He'd never admit it anyway. For Neo, being anything but balls to the wall was a weakness and Neo didn't do weakness.

I stood. "Want something to drink?"

I squeaked when he wrapped his arms around my waist and pulled me into his lap.

His hard dick pressed against my ass, close enough to my pussy to make me wet all over again.

"No, I want your ass in my lap." He nuzzled my neck, then raised his head to stare accusingly at Oscar and Rock. "Willa smells like shampoo. And soap. And dick."

Rock shrugged. "You weren't here."

One of Neo's hands snaked up my pink T-shirt while the other slipped into my Wednesday underwear. "You let these two assholes fuck you without me?"

"Like Rock said, you weren't here." I tried to keep my voice steady but my breathlessness gave me away.

I'd just been fucked into oblivion by Oscar and Rock but I was more than ready to straddle Neo and take his dick right there in the kitchen.

What a slut.

He slipped two fingers inside me and stroked the walls of my cunt. His cock was huge under my ass and I wriggled against it, seeking the completion my body craved.

"Maybe you should've waited," he said, working my pussy with his fingers.

"Maybe you should've come home sooner," I said, grinding against his fingers, another orgasm sparking to life between my thighs.

"Jesus fuck," Rock said, his gaze glued to me and Neo. "If you two don't stop I'm going to overcook the pasta and burn the sauce. Fucking store-bought pasta and sauce. My ego will never recover."

"Can't have that," Neo said, withdrawing his fingers. "I'm starving."

My body screamed its frustration. "Fucker."

His laughter was dark, knowing, and sexy as fuck. "That'll teach you not to party without me."

I looked at the shopping bags piled on the floor, hunting for a distraction from the frustration of my aborted orgasm. "It looks like you partied plenty without us."

"I'm willing to bet you had more fun than I did," he said. "But be a good girl and get the shopping bags and I'll show you what I bought."

Fuck me. Why did he have to call me a good girl?

The only thing I liked more than Neo calling me a

good girl was when he called me a good girl with his cock in my mouth.

I scrambled off his lap and retrieved the shopping bags, setting them next to him on the floor, and he spent the next fifteen minutes unpacking his purchases, which included several outfits for me and some things for Rock and Oscar.

"Thank fuck," Rock said, taking a package of underwear and stack of jeans and white T-shirts out of Neo's hands. "I owe you."

"It was selfish," Neo said. "I was going to throw myself over the falls if I had to hear about your chafing balls one more time."

"I never thought I'd say this," Oscar said, "but I'm equally happy to see the underwear."

"Dinner's ready," Rock said, opening the oven and removing a sheet pan with slices of white bread that he'd buttered and sprinkled with garlic salt. "And I use the word *dinner* loosely."

My stomach rumbled at the smell of tangy tomato sauce and buttery garlic bread. "It smells good to me."

Rock bent to kiss me, his tongue darting out to tease my lips before he pulled away. "You're either very easy to please or you have a terrible palate."

We spent the next hour eating dinner and giving Neo the details of my conversation with Mrs. Giordana. Then he told us about his conversation with Hawk and Oscar and Rock asked a bunch of questions about the guns.

"I called Rafe on the way home," Neo said, pushing away his plate.

"Why Rafe?" Oscar asked.

"We can't stay here," Neo said. "Not without our computers and stuff. And even if we had them, the Wi-Fi blows. These binders are all we've got to figure out what happened to Emma and the other girls and we can't do any research here."

"You're saying we're going back to the house?" I asked.

"I'm saying the house is the best of all our shitty options," Neo said. "From what you said, there's no smoking gun inside those binders. Figuring out what's going on is going to take a while, and school starts again in two weeks."

"I can't even think about school right now," I said.

Oscar reached for my hand under the table. "I get that, but Neo's right. We're at a disadvantage here, even with all of Daisy's help. We're better off at the house, where we have access to our tech and more control over who comes and goes. We'll figure out what to do about classes."

"I love the idea of going home, but I don't love the idea of making it easy to find us," Rock said. "Especially after those assholes broke in before we went to the island."

"That's why I called Rafe," Neo said.

"It would take a small army to adequately protect the house," Oscar said.

"Which is why we'll need to stay here a few more

days," Neo said. "It'll take Rafe that long to pull together the resources we need."

"I'm surprised Rafe will even give us any of his men after what happened," I said, remembering the three of his men that had been killed during the home invasion that had sent us to the island. "But I'm guessing you're going to tell me he owes you a favor."

"Or five," Rock said.

I sighed. There was no point trying to unravel the mystery of the Kings and their lives before I'd come to Aventine. Maybe someday we'd have the time to really talk, the way new lovers talked.

Right now we were too busy trying to stay alive.

"How long will it take Hawk to deliver on the guns?" Oscar asked.

"A day or two," Neo said.

"Won't we be back in the house by then?" I asked.

"Hard to say," Neo said. "It depends on how long it takes Rafe to get enough men to cover the woods around the house. I'm not risking a repeat of that fucked-up home invasion. But we'll need the guns anyway."

"You already have guns at the house though right?" I asked.

"I think this is one of those *the more guns the better* situations," Rock said, picking up my plate and taking it with his to the sink.

"Exactly," Neo said. "You left the keys in the Mercedes

right? Daisy will be by to pick it up first thing in the morning."

"Yep, as instructed," Oscar said. "It's not the Porsche, but it is one nice car."

"Not like she can't spare it," Neo said.

"What's her story?" I asked. "If it won't betray her confidence, I mean."

I was definitely being nosy, but I couldn't pretend not to be curious.

Oscar glanced at Neo, who gave him an almost imperceptible nod.

"She was part of a crazy murder that happened here a few years ago," Oscar said.

"That happened *here*?" I wasn't easily spooked but the big house in the middle of nowhere at the top of the falls was the actual definition of spooky. The idea of spending the next few days there knowing a murder had occurred within its walls wasn't exactly comforting.

"Not at the house," Rock said. "In Blackwell Falls."

"You're kidding." It was impossible to believe the warm girl with haunted violet eyes that had done so much to help us was a murderer.

"Well, she didn't actually do the murdering," Oscar clarified.

"Maybe you should just start from the beginning," I said.

"Daisy's older brother was murdered at the base of the

falls," Neo said. "When the cops got there, Daisy was standing over the body with three friends of hers. Daisy was holding the knife that had killed her brother and the men that were with her were covered in blood."

I looked at Oscar. "I thought you said she didn't do the murdering."

"She didn't," Oscar said. "At first they claimed none of them had done it. Said they'd found Daisy's brother already dead at the falls. But then one of the guys confessed and the other two said they'd helped him do it."

"They all went away for the crime," Oscar said. "Except for Daisy, probably because her dad is as rich as Midas."

"And because of the three dudes who confessed to the crime," Rock said.

I shook my head, trying to reconcile this new information with the image I already had of Daisy. "So wait, Daisy was a murder suspect until three guys confessed and went to prison for it?"

"That about covers it," Rock said.

"It was a big deal in Blackwell Falls for months," Neo said. "The story is kind of a legend now. The newspapers called the three guys 'the Blackwell Beasts.'"

"Wow," I said. "I don't know what I'd expected when I asked about Daisy but it definitely wasn't this."

"The three guys were assigned a court-appointed attorney, but Daisy's dad hired the best criminal lawyer in the country," Neo said.

I didn't know what to say. Was Daisy a murderer who'd let three guys take the fall for her?

It was hard to believe but I'd learned the hard way that people could surprise you in all kinds of ways, and not all of them were good.

The kitchen fell into silence until Neo pushed back from the table and stood. "We should cut the lights. It's dark."

They told me about a notorious murder that happened at the base of the falls and now it was time to turn the lights out for the night?

Great.

"I'll get the candles," Rock said.

He sounded dejected and I couldn't blame him. We'd been chased and shot at — twice — and were in hiding in the middle of nowhere.

"Any ideas for how to pass the time?" Oscar asked.

Neo grinned. "I'm sure I can think of something."

I rolled my eyes. "It's only six o'clock. I think I saw a jigsaw puzzle in one of the cupboards. I'll go get it."

I was halfway down the hall when Neo cut the lights.

My burner phone wasn't fancy enough for a flashlight but I used the dim light on the display to navigate my way to the empty bedroom where I'd seen the puzzle. The winter wind rattled the old windowpanes and I thought I could hear the falls like a deep sigh far below the cliff. For the first time since we'd arrived at Daisy's house, I felt the thrum of fear.

We were completely and utterly alone.

Chapter 21

Willa

Two days later we were still studying the binders, daylight waning, the sinking sun casting weak light across the shoddy living room Neo and Oscar had made by carrying in two love seats from the bedrooms.

The sofas were small and cramped, with carved wood legs and stiff backs, but it was nice to have somewhere to sit besides the kitchen and the bedroom. The former was small with only the table and the latter always led to something besides just hanging out.

One of the many things I'd learned about myself over the past few months was that I couldn't to be trusted with the Kings near a bed. Actually, I couldn't trust myself with the Kings anywhere, but the bed made it way too easy.

"I don't know what we're even looking for at this point," I said, leaning back against one of the love seats.

My vision was blurry from looking at the information in the binders and I was no closer to figuring anything out than I'd been when I'd left Mrs. Giordana's house with them.

"I don't know either." Oscar's head was still bent to one of the binders, a lock of his dark hair falling over his forehead. I resisted the urge to push it back. I knew how silky it would feel in my fingers but I also knew we'd end up fucking on one of the tiny love seats if I touched him.

If I touched any of them.

And that was the other thing, I was still figuring out how to navigate this relationship-with-three-friends thing.

I knew Neo had a jealous streak in spite of his willingness to share, and I was careful not to play favorites — in the bedroom or out.

"Well, at least now we know that each binder has the information for one of the cabins," Rock said next to me on the floor. "They each have the map that Willa took a picture of the first time she went to Dean Giordana's house, but after that, it really does seem like it's just a bunch of land surveys and financial stuff."

"I feel like the financial stuff should be making more sense," I said, returning my focus to the binder spread out in front of me. It was for the cabin labeled RAA, and I was looking at a page of what looked like wire transfers from a company of the same name to an escrow company of the previous owner.

I was surprised to feel Neo's hand on the top of my head. He was sitting on the love seat above me, and I could admit I enjoyed leaning against his strong legs a little too much.

He stroked my hair and I couldn't help thinking there was something... *affectionate* in it?

Ugh. Pathetic.

We'd broken the seal on our physical relationship, and he'd shown he cared through his determination both to see me at the hospital after he'd regained consciousness and to protect me from Roberto's men.

But there was still a part of him that felt unreachable, and the part of me that was a dumb bitch desperately wanted to break through.

"The names are the key," Neo said. "The numbers will never be anything but numbers, but the names of the cabins have to mean something."

"Agreed," Oscar said from the other love seat.

Rock looked at Neo. "And you're sure none of these other names mean anything to you? Maybe if we could prove that Roberto owns them all we could get the police to search the woods for the missing girls."

I'd admitted that I knew Emma was probably dead, but the thought of her buried in an anonymous grave in the woods with the other missing girls still hurt.

"Not a thing," Neo said. "I could do a more thorough search of his known assets if I had access to a computer."

"Any ETA from Rafe?" Oscar asked.

"Later this week," Neo said. "He estimates we need at least twenty men, probably more like twenty-five, to cover the woods around the house."

Just the thought of it was enough to cause an impending panic attack.

The Kings were right: we couldn't stay here.

But when we did finally get back to the house, we'd be in real danger. So much danger that we'd be surrounded by a small army at the house, all of them trying to keep Roberto and his men from killing us.

"I'm not gonna lie, I'm looking forward to having lights at night again," I said. "And takeout." I looked at Rock. "No offense. You know I love your cooking. But I really do miss takeout and *Love or Money*."

I'd never been more in need of our favorite reality TV show, a greasy pizza, and a cuddle sesh on the sofa at the house with the Kings.

Neo got to his feet. "Speaking of lights, we should cut the power. The sun's almost down." He looked meaningfully at Oscar and Rock. "Don't you two have an errand to run?"

Rock looked momentarily confused before understanding lit his blue eyes. "Right! We do."

I narrowed my eyes at them. I was definitely missing something. "What errand?"

"That's for us to know and you to find out," Rock said with a grin.

What the fuck were they up to? We weren't supposed to leave the house unless it was absolutely necessary.

"Seriously," I said, "you guys are freaking me out."

Oscar pulled me to my feet and wrapped his arms around me.

Rock looked at me like I was the sun, moon, and stars all in one.

Neo, like I was a rare jewel, one he would kill to protect.

But Oscar seemed to see into all the shadowed crevices of my soul. Like he saw all the things I tried to hide from everyone and wanted me anyway.

He pulled me closer and smiled. "Happy New Year's Eve, tiger."

Chapter 22

Willa

The errand was pizza.

Hot, cheesy, delicious pizza.

Oscar and Rock drove three towns over to pick it up in the Buick, careful to make sure they weren't followed. By the time they got home with it, Neo had unveiled several bottles of champagne he'd bought when he'd met Hawk, storing them in the trunk of the Buick so it would be a surprise.

He'd also bought me sexy lingerie, another surprise he'd saved after his meeting with Hawk.

I opened the bags excitedly, excited to ditch my Friday panties.

He watched me pull a sea of satin and lace from the bags, looking sexy as fuck as he leaned back on the sofa.

Manspreading might've been bad form on a bus or subway, but watching Neo eye me with undeniable hunger, muscular legs spread wide to reveal his bulging dick, was the turn-on of the century.

He insisted I choose something for our New Year's Eve party, and by the time I emerged from our shared bedroom wearing a demure but barely there pink baby-doll nightie, Rock and Oscar had returned with the pizza.

Rock stopped in his tracks when he spotted me, then rubbed his hand over his face. "Fuck me," he said. "And by *fuck me* I mean seriously, please, fuck me."

I laughed, feeling a little embarrassed by the attention.

Oscar's dark eyes were molten with appreciation and Neo surveyed me from the sofa like a lion about to pounce on an unsuspecting gazelle.

I couldn't really blame them. The nightgown's thin straps easily held up the tiny garment. My tits were on full display through the sheer mesh cups, and while the bottom fell in full pleats, it ended in a ruffle that barely — and I did mean barely — covered my ass, hanging out for everyone to see in the tiny lace thong that matched the nightgown.

"I'm not fucking anybody until I get my hands on that pizza." My mouth watered at the smell of warm dough and melted cheese.

"You're the boss." Oscar grinned. "For now."

We opened the boxes right in our makeshift living room while Rock went to get plates.

Oscar poured a fresh round of champagne into the coffee mugs Daisy had brought with the dishes, and we spent the next hour demolishing three pizzas —sometimes I forgot how big the Kings were; they ate like they fucked, like ravenous beasts — and powering through two bottles of champagne.

Neo had long since cut the lights and the room felt cozy and warm, candles flickering from the floor and the dresser in the corner.

It had started to snow, but it was impossible to see the crystalline flakes falling from inside the dark house. The only sign of the weather was an occasional howl of the wind rattling the old windows.

"I wish we could watch a movie," Oscar said. "Or even just listen to music."

"It's so quiet here," I said, leaning my head back against the sofa on the floor where I was sitting. "It feels like the rest of the world is a million miles away."

"I wish it was," Rock said.

I knew what he meant. In between our peaceful moments together — moments like this — I was all too aware that Roberto was nipping at our heels.

And not just him. I knew in my bones that whatever he'd done to Emma and the other missing girls, he hadn't done alone.

We had other enemies. We just didn't know who they were yet.

"Let's play a game," Neo said.

There was something dark in his voice that sent a

shiver through my body. Anticipation? Fear? Sometimes with Neo they felt like one and the same.

"What kind of game?" I asked.

He looked up at the high ceilings and scanned the room, his eyes unreadable in the dark. "We have this big house at our disposal and we haven't explored hardly any of it. What better place to play hide-and-seek?"

"Hide-and-seek?" I repeated.

"I like it." Oscar's eyes glittered with excitement. "Willa can hide. Naked. We'll seek."

Chapter 23

Willa

"I can't believe I'm doing this," I said, standing naked and shivering in the drafty third-floor room.

Oscar flashed me a roguish smile. "I can't believe we're actually telling you to hide from us looking like that."

I looked them over. "This feels unfair. If I have to be naked, you should have to be naked too."

"She has a point," Rock said. "It wouldn't be very feminist of us to expect Willa to be the only one playing naked."

Neo rolled his eyes. "For fuck's sake," he muttered, reaching for the button on the jeans he'd bought at the mall.

I watched with satisfaction as they stripped off their clothes, slowly revealing their magnificent bodies, somehow even more appealing in the candlelight, sculpted to perfection, their dicks hard between their thighs.

I knew what they felt like inside me — in my cunt, my ass, my mouth — and that made the sight of them even more of a turn-on.

They looked like naked gods, the candlelight exaggerating every shadow, every muscle, casting their faces in an evil glow that made me wet.

"Why do I have to hide?" I asked.

Neo crossed his bulging arms over his chest. "You've already negotiated to your limit. You run. We hunt."

The thought of them hunting me through the abandoned house sent a terrified thrill through my body. It wasn't like they were going to hurt me, but something about the thought of them hunting me down, wondering what they would do to me once they found me, caused fear to mingle with the lust already coursing through my body.

"Fine," I muttered. "But this house is huge. If we're allowed to use the whole thing, I need a good head start."

"I'm fine with a good head start," Oscar said. "But I think we need some ground rules."

"What kind of ground rules?" I asked.

"No basement, no attic, and nothing outside," he said. "The first two would probably give you tetanus and I don't want to worry about you freezing to death in the snow or going over the cliff into the falls."

A chill ran up my spine. "Fine with me."

"Sounds good," Rock said. "Only the three floors of the house."

"We'll give you three minutes," Neo said.

"Three minutes? It'll take me two just to get to the ground floor," I said.

"Then run faster." His eyes bore into mine across the candlelit room. "Three minutes, Jezebel."

I recognized the note of coldness in his voice.

It meant he was in charge. It meant I was at his mercy.

I should have hated it. I should have rebelled. Instead, I had to tamp down the roar of sexual hunger that swept through my body.

I lifted my chin. "Turn around and start counting."

Chapter 24

Willa

I headed for the staircase even before they started counting.

Maybe their bare asses should have been funny, but coupled with their muscular backs and broad shoulders, not to mention the dark house looming all around me, I felt like a rabbit set loose for a den of foxes.

They'd made it to the count of ten by the time I hit the stairs. I flew down the first flight, holding on to the banister as I spun onto the second.

It felt subversive to be racing through the house ass-naked but weirdly liberating too. We were teetering at the top of the falls in the giant house, far from town, a winter storm howling outside.

The moon must have been hidden by clouds because it was dark as fuck, and I was relieved to hit the ground floor, free of the sweeping staircase that could have been deadly in a fall.

Somewhere on the last flight of stairs, I'd left behind the sound of the Kings counting. I had no idea how far along they were but adrenaline raced through my veins as I sped down the long main hall on the first floor.

I glanced through the open doors of rooms as I passed, ghostly shapes of covered furniture lurking in the shadows.

I turned into some kind of formal living room and contemplated hiding under what looked like a grand piano near a bank of windows, but it was too obvious. If it got my attention, it would get the Kings' attention too.

I needed something hidden but so mundane it blended into the rest of the house.

I reentered the hall and heard footsteps pounding down the staircase.

"Here kitty kitty kitty." Rock's voice sounded sinister echoing through the empty house.

I fled down the hall for the back of the house. I hadn't explored it at all, and Daisy had only shown us the third floor, plus the boiler room to Neo. I had no idea what I was running into, but a few seconds later I pushed through a large swinging door and found myself in a massive kitchen.

And I did mean massive.

The luxury kitchen in the Kings' house was huge but this room was at least twice that size, with what must have been a large table at its center covered in a dusty white sheet.

"I hope you have a good hiding spot, tiger," Oscar called from the front of the house. "You have no idea what we have planned for when we find you."

The blood was rushing in my ears, my heart beating wildly. My brain didn't know the difference between a real threat and a pretend one, and who could blame it? I'd thought the Kings were my enemies and they'd ended up being my only allies. I'd thought I could trust my mom and she'd turned her back on me.

My sense of safety was all kinds of fucked up.

I was in full on survival mode, panic fighting its way up my throat as I frantically searched for a place to hide.

And underneath it all, as sick as it was, I was horny as fuck.

I was being chased through the house by the three hottest most dangerous men I'd ever known, and I knew all too well what they'd do with me when they found me.

That my instinctual fear mingled with sexual desire was just one more sign that I still had a lot of things to learn about myself.

Somewhere not far enough away, Rock made a whispering sound like he was calling to a lost cat. "I think our kitty cat is lost, boys."

I scanned the kitchen, my gaze landing on a door to one side of the room. I had no idea what it was, but the kitchen wasn't exactly overflowing with hiding spots, so I ran toward the door and flung it open.

I'd just closed it behind me when I heard heavy footsteps enter the kitchen I'd just vacated.

I glanced frantically around the dark, narrow room I'd entered but couldn't make out anything except a bank of cabinets.

I reached out hesitantly, not wanting to make any noise, and came in contact with a smooth dusty surface that felt like butcher block.

Was I in a butler's pantry? That would make sense. Rich people had them in the old days to hide all their extra dishes and supplies.

My eyes were adjusting to the darkness. I could make out a row of lower cabinets fronted with round wooden knobs.

I headed for the ones at the back of the narrow room and eased open one of the lower doors, hoping it would be big enough for me to crawl into.

I tried not to think about all the dead bugs and mouse droppings that might be inside the cabinet. It was disgusting but I was also fully immersed in the game and determined not to be found.

I wedged myself into the tall lower cabinet, thankfully just big enough to hold my body if I leaned forward over my knees.

I pulled the door closed behind me and heard someone step into the room.

I tried to slow my breathing. It sounded so loud in the confined space I was shocked it couldn't be heard outside my hiding spot.

"Oh Jezzzzebel..." Neo's voice sounded almost soothing, just the slightest hint of threat under the words. "I know you're in here."

My mind and body were hella confused. I was terrified at the same time my cunt was slick with need.

"You know you can't hide from me," Neo said, his voice low and dangerous right on the other side of the cupboard where I was hiding. "I can smell you. I can feel you."

I held my breath.

The cupboard door flew open and I was pulled from inside by a pair of strong hands.

"Got you."

Chapter 25

Willa

He pulled me to my feet and pushed me against the bank of cupboards inside the tiny room.

The press of his naked body against mine was the best kind of shock, like being electrified from the inside out, every nerve tingling with hunger that was only amplified by the fact that I could barely see him.

"You owe me one, Jezebel."

His hands were all over me as his mouth crushed mine in a brutal kiss.

I moaned, letting him pillage my mouth, because that was what Neo did when we were alone. He was an invading force that occupied my body. There was no room for hesitation or dissent.

Not that I wanted to dissent.

The force of Neo's hunger swept everything else out of my mind and body and I was all too happy to be left vacant, no room for anything but his hands and mouth and dick.

I wrapped my arms around his neck and molded myself to his hard body. His cock was huge and rock-hard against my stomach and I reached down and took it in my hand.

He growled into my mouth as I stroked, then spun me around fast to face the bank of cabinets.

"I don't think you understand the game, Jezebel." His breath was hot against my ear. "I'm the predator. You're the prey. And you've been caught."

He wedged his knee between my thighs, spreading my legs.

His dick was pressed against my ass, every movement of his body making me hotter and more desperate to feel him inside me.

He slid a hand between my thighs and stroked through the wet folds of my cunt. "I knew it. You're fucking soaked." He circled my clit and spoke against my neck. "You love this, don't you?"

"Yes," I gasped, riding his hand. I was already close to coming, the darkness around us and the hot press of his body creating one hell of an erotic fantasy.

"You can let Rock baby you," he murmured. "Oscar can comfort you. But nobody fucks you like I fuck you."

He drove into me from behind all at once.

I cried out from the pure pleasure of it, holding on to

the edge of the cabinet, beyond caring that we were fucking like two wild animals in a dirty dusty closet.

His hands closed around my tits. "Fuck, your pussy is good. So hot and tight."

He dragged out of me and I pressed backward, letting him know I wanted more.

The slap of his hand against my bare ass made me yelp.

"I decide how fast we go, Jezebel. Your job is to take it like a good little bad girl," he said. "Tell me your job."

He was poised at my entrance, obviously waiting for me to answer to give me more of what I wanted.

It was a testament to how much I wanted it that I obeyed. "I have to take it like a good little bad girl."

Somewhere in the back of my mind I knew I would hate myself later for saying the words, but right now, I could barely get them out around my hunger for him.

"Yeah you do," he said, driving back into me.

He moved faster behind me, fucking me in a frenzy, like he couldn't bury himself inside me fast enough, his fingers pinching my nipples while he squeezed my tits.

I was lost in a world of private pleasure, the confined darkness adding to the feeling that we were alone and spinning through space with nothing but our bodies and the need for release.

I panted as my orgasm built, rocking my ass against him as he slid into me, stretching me wide and hitting my cervix with his gargantuan dick.

His palm landed with another slap on my ass. It was probably meant to be a punishment for daring to move or trying to set a pace, but if this was punishment I was a fucking masochist because it threw me over the edge, into the abyss of my climax.

"Oh my god..." The orgasm hit me like a freight train, slamming through my body as Neo groaned behind me.

"Fuck yes," he said, pounding into me. "I love to make that sweet pussy come."

He groaned long and low, animalistic and guttural, and I knew he was coming too, spilling into me as I shuddered around him, the slapping of our bodies and our panting breath the only sound in the darkened room.

When it was over, he spun me around to face him and took my face in his hands.

His eyes were glittering chips of amber as he stared down at me with fevered possession. "Every time you fuck them without me, I'm going to take you alone."

It was a threat. And a promise.

And fuck me if I didn't mind either.

Part Two

Chapter 26

Neo

I scanned the trees surrounding the house as we emerged from the lined driveway leading to the house. I'd been tense ever since we left Daisy's place after packing up the few things we'd accumulated during the week it had been our home.

If it had just been me, Drago, and Rock, I wouldn't have given a fuck. My father's men could come for us and the chips would fall where they may.

But this wasn't just about us.

I glanced in the rearview mirror at Willa, sitting in the backseat next to Drago, her still-battered face turned to the window as we approached the house.

A storm of protective fury blew through my body at the sight of her. I was beyond caring what my father did to me, but I would protect Willa with my dying breath.

I thought about the ring stashed in my bag and hoped I'd figure out the right time to give it to her.

To ask the question that was burning a hole in my fucking heart.

I used the smart phone home app I'd downloaded to my burner to open the garage door and returned my attention to the woods as I waited for it to rise.

Rafe had given me assurances that the property was teeming with trained guards, but as soon as I got Willa settled I'd be out there counting for myself, making sure there were more than enough men to fight off anything Roberto sent our way.

Willa would have the illusion of freedom now that we were back home, but I wasn't taking any chances with her safety.

"It's weird being back right?" Willa asked.

"As fuck," Rock said from the passenger seat.

"I feel like everything should be different, like a hurricane or tornado made us leave and everything should be trashed or something," Willa said.

I knew what she meant. We'd abandoned the house like a sinking ship after the home invasion, grabbing whatever we could carry with the little bit of time we had. We'd already worked through the night to bury Roberto's men — the men who'd dared to come for Willa under our roof — and we hadn't known how much time we had before he sent reinforcements.

We were returning to the scene of the crime — the ones committed against us and the ones we'd committed to protect Willa.

Rock and Willa were right. It was strange as fuck.

I pulled forward into the garage and we waited for it to close behind us to get out of the car.

"Let's get everything inside," I said. "I need to talk to Rafe."

He'd already cleared the house and was waiting outside to brief me on the new security measures.

"Fine with me," Willa said. "I can't wait to sleep in my own bed."

I was buoyed by her choice of words. She was happy to be back. This was her home too.

Then I remembered that she didn't plan to stay and the knowledge tore through me like a fucking machete.

Drago and I grabbed our stuff from the trunk of the Buick and we headed for the door leading to the house.

I'd never been so glad to see our cars and bikes lined up in the garage, and I looked them over like long-lost pets. The Buick had gotten us through the last week but it was slow as hell and even more boring. I was looking forward to passing it off to the Blades' chop shop.

"Hello baby," Drago cooed, running his hands along the Porsche as we headed for the door to the house. "I fucking missed you."

"Oh my god," Willa groaned.

"What?" Drago asked. "Next to you, this car is the sexiest fucking thing I've ever owned.

Willa glanced back at him, her green eyes flashing. "You must be high. You don't own me."

Drago grinned. "That's not what you were saying last night when my dick was in your ass."

Willa flushed and I had a flash of our tangled bodies and the hours we'd spent fucking her every which way while we'd been trapped at Daisy's house. It had been the perfect place to regroup, to heal and recover in more ways than one.

The fact that we'd had unlimited time to fuck Willa was one hell of a bonus.

She laughed. "You're the worst."

We filed into the kitchen and I disarmed the alarm. Rafe had installed a backup generator in the house's basement, an insurance policy against another cut to our power. Now, someone would have to gain access to the house to take out the power, and they couldn't gain access to the house as long as the alarm was armed.

Drago looked at Willa. "I guess now you can get rid of your days of the week underwear."

"I don't know," she said, "I think I kind of like them."

"That makes two of us," Rock said. "I can't say the same about my caftan. I don't think I'll ever be able to look at that thing without feeling my balls itch."

"I'd be more than happy to host a ritualistic bonfire to burn the fucking thing if it means I never have to hear about your balls again," Drago said.

Willa headed for the stairs. "I can *not* have another conversation about Rock's balls. I'm going to take a shower."

"I'll come— " Drago and Rock started at the same time.

"Not this time," Willa said without turning around. "I just need one shower where all I do is get clean."

My dick hardened at the mention of a shower with Willa like some kind of horny Pavlov's dog. I couldn't count the number of showers we'd spent fucking Willa at Daisy's house. I wasn't sure I'd ever be able to take a shower again without getting hard.

"I'm going to talk to Rafe," I said, heading for the doors leading to the patio area off the kitchen.

It was cold and overcast, the pool covered for winter, the patio furniture put away for the season. I stepped onto the snow covered lawn and made my way toward the tree line.

I was halfway there when a black-clad figure emerged from the woods.

He walked toward me and I saw that it was Rafe in full winter tactical gear, strapped with a semiautomatic weapon.

"Welcome home," he said. His brown hair was tucked

under a black hat, and his face looked older in the cold. I knew he'd served as an Army Ranger and his eyes definitely said he'd seen some shit.

I shook his hand. "Thanks. Wouldn't be here without you. Literally."

"Least I can do after what happened last time," he said.

I'd apologized for the loss of his men in the home invasion and had been surprised to find that he felt responsible. He owned and operated the best security company on the Eastern seaboard and considered it a personal failure that someone had gotten through his men.

"No one to blame but the guys pulling the trigger," I said. "What do we have out here?"

Rafe turned to face the trees and whistled. Similarly dressed men emerged from the woods a few at a time, stepping out of the tree line and standing with their weapons as they faced the house.

"Twenty-five men armed, trained, and ready to rumble," he said. "Plus the new generator in the basement attached to the Wi-Fi and alarm system. I also added four new cameras at the perimeter feeding to your CCTV."

I looked at the men surrounding the house and thought about the new security measures, hoped they would be enough to protect Willa until we could figure out who was working with my father and eliminate them as a threat.

"Thanks," I said.

He opened his mouth to say something, then seemed to think better of it.

"Something else to say?" I asked.

He shook his head and rubbed his jaw. "I'm confident you're covered here. It's everywhere else I'm worried about."

Chapter 27

Willa

I f someone had told me four months earlier that I'd be happy to be back at the Kings' house, I would've told them they were insane.

But I couldn't lie. It felt like home.

I dropped the few things Neo had bought for me at the mall on the floor of my room and collapsed on my bed with a sigh. My bedroom felt huge and luxurious after being crammed into one bedroom with three giant guys.

Not that I was complaining about the bedroom part.

I'd had a whole week of the best sex of my life with three of the hottest guys on the planet.

And not just sex.

We'd talked and laughed and done jigsaw puzzles and cooked in the tiny cramped kitchen and it had felt more like a much-needed getaway than a necessary hideout.

We'd also gotten a lot of sleep without TV or other

distractions, something our wounded bodies had seriously needed. Rock's arm was still in a cast but the gunshot wound on Neo's chest and the one on Oscar's thigh were getting better.

We were all still a little banged up, but our bruises and cuts were healing, and I was happy to look in the mirror and see that my own face wasn't quite as battered. Best of all, I could breathe and laugh without my chest hurting.

We'd survived Roberto's attempted assassination, thanks to the Kings' preparation and Daisy's help.

Now we just needed to figure out who else had been involved with the missing girls.

Then we had to bring them down hard.

I sat up with a sigh and stood to strip off my clothes. I padded barefoot into the bathroom and turned on the hot water in my luxurious shower, moaning with pleasure when I stepped under the powerful spray.

Daisy's house had been a godsend but the water pressure sucked and as much as I'd loved being fucked in the shower by the Kings, being alone in my spacious private shower felt like the ultimate luxury.

I shampooed my hair and soaked my body with the fancy products stocked in my bathroom, inhaling their delicate scents. I'd lived with the cheap stuff when I'd been traveling, so it wasn't like I was some kind of product snob, but I'd gotten used to living the high life with the Kings and I had to admit, after a week of roughing it, it was bliss.

I stepped out of the shower and dried myself off with one of the thick bath towels stacked in my bathroom. Then I wrapped my hair and pulled on my softest velour tracksuit. I added my thickest socks — it looked like it was about to snow again — and collapsed on my bed. I was asleep in seconds.

When I woke up hours later, my room was cast in a faint blue glow, the winter sun nearly set.

I had a moment of disorientation before I remembered I was back in my bedroom at the Kings' house. I lay there for a few minutes, reveling in how clean and comfortable I felt after my shower and in my own clothes.

I'd been off-grid for over a week. Claire and Mara would be worried, especially Mara. It was rare for us not to text on the daily and we'd already had sparse communication from the island.

I wondered if the new phones Neo ordered had arrived. Part of me wasn't ready to rejoin the real world — I knew what carnage awaited us — but I also didn't want to worry my two closest friends.

I threw off the covers and sat up, reluctantly getting out of bed. My stomach was rumbling and I felt crazy dehydrated. I needed food and the biggest glass of water known to man.

I made my way down the back stairs, comforted by the sound of someone in the kitchen and the smell of cooking meat. I assumed it was Rock, but when I stepped off the staircase and into the kitchen I saw that it was Reva.

She looked up when I entered the room. "Well, aren't you a sight for sore eyes!"

I lunged for her and squeezed her tight. "I'm so happy to see you!"

I might have been a little overenthusiastic.

She staggered backwards a step and laughed, tightening her hold on me. "You sure know how to make a girl feel welcome."

"You have no idea how much I've missed you," I said, releasing my hold on her.

She smoothed my hair and took my cheeks in her hands, studying my face. "No offense honey, but it shows."

I laughed. "It's been a tough few weeks."

"Rock said you've been roughing it so I made you a big dinner," she said. "Meatloaf and mashed potatoes, plus my famous chocolate cake for dessert."

I knew it would all be awful — all of Reva's cooking was awful — but right then, I didn't even care. I was just happy to be back in the Kings' big kitchen with Reva's comforting presence.

"Sounds amazing," I said. "I hope you made a lot because the Kings really love your meatloaf."

I bit back a smile, looking forward to the moment when Reva would force extra helpings of her meatloaf onto the Kings, who would be too polite to turn it down.

"You know it, sugar," she said. "Can't have you and my boys going hungry."

I smiled. "You take such good care of us."

"It's my pleasure to do it," she said.

"Speaking of, why is that?" I asked, walking to the fridge.

It was a question I'd been wanting to ask for a long time. Now it felt like Reva knew everything about our absence from the house.

And that meant she probably knew everything about everything.

What I didn't understand was why she was so loyal to the Kings. I was sure they paid her well and everything, but her loyalty felt like more than a paycheck.

I uncapped one of the two bottles of water I'd taken from the fridge and guzzled half of it in one go.

"Let's just say I got myself into a marriage with the wrong kind of man," she said. "When it all became too much I needed a little help making him disappear."

"So they killed him for you?" I asked.

The thought of the Kings killing someone no longer shocked me. I'd seen them do it with the men who'd invaded the house before we went to the island, had watched Neo and Oscar return covered in dirt after burying the bodies.

Reva laughed. "Oh honey, I didn't need help with the killing. Just the disappearing."

Now I was surprised. "You killed him?"

"Tried everything else," she said, opening the oven door to peek at the three loaf pans lined up inside. "Anyway, the boys made sure there weren't too many questions, and if there were, no one would find any answers. Then they gave me a gig working here at the house. My ex was an asshole but he did have a paycheck, and I'm sorry to say, I don't have much in the way of marketable skills."

I looked at the sweet Southern woman who spent all her time taking care of us and tried to imagine her murdering her husband. How did she do it? Frying pan? Smothering him with the pillow in the middle of the night?

I wanted to ask but it seemed like bad manners, and even though there was a time for bad manners, this didn't seem like one of them.

"I'm sorry you went through all of that," I said instead.

She turned off the heat under a pot of boiled potatoes. "Don't be. I learned that the worst things that happen to us in life usually end up leading us to the best places."

It was hard for me to believe with Emma missing and probably dead, with the other girls missing and probably dead. My dad was gone, also probably dead, and my mom had turned her back on me for an abusive psychopath.

But I didn't want to ruin Reva's silver lining.

"Well, I'm glad you found your way to the Kings and to me," I said.

She smiled. "Me too. I might never have known what a good cook I was if I didn't have to cook for those boys."

I plastered a smile on my face and nodded because I wasn't about to burst her bubble. "For sure."

I caught a flash of light near the trees surrounding the house and moved closer to the window to gaze out over the property.

"You won't have to worry about a repeat of that incident before you left the house," Reva said behind me. "This place is battened down like Fort Knox."

I wasn't surprised she knew about the home invasion or the added security in the woods.

I'd been right: Reva clearly knew everything.

"It's weird to think of them out there, isn't it?" I asked without turning around. The light I'd seen disappeared, either shut off or pointed in another direction.

"Not as weird as worrying about the four of you unprotected here," Reva said.

"You have a point," I said. I turned around and moved away from the window. No point obsessing over the fact that the woods were teeming with Rafe's men. I would have to get used to the idea. "Where are the Kings?"

"Sleeping probably," she said. "Rock and Oscar went upstairs right after I got here. Neo was talking to Rafe for a while, but he went upstairs afterwards. They left that for you."

I followed her gaze to the new phone, still in the box, on the island.

I had mixed feelings about opening it but I reached for it anyway, thinking about Claire and Mara. It was time to get back to reality.

Ready or not.

Chapter 28

Willa

We'd been home about a week when I heard a commotion in the kitchen. I put my book down and got up from the couch, then slapped Oscar's hand away as he pinched my ass.

We were all enjoying the luxury of having so much space and I'd taken to reading on the sofa while the Kings played video games.

"Don't be long," Oscar said, leering at my ass, hanging out of my booty shorts.

They were totally inappropriate for January but the house was warm, probably because the Kings were just as happy as I was to be in a well-insulated house after our time at Daisy's.

"Yeah," Rock said, his gaze still on the video game he and Oscar were playing, "you know how Oscar likes to give you spankings."

It was pathetic that just the thought of it made me wet.

Sometimes I really hated myself.

I followed the sound of Neo's angry voice and a tinny voice coming from the intercom at the gate.

"What's going on?" I asked.

He'd been working out in the gym, trying to stay in shape between fights, and I tried to focus on the fact that he was glaring at me instead of the fact that his chest was bare over basketball shorts, sweat glistening on his muscled pecs.

Fuck me and fuck me again.

"Claire is at the gate," he said accusingly.

I bit my lip. This was definitely my fault. I'd texted Claire and Mara with my new phone, making up some bullshit excuse about why I'd been incommunicado. I'd had a feeling neither of them bought it but I didn't dare tell them the truth for fear of involving them in what was obviously a deadly situation.

That Claire was at the gate — demanding to be let in from the sound of it — was just a testament to her loyalty. I didn't doubt that if Mara were closer, she'd be down at the gate demanding to be let in too.

I shrugged. "Let her in."

"If we let her in, we have to explain the security situation," Neo said.

"Obviously," I said. "But what's the alternative? I mean, we have no idea how long it's going to take to figure out who's working with your dad. Don't you think people will get suspicious if we lock ourselves on the property and refuse to tell anyone why?"

His expression grew stormy. "We didn't discuss this."

"I know," I said. "But it's not the first unexpected thing to happen and it probably won't be the last, so we're probably going to have to roll with the punches here. We can trust Claire."

"How can you be sure?" Neo asked.

"Because she's Claire," I said, reaching for the intercom.

Neo had my wrist in his hand before I knew what was happening. He backed me against the wall next to the intercom and pressed his hard body against mine.

His dick was like granite, grinding into my stomach as he stared down at me. "Maybe I don't want to let her in. Maybe I want you all to myself."

I heard the truth in his words. He was always willing to share with Rock and Oscar, but I often caught him staring at me with possession, and more than once when I slept alone, I woke up to find him watching me in my sleep, his eyes burning through the dark.

"You're going to keep Claire out there by the gate in the cold so you can fuck me alone in the kitchen?" I asked.

He closed a hand around my throat, his thumb stroking my pulse, and murmured against my neck. "Don't tempt me, Jezebel."

He used his free hand to punch a button on the intercom. "Let her in."

Chapter 29

Willa

Claire greeted me with relief and giant smothering hugs that were all too welcome given all that had happened since I'd last seen her before the cliff jump at the quarry.

She immediately took my hand and dragged me upstairs where we could talk alone, but I knew I was never really alone in the Kings' house, and I loaned her a swimsuit so we could sit in the hot tub instead.

We walked to the kitchen in our suits, passing the Kings, who were raiding the fridge for snacks. I made it clear this was a girls-only excursion and Claire and I stepped outside and walked carefully across an inch of slushy snow on the patio.

Getting the cover off the hot tub was easy enough and five minutes later we were sinking into the hot water, bubbles gurgling from the jets.

"I swear I wasn't angling for a hot tub invite," Claire said, tipping her head back. "But I am *definitely* not complaining. This feels amazing."

I laughed. "Definitely better than being cooped up inside."

"Tell me about it. It's only January and I already have cabin fever, especially after the last two weeks at home," she said. Her copper curls were already damp from the steam, her hazel eyes sparkling even in the faint light from the patio.

"It wasn't nice to see your family for the holidays?" I asked.

She rolled her eyes. "We are not talking about my boring family when you have been totally MIA for the past two weeks."

"I've been texting you!" I objected.

"You're hiding something," she said. "I know we haven't been friends for long, but I like to think we *are* friends. You've been putting me off for coffee at Cassie's for the past week, so either you're knee-deep in King dick or something's up. Probably both, in which case you owe me a *lot* of details."

It said a lot about my situation that I was more tempted to tell her about the King dick than all the other shit that was going on, especially since I'd once sworn I would never — and I did mean never — sleep with Neo.

But somehow, I didn't think that was going to cut it.

"I found out what happened to Emma," I said. Then I shook my head, because that wasn't quite right. "Not what happened to her exactly. More like I found out who happened to her."

Clara furrowed her forehead. "I'm not following."

"If I tell you, you have to swear you won't tell a single soul. Not Erin, not Quinn, no one."

I really didn't want to tell her anything, but she was right. We were friends. In fact, other than the Kings, she was the best friend I had at Aventine. As scared as I was to involve her with what was going on, I knew her: she wasn't going to give up until she had the truth.

She held up a hand like she was taking an oath. "I swear."

"Neo's dad was involved," I said.

"Involved how?"

"That's the part we don't know yet."

I told her everything. I told her how Emma had come to the Kings for help and then disappeared. I told her about going to see Mrs. Giordana and the binders with the maps of the woods and the cabins.

Then I told her about the home invasion and our escape to the island, followed by Roberto's assassination attempt on all of us.

The only thing I didn't tell her was how we'd holed up at Daisy's abandoned house, because that wasn't my secret to tell.

When I was done, she was staring at me with wide eyes through the steam in the Jacuzzi.

"Whoa," she said. "Neo's dad tried to kill you? All of you?"

"Twice, technically." His men had come way too close to getting us in the hospital.

"How is Neo taking it?" she asked.

I thought about all the things I knew about Neo and his father.

They weren't my secrets to tell either.

"I don't think it came as much of a surprise unfortunately," I said.

"Well, I guess now I know why there was a scary-looking man with a gun standing at the gate, acting like I was requesting an audience with the queen," she said.

"That would be why," I said. "And there are more like him in the woods, plus a generator to make sure no one can cut power to the alarm system again."

"What are you going to do now?" Claire said.

"I don't know," I said. "I just know Roberto wasn't in on this alone. There's no way he could have coordinated the disappearance of all those girls on his own," I said. "I feel like the answer is staring us in the face in those binders, but the cabins are all recorded as being owned by shell companies."

"Ugh. Say no more," she said.

Shell companies for our families were the modern

equivalent of mobsters who used to bury their cash. They were next to impossible to find unless you had some idea where to start.

"What about school?" Claire asked. "If the security set up here at the house is any indication, it kind of seems like you're not going anywhere."

"I'm sure the Kings would prefer it that way, but I'm definitely going back to school after the break," I said.

Claire lifted her eyebrows. "Do they know that?"

"Not yet." I'd been trying to think of the best way to bring up the subject. I knew the Kings were going to fight me, but there was no way I was staying imprisoned in the house for the next however many months it took us to figure out who was working with Roberto. I wasn't stupid enough to think we were out of danger, but the odds of Roberto trying to hit us on campus were slim. It was the only place other than the house that I felt like we were safe. "But they will."

Skepticism was written all over her face. "If you say so. They seem like bulldogs when it comes to you, but you know them better than I do."

She wasn't wrong, but I could be stubborn too.

"Let's talk about something else." It was bad enough that I would have to approach the Kings about going back to school. Why torture myself by talking about it with Claire? "How was your holiday?"

She rolled her eyes and sank lower into the water,

holding on to the edge of the hot tub behind her to stretch out her legs. "Like I said, boring. Except for the part where I found out Liam is going to be working in town for the next few months."

Liam was one of Claire's many brothers, but he usually worked with a crew out of Boston.

"Really? Why here?"

"It's so gross I don't even want to say it out loud," Claire said.

I laughed. "Well now you have to tell me."

Water dripped down her arms as she covered her face with her hands. "He's working at St. Andrew's."

"Is that... a church in town?" I asked.

She peered through her fingers. "You're kidding right?"

"I'm obviously missing something here," I said.

She dropped her hands back into the water. "St. Andrew's is the sex club in town."

I shook my head. "Okay, I feel like I'm missing a lot of somethings now. There's a sex club in town? And it's called St. Andrew's? And your brother is working there?"

"Yes to all of the above."

It took me a minute to connect the name of the club to the BDSM prop of the same name and I immediately conjured an image of the X-shaped piece of equipment used to strap someone down for fun and games.

Witty for a small town like Blackwell Falls, especially given the local conservative Catholic population.

I hoped they'd never gone to St. Andrew's to pray.

"How did I not know there was a sex club in Blackwell Falls?" I asked.

"Probably because the Kings want to keep you all to themselves," Claire said.

I couldn't argue that point.

"Why is your brother working there?" I asked. "Or do I not want to know?"

"It's just business," she said. "He's not *working there* working there."

"Got it," I said.

Our families liked to pretend like there were differences between them, but one thing was true of all of them — they were into all kinds of shit.

It didn't matter if it was the Italians, the bratva, the cartels, or the Irish — they all had controlling interests in everything from restaurants to finance companies to strip clubs.

And yes, sex clubs.

I grinned at Claire through the steam. "I guess it'll only be weird for you if you show up at St. Andrew's."

"That's the thing," she said. "Everybody goes to the Spring Fever masquerade at St. Andrew's. It's a tradition! Now I have to decide if I'm still going to go even if it means running into my big brother."

"Yikes," I said.

"Exactly."

Just a few months ago, I'd thought the strangest thing about Blackwell Falls was that Aventine, a private college for the kids of Mafia families, was the strangest thing about it.

Now I was starting to feel like it was just the tip of the iceberg.

Chapter 30

Willa

I was lying on the couch, my head in Oscar's lap, my feet across Rock's thighs, when I decided to make my move. It had been a week since Claire's visit and I'd been angling for the right moment to mention school to the Kings.

We'd just finished a two-episode *Love or Money* binge and the Kings seemed to be relaxing into the safety net provided by Rafe and his men.

Plus, school started next week, so it was kind of now or never.

"I never thought I'd say this," I started, "but I'm actually excited for school to start again."

In all my private rehearsals for the conversation I'd decided I may as well shoot for the moon with my opener.

Maybe they'd surprise me and just go along with my idea.

"I don't know why you'd be excited," Neo said from the chair across from the sofa, his voice cold. "You're not going back. Not until we find out who's working with my dad."

He never joined us on the sofa, preferring to watch me from afar, an amber-eyed falcon tracking a field mouse.

Except I was no mouse. I never had been.

"Your dad isn't going to execute — no pun intended — the hit on us on campus," I said. "It would be way too risky. The other families would lose their shit."

"Still not going back," Neo said.

Oscar stroked the hair back from my head. "We're just looking out for you, tiger. After what happened when we left the island, and again at the hospital, we can't take any chances."

"Agreed," Rock said, massaging my feet like it was some kind of consolation prize.

Traitor.

"It's actually not a request," I said. "You can't keep me prisoner here."

The tracker around my neck was one thing. I'd agreed to wear it. I hadn't signed up for indefinite house arrest, and I wasn't going to let Roberto take one more thing from me.

"Actually, we can." Neo flashed me a chillingly evil grin. "You might even enjoy being our prisoner."

Fuck me. He was right but it wasn't like I was going to tell him that.

Time to pull out the big guns.

I pretended to stretch, arching my back to give them a prime view of my braless tits under the skimpy tank top I was wearing over boxer shorts.

When I opened my eyes, their lust was so apparent I felt like I'd already been fucked.

They were hardly breathing when I slid my hands up my tank top to cup my tits.

I pinched my nipples, hard just from the knowledge that the Kings were watching, and parted my lips, wiggling my ass a little just to prove I was turned on.

It wasn't just for show. I'd felt slightly self-conscious at the thought of using my feminine wiles as a negotiating tool, but now that the Kings' hungry eyes were roaming my body, I was starting to wonder if I'd gotten in over my head.

Rock's hand slid up my calf. He got to my knee before I slapped his hand away.

"If I don't get what I want, you don't get what you want."

"Ow," he said. "That was a hard slap."

"Do you really think this is going to work, tiger?" Oscar asked. "Not to be indelicate, but we all know you're a horny little thing."

"Oh, I'm definitely horny," I said a little breathlessly. I slid one of my hands into my boxer shorts while I continued playing with one of my nipples. "Lucky for me, I can take care of that myself."

"If you think we're going to risk your safety because of this little show you're putting on, you're underestimating us," Neo said.

I met his gaze while I stroked through my wet folds. "Hmm-hmm," I murmured. "You're totally immune to my charms."

He had a point. A little tease wouldn't make them throw caution to the wind. They were right: I was too horny for that to be a long-term strategy. All they had to do was unleash their big dicks and I was fucked.

Literally.

But if we were going to negotiate, I might as well make it fun, and who was to say my little show wouldn't be the cherry on top that would push them over the edge.

Not that there was actually a cherry at this point.

My tank top rode up to expose my tits and I squeezed one of them while making circles on my clit with my other hand.

"Oh my god," I moaned. "I'm so wet."

Rock groaned on the other end of the sofa and scrubbed his face. "Fuck me."

"I'd love to," I said, stroking my cunt. "I can just imagine you fucking my ass. Or maybe my mouth."

Fuck him? Fuck me.

I hadn't expected it to be so hot to get myself off while they watched, forbidden to touch.

"Jesus fuck," Rock said.

"You act like we're the only ones missing out, tiger," Oscar said, looking down at me. "You forget that I know how much you love to feel my pierced dick buried in your sweet little pussy."

I moaned, sliding two fingers inside my soaking cunt. "I do really like that." I met Neo's gaze and was surprised I didn't spontaneously combust from the heat in his eyes. "Especially when Neo's cock is in my ass."

"This is ridiculous," Neo grumbled. His dick bulged in his jeans and he shifted uncomfortably in the chair.

"I agree," I gasped, an orgasm building at my center. "Roberto isn't going to fuck with us on campus and you know it."

"You're crossing a dangerous line mentioning my father while you get yourself off," Neo said, his expression murderous.

"I'd be screaming *your* name if you'd just listen to reason," I said.

"She has a point," Rock said. "And I'm not just saying that because my dick is about to explode."

"If we give in now," Neo said, "what's to prevent her from playing this little game the next time she wants something? Something more dangerous?"

I used my thumb to stimulate my clit while I plunged my fingers into my cunt. A strangled moan tore from my throat as my orgasm built. "You have my word this is the last time I'll make myself come to get what I want. You better hurry though, because I *am* going to come, and afterwards, I'm going to take a shower. Alone."

Oscar adjusted his visibly hard cock inside his sweatpants. "We can make her agree to certain rules." Was he sweating? "One of us walks her to and from every class, plus lunch. She doesn't even go to the bathroom without one of us outside."

"Good thinking," Rock said hurriedly, his eyes locked on my exposed tit. "We could even station one of Rafe's men in the parking lot in case we need quick backup."

"Mmmmm," I moaned, working my clit faster. "These all sound like good compromises." I looked at Neo as my orgasm built. "What do you think?"

He stared me down, our gazes locked as I climbed the peak to my climax.

"Hurry!" I gasped. "I'm going to come."

I was trying to hold off my release. They weren't the only ones who wanted to fuck now, and if I reached orgasm without their agreement, I would have to follow through on the solo shower on principle.

"Fine," Neo said. "We'll go back to school with all the rules we just discussed. And you keep your tracker on 24/7."

"Fuck," I moaned, giving all the attention to my clit as I imagined them all inside me. "I'm coming."

I cried out as the orgasm washed over my body, closing my eyes as I shuddered, lost in the pleasure I'd given myself with the help of their obvious lust.

When I opened my eyes, there was a moment of silence, all three of them staring at me like it was Thanksgiving and I was the awaited feast.

Neo's expression was stormy. "You're going to pay for that, Jezebel."

He stood and stripped off his clothes, his giant dick springing free.

Rock followed suit, although a little more slowly with one arm in a cast. Oscar stayed where he was, my head in his lap, but I could feel his hard dick at the back of my head.

Neo stalked toward the couch like a mountain lion. He reached down, took a hold of my shorts, and tugged.

They ripped like a piece of paper, lying open to reveal my lace underwear.

He knelt on the couch and grabbed my hips, and I locked my arms behind his neck as he lifted me up and sat on the couch so that I was straddling him.

Oscar wasted no time standing and taking off his clothes while Neo's gaze burned into mine. His cock was nestled against the thin fabric of my panties, stoking the embers of my desire as it pressed against my still-throbbing cunt.

"Get the lube," he ordered no one in particular.

Oscar left the room and returned with a clear bottle.

Behind the couch, Rock stroked his cock inches from my face, making his intentions clear while Neo lifted my tank top. He tossed it somewhere into the room, then closed his mouth around one of my tits.

I sank into the warmth with a moan right before he bit my nipple.

Hard.

"Ow! Fuck!" I threaded my hands into his thick hair and yanked. "That hurt."

"Not as much as it hurt to watch you make yourself come," he said against my tit. "I promised you were going to pay."

He reached down and pulled my underwear aside and I gasped as his dick came in contact with my pussy.

"Fuck, Jezebel," he said. "You are fucking *wet*."

Behind me, I felt the tip of Oscar's pierced dick against my ass. He must've been on his knees because when I turned my head his face was close enough to mine that he leaned in to give me a passionate kiss.

Neo grabbed on to my ass cheeks and spread me wide, causing his cock to slide between my folds, his head bumping against my clit.

Oscar broke our kiss and I felt Neo's dick press against the entrance to my cunt.

They were poised to enter me from two different directions and I was more than ready for it. Then Rock moved closer to the back of the couch, stroking his shaft as he offered me the head of his cock.

I closed my lips around it eagerly just as Neo sank into my cunt.

"Fuck yes," he groaned. "Nothing feels as good as your tight pussy."

I moaned around Rock's cock as he sighed with pleasure.

"Spread her wider for me," Oscar said, his breath hot on my shoulder.

Neo spread my ass cheeks wider, sinking deeper into my cunt, my clit rubbing against his base, and Oscar's pierced dick slid all the way into my ass, the barbell on Oscar's head stroking my walls on the way in.

I was completely filled with them: Rock fucking my mouth, Neo's massive cock buried in my cunt, Oscar's dick filling my ass.

It was almost too much pleasure to bear and another orgasm roared to life inside me as I moaned around Rock's cock. I was already close to coming again, my body primed and ready after the show I'd given the Kings, the sweet completion of finally having them inside me.

Rock hissed when I took him to the back of my throat. "Goddamn, kitten. I fucking love the way you take it all."

I held on to Neo's shoulders for leverage, bouncing faster on his dick, seeking the promised release. I was only vaguely aware that Oscar was pounding into me from behind, that it was going to hurt tomorrow.

Right then, I didn't care about anything but coming and feeling them come right along with me.

"I think Jezebel here wants to come," Neo grunted, still holding my ass cheeks open for Oscar.

"Good thing," Oscar said, "because I'm about to blow in her luscious ass."

Rock fucked my mouth faster, hitting the back of my throat as Neo and Oscar filled me everywhere else. It was pure bliss feeling all three of them sink all the way into my body only to drag out and drive in again and I panted as my orgasm gathered speed at my core.

"Fuck!" I said. "I'm going to come!"

Neo let go of my ass and cupped my tits, pulling one into his mouth and sucking as Oscar's hand came down on my ass.

It was the final straw and I tumbled over the edge into release.

Rock groaned, spilling into my mouth, and the taste of his hot salty semen only made my release more powerful, my body clamping down on Neo's and Oscar's dicks as they let go.

"Fuck yes, Jezebel," Neo growled.

Oscar drove into my ass hard and fast. "So. Fucking. Good."

It felt like my orgasm went on forever, my body exploding like a collapsing star, pleasure washing over me in waves until I was spent.

Rock removed his dick from my mouth and bent to kiss me. "Best blow job of my life."

"I bet you say that to all the girls," I said.

He chuckled and collapsed on the couch next to Neo.

I was still straddling him, his dick still hard inside me. He was a machine — a literal fucking machine — and I wasn't about to complain.

Oscar sat on the other side of him and pulled me off Neo's dick and across their bodies.

We were naked and sweaty, my upper body cradled by Oscar, Neo's lap under my ass, Rock back in position with my legs over his thighs, albeit a lot more relaxed than he'd been when I'd started this whole game.

Neo scowled down at me, worry furrowing his brow. "We didn't give in because of your little show."

"I know," I said, looking at him through half-closed eyes.

"If I thought we couldn't protect you, there's nothing we wouldn't do to keep you safe, including locking you up here," he said.

"I know."

There was something else in his eyes. Something that had been lurking between us for weeks.

Something I knew he'd probably never say.

But it didn't matter.

I know, I thought, looking into his eyes. *I know.*

Chapter 31

Willa

I followed every rule on our first day back at school. The fact that we'd come to an agreement in such an unusual way changed nothing. I knew the Kings would find a way to keep me home if I didn't honor our agreement.

Besides, there were worse things than being escorted around campus by my guys.

Whoa. Back the fuck up.

When had I started thinking of them as mine?

Problematic, but a worry for another time.

Class with Professor Ryan was as strange as ever, and I avoided his eyes even though his face was back to normal after the beating he'd taken at the hands of the Kings.

I had to negotiate with two of my teachers to make up finals I'd missed thanks to our hurried escape to the island, but thankfully, they were understanding about my *family emergency.*

I thought everyone would be talking about the cliff jump, then remembered that they'd had another week of school while the Kings and I were on the island.

Everyone had moved on to discussions of their vacations and I eavesdropped on conversations about Italy and Aspen, grateful I'd spent the time alone with the Kings. Our time on the island had ended horrifically, but the two weeks before that had been perfect and I wouldn't trade them for all the luxury vacations in the world.

By the time Oscar picked me up for lunch, I'd settled back into my old routine. Surrounded by homework assignments, dating gossip, and lectures, it was almost like the last month hadn't happened at all.

I emerged from English to find him leaning sexily against the brick wall, his camera raised.

I heard the click of the shutter as he took a picture of me.

"You have to stop doing that," I said. He'd been taking pictures of me constantly since being reunited with his Canon at the house. According to him, it wasn't as good as the Nikon he'd lost during Roberto's assassination attempt, but that hadn't stopped him from using it 24/7. "I'm starting to feel like I have a paparazzi problem."

He lowered the camera, and his rogue lock of dark hair fell over his forehead. "I'm making up for lost time. I lost a whole week taking pictures of you while we were at Daisy's house."

I locked my arm in his and he leaned down to kiss me. It was probably meant to be quick, but then his tongue met mine and the next thing I knew, I was shoved up against the brick wall, breathing heavy with Oscar's hard-on pressing against my stomach through my shirt.

His tongue stud did crazy things to my body and it took all of 3.5 seconds for me to contemplate reaching into his pants for his dick even though we were in public.

Then he pulled away and grinned down at me like he knew exactly what I was thinking. "Ready to eat, tiger?"

It was obvious that he wasn't talking about lunch.

"I said I'd let you walk me to class," I said. "I didn't agree to sexual innuendo."

He leaned down to murmur in my ear and I got a heady whiff of leather, black coffee, expensive cologne. "Consider it a bonus."

We made our way out of the building and continued onto one of the paths connecting the lecture halls to the Admin building. It was cold, the sky crystal clear overhead, and I tucked my chin into my jacket as we hurried across campus.

Oscar was watchful, the stiff set of his shoulders giving away his wariness. I still didn't think Roberto would make a move on campus, but I had to admit, I felt better with the Kings on alert.

I sighed with relief as we stepped into the Admin building, the warm air a welcome caress on my freezing skin. The halls were packed with students, most of them walking to and from the cafeteria, heads bent in conversation or laughter.

I relaxed a little, glad all over again that the Kings had agreed to let me go back to school. After weeks of chaos, I was in need of some serious normalcy.

We were approaching the doors to the luxe cafeteria when I saw Interim Dean Garcia standing outside, greeting students as they entered.

I'd only met her once, right after Dean Giordana had died in the fire at the cabin.

But she'd given me a strange feeling then and I had the same feeling now when her gaze met mine, like I was meeting the eyes of a friend through a crowd.

Recognition.

But that didn't make sense. She was just an administrator, someone hired by Aventine's board of directors to run the school until Dean Giordana could be permanently replaced.

Still, nerves twisted in my stomach as I approached her, her slim figure elegantly draped in a skirt suit that showed off surprisingly nice legs for her age.

"Willa," she said, smiling warmly, "how nice to see you. How was your holiday?"

"Um, it was nice, thanks. How about yours?"

"Restful, thankfully." I still thought it was weird that she knew my first name, but then she turned to Oscar and used his so maybe I was just being paranoid. "And how about you, Oscar? Did you enjoy the break?"

"Definitely," he said, pulling me past her into the cafeteria. "Have a good one."

"Okay," I said to him when we were out of earshot, "rude."

"She gives me the creeps," he said.

The cafeteria was a riot of noise and conversation, the dark wood-paneled walls and high-end dining tables and chairs no match for a bunch of hormonal twenty-somethings reunited after weeks spent with their parents and siblings.

We got in line and I grabbed my favorite Cobb salad while Oscar got a burger and fries, then we made our way to my usual table with Claire, Erin, Quinn, and a handful of other girls who were friendly but not friends.

I expected Oscar to peel off and join Rock and Neo at their usual table with the assortment of groupies who routinely draped themselves over the Kings, but when I looked over, their table was empty.

I didn't get a chance to ask why, because a second later Oscar looked past Claire, Erin, and Quinn at the other girls at our table.

"Time for you to go," he said to them.

I gaped up at him. "Wow, you really are rude today. You can't just order them to leave."

"I can. I did." He looked back at the girls. "Nothing personal."

"I'm sorry," I said to the girls as they gathered their things and stood to leave. It was already clear from the tone in Oscar's voice that it wasn't a request, and even on a good day, no one was eager to defy the Kings.

He took one of the open seats and I claimed my usual place next to Claire, who was staring wide-eyed at Oscar.

"I mean, you're always welcome at our table, but what's the occasion?" Claire asked.

"The occasion is we sit here now." The answer came from Neo, looking scary as fuck as he slid into the vacant chair next to Oscar.

I was glad the girls had left when they did. Better to face Oscar than Neo, who looked more than ready to take on anyone who so much as looked at him the wrong way.

Rock came next, ambling over like he didn't have a care in the world despite his broken arm, all tanned blond gorgeousness and blindingly white teeth.

"Hey there, ladies," he said, sitting next to Neo. "You don't mind do you?"

"Would it matter if we did?" Quinn asked, her dark brows raised in amusement. Her curls were pushed back from her forehead with one of her colorful scarves, her makeup on point as usual, highlighting her perfect bone structure and gorgeous brown eyes.

"No, but I try to be polite," Rock said.

I sighed and turned to Quinn and Erin. "Hey. How was your break?"

"It was fun," Erin said. Her short hair had grown out a little since I'd seen her last, giving her elfin features an adorably shaggy frame. "We went skiing in Park City."

"That sounds fun," I said.

"I was in Bermuda until two days ago," Quinn said.

"Lucky bitch," Claire said.

I laughed. "Seriously."

The only thing better than being on an isolated windswept island with the Kings would be being on a tropical beach with warm water and umbrella drinks with the Kings.

"You're just in a bad mood because Liam is working at St. Andrew's," Quinn said.

"Wouldn't you be in a bad mood if your brother was working at the town sex club?" Claire asked.

"Oh I'd kill myself," Quinn said.

"I just don't understand why they would transfer him from Boston to Blackwell Falls," Erin said. "Isn't that, like, some kind of demotion?"

Erin and Claire both came from Irish crime families. They'd grown up together, which was probably why they bickered like sisters most of the time.

Claire rolled her eyes. "It's not a demotion. They're just cycling him through RAA's holdings. They do that with everybody. You know that."

It took me a minute to register what she'd said. Then, I wondered if I'd imagined it.

"What did you just say?" I asked.

She waved away my question. "It's what they do in our family when they're training soldiers for leadership. They cycle them through all the major holdings so they have a handle on the business operations at a high level."

"You said RAA," I reminded her.

"That's because all our holdings are funneled through shell companies," she said. "Come on, Willa. You know this. All the families do it."

I felt like time had stopped. The noise in the cafeteria receded as the reality of what she was saying made its way through the shock echoing through my mind.

"You're saying RAA is one of the Irish family's holding companies?" I asked.

"It's the one that owns most of our properties," she said. "There are others for finance and such. Is this really a surprise to you?"

I spent more hours than I could count poring over the binders from Dean Giordana's study. The names next to the cabins around Aventine — cabins like the one owned by Roberto Alinari — were burned into my memory.

Genarro.

Neon Corp.

Global LTD.

RAA.

I put down my fork and looked at Neo, who must've had some kind of instinct for big moments, because he was already staring at me.

I tried to keep my voice steady. "I need to talk to you alone."

Chapter 32

Oscar

We flew up the snow-covered trail, the headlights of our snowmobiles cutting a path through the darkness. Ahead and behind us, I heard the whine of engines as the other houses made their way towards the quarry.

The pressure of Willa's arms around my waist, her thighs pressed against mine behind me, called forth the possessiveness I usually tried to ignore.

One word beat a rhythm through the noise of the snowmobiles.

Mine.

It wasn't true. A more accurate word would be *ours.*

It didn't have quite the same ring to it. But I could live with it.

Up ahead, Neo eased off the gas, the snowmobile he was driving slowing as we approached the clearing at the top of the cliffs. Rock hadn't been thrilled about being his passenger, but he hadn't had much choice given his broken arm.

I slowed down and cruised to a stop next to Neo's snowmobile, satisfied by the fact that the guys we'd sent up to prepare the site had done their job. A clearing had been shoveled in our normal spot and a massive fire already raged in the center, sparks drifting upward into the dark winter night.

A crowd had already gathered, everybody bundled in winter clothes, some of them drinking from thermoses while others tipped flasks to their mouths.

No one was up for dragging coolers through the snow.

I cut the engine on the snowmobile and waited for Willa to climb off, then immediately missed the heat of her body against mine.

I couldn't fucking get enough of her. I didn't want to break the habit even though it was going to hurt like a motherfucker when she left.

I climbed off after her and turned to remove her helmet. She looked adorable bundled up in snow clothes, her hair tousled, and I pulled off one of my gloves to touch her face.

Her skin was cold against my warm palm and I rubbed my thumb along her full lower lip before kissing her.

She opened for me, her tongue dancing with mine, and I immediately got hard because that was what always happened when Willa touched me, kissed me, so much as fucking looked at me.

I broke the kiss and smiled down at her. "That's going to get us into trouble."

"I think I'm starting to like trouble," she said.

She meant it to be lighthearted but the words scared the fuck out of me. We'd been determined to remind Willa of who she was. Remind her that she wasn't meant to be some wallflower hiding in Emma's shadow.

We wanted her to remember that she was strong. Now she had and I couldn't help feeling like we'd lifted the lid on Pandora's box.

Maybe we should have sent her away a long time ago. Maybe it would've been better if she'd stayed afraid. Now she was determined to see the hunt for Emma's killer — we all knew she was dead, Willa included — through to the end.

That scared the fuck out of me too.

"Let's go you two," Neo barked, hanging his helmet on the handle of his snowmobile.

He was right. We had business to attend to.

Important business.

But even if that hadn't been true, I knew Neo would have been eager to put distance between me and Willa. He was willing to share but it was pretty common knowledge that in a perfect world, Willa would belong only to him.

I understood the sentiment and I was pretty sure Rock did too.

For fifteen years, Willa had belonged to us all, a communal muse who lived in our dreams.

Now that she was with us, a living breathing embodiment, it wasn't always easy to share. Deep down I knew it wouldn't be the same without my brothers, but fuck if I didn't sometimes want her to myself.

"I thought you said there were other locations for the games in winter," Willa said as we crunched our way over the snow to join the others gathered around the bonfire.

I lifted my camera and snapped a picture of her, then grinned as she rolled her eyes.

She looked hella cute in pink snow pants and a matching pink coat with fur trim on the hood, not to mention her furry boots, which conjured up all kinds of sexy images of her in them and nothing else.

"There are," Rock said.

"Then why are we here?" she asked, taking in the clearing and fire. "It looks like a lot of trouble."

"This is where all the most important games have happened," Neo said. "And this is the most important game of all."

Willa nodded her understanding. She knew as well as anyone how important the next step would be.

Neo greeted the other houses on the way to the other side of the bonfire. There was no music this time, as if the other houses, the ones who'd gotten here before us, knew something was up.

"See you on the flip side, kitten," Rock said, leaning down to give Willa a quick kiss on the lips.

I followed him and Neo and watched as Willa made her way to a group from the Queens' house on the other side of the fire.

Another pack of snowmobiles roared to a stop next to the ones parked at the edge of the clearing. I knew even before their drivers pulled off their helmets that they were from the Knights' house.

The Russians were all fucking huge.

Alexa climbed off the back of one of the snowmobiles and followed the men to the bonfire.

For the first time I had doubts about our strategy. I wanted to believe the other houses would care as much as we did about the missing girls, but what if they didn't?

What if they saw Emma Russo — daughter of the Italian family, of a traitor no less — as not their problem? What if they saw the other Bellepoint girls as disposable?

It would be depressing as hell, but beyond that, we would have tipped off the wrong people to what we had discovered.

I stuffed the thoughts down. We didn't have a choice. We had to try and get the other houses behind us if we wanted to catch the men — and they were almost certainly men — who had killed Emma and the other Bellepoint girls.

"Hear ye, hear ye," Neo shouted.

Everyone got quiet, their gazes swiveling to where he stood at one side of the fire.

"It's time to talk game four, and in case this meeting spot hasn't tipped you off, this one is important," he said.

I met Willa's eyes across the clearing. This was it. After this, everyone would know what we had discovered.

They would either become our allies or our enemies.

And looking at Willa, her face finally healed from Roberto's assassination attempt, my instinct to protect her more powerful than my own survival, I wasn't sure we could handle any more enemies.

Chapter 33

Willa

Neo paced in front of the fire, his expression dark. I had no idea what he was going to say, how he was going to bring the other families to our side.

Maybe he didn't know either. Maybe that's why he seemed at a loss for words, a first as far as I was concerned.

He turned to face the crowd, silent and tense, like they knew something was about to change.

"*Famiglia oltre il sangue.*" He didn't shout it like he usually did. They were just words, spoken with a silent weight.

Everybody looked at each other uncertainly, clearly not sure whether this was one of those times when they were supposed to shout it back.

"We say it, but do we mean it?" Neo asked them.

Asked us.

"What is going on?" Quinn murmured next to Claire.

I hadn't told a single soul what we'd figured out since Claire dropped the bomb about RAA in the cafeteria.

Not Claire. Not Mara.

No one.

The Kings and I had decided it was too risky to let the rumor mill take control of the narrative. We needed to get in front of it, deliver the message to everyone at once and get a read on their reaction.

"What if we had to choose?" Neo asked them. He scanned the crowd, meeting the eyes of our peers. "What if we had to choose between family — the ones who sent us here — and honor? What if we had to choose between the families that sent us here and this one, this family?"

Claire met my eyes and lifted her eyebrows in silent question.

I shook my head and looked down at the ground. I felt bad about keeping her in the dark, especially since she was the one who'd helped me put the final piece of the puzzle into place.

"You all know that Emma Russo disappeared two years ago," Neo continued. "She wasn't technically a student at Aventine, but she was one of us, and she was last seen on our campus. What you may not know is that she wasn't the first girl to go missing here. Other girls have gone missing from Bellepoint over the years, made to look like they left voluntarily."

"What the fuck does this have to do with our game?" one of the Rooks yelled from the crowd.

Neo's eyes flashed. "It has everything to do with our game. Because in a minute I'm going to ask you all to do something you've never been asked to do before. Something that will make you a traitor to your families."

A murmur rolled through the crowd and I heard someone say, "What the fuck?"

"It's come to my attention that someone in the Alinari Mafia family is responsible for the disappearance of Emma Russo, and probably the other girls too," Neo said.

A collective gasp rose from the crowd like a gust of wind.

"But my family isn't the only family responsible," Neo said.

My heart pounded in my chest like a war drum. After this, the target on our backs would be bigger than ever.

And Roberto wouldn't be the only one aiming for it.

Neo looked at the crowd, his gaze settling on the leaders of every house but the Queens.

Alexa Petrov was a massive bitch but her father was the head of the Russian family, and the other Queens had loyalties of their own. In this game, they would have to work with the Rooks, Knights, and Saints.

"There is at least one member of every family represented here who's been party to the disappearance of Emma and the other girls." Neo let that sink in for a minute before he continued. "Take that in. Someone in your families has been kidnapping girls up here, probably killing them, and they've been doing it for years."

"Yo, this is bullshit," one of the Saints shouted. "I don't give a fuck who you are, you keep talking shit about our families you're going to be the one who disappears."

I held my breath, half expecting Neo to lose his shit. Instead, he nodded slowly, his gaze burning with conviction.

"You're with the Rojas family out of Columbia, right?" Neo asked the guy who'd spoken.

He nodded and held up two fingers in a peace sign. "Rojas forever."

His buddies jostled him good-naturedly before Neo spoke again.

"Your shit is held under Neon right?" Neo asked. "All your big shit anyway."

The guy looked stricken. "So?"

The fake companies set up by each of the families weren't common knowledge, but it hadn't been difficult to connect the dots once we knew what we were looking for.

"Before the fire that killed Dean Giordana, there were four cabins in the woods surrounding Aventine," Neo said. "We have reason to believe the missing girls were taken there before they were killed. The one that burned down was owned by the Alinari family. The other three are owned by Neon Corporation, Global Limited, and RAA Holdings."

The last couple words in his sentence were drowned out by the commotion as everyone realized that he was implicating their families in the disappearance of the girls.

Neo held up a hand to quiet everyone. When that didn't work, Oscar let out a piercing whistle.

"Shut the fuck up!" Oscar shouted.

"I don't know why this would be so hard to believe given all the other shit our families are into," Neo said. "But I figured it would be a hard sell, so Rock is going to hand you a map of the cabins."

Rock reached into his parka and removed a roll of papers held together by a rubber band.

"Each of the cabins are labeled with the names of the recorded owners, all of which are shell companies owned by our families," Neo said. "I don't know what the fuck has been going on up here, but I can take a guess, and even with all the shady shit that's a part of our business, I don't want any part of kidnapping and murdering girls. I'm hoping you don't either."

"This doesn't prove anything," one of the Knights said, looking up from the piece of paper Rock had given him.

"No," Neo said. "The proof is up to you. And that brings me to game number four."

"I'm so confused," Erin said. "What is he saying?"

Claire rolled her eyes. "He's saying someone in all of

our families is involved in the disappearance of the missing girls." She looked at me. "You figured it out because of what I said about Liam working for RAA, didn't you?"

I nodded. "Sorry I couldn't tell you sooner. I wanted to check my theory with the Kings and then we were worried word would get out before we could give everyone the details."

She reached for my hand and looked at me, her eyes full of sympathy. "Emma... I'm so sorry, Willa."

I had to force air into my lungs against the crush of grief that threatened to collapse them.

Deep down, I'd always known something terrible had happened to Emma, but there had always been a sliver of hope that it was something else. Maybe she'd disappeared on her own after all, like my mom said. Or maybe she'd wandered off a cliff on her way back to Bellepoint.

It wasn't that I loved either of those possibilities, but somehow they'd seemed less horrific than the possibility that someone had taken her.

That they'd hurt her.

That they'd killed her.

I squeezed Claire's hand because I didn't trust myself to say anything.

"Game number four is mandatory," Neo said. "Anyone who doesn't complete it by the end of the year forfeits this game and all games for the next five years."

I'd thought the earlier commotion was chaotic but it

was nothing compared to the shouting and shoving that ensued next.

"You can't do that..."

"Who does he think he is?"

"Fuck him."

Neo's expression remained determined. "Game number four. Each house must ferret out the person or persons who participated in the kidnapping and murder of Emma Russo and the other girls from Bellepoint. Once confirmed, each house will bring us the name or names."

"This is so weird," Erin said. "Usually the games get more dangerous as we get closer to the end of the year."

"Oh my god," Claire said, clearly exasperated. "How can someone so dense manage to survive in this world?"

Usually I felt sorry for Erin when Claire treated her like a dumbass, but in this case I couldn't really blame Claire for her frustration.

"This is the most dangerous game of all," Quinn explained. "If someone catches any of us digging for dirt on our own families, we're dead."

Erin's eyes widened. "Oh..."

"This could get us killed," Yury, one of the big Russians, said.

"So can jumping off the cliff into the quarry," Neo said. "So can almost every game we play at the end of every year. This time it's for a good cause, and we're giving you extra time because we know it might take a while."

"Gee, thanks," someone muttered.

"I know this isn't easy, and we all know this one isn't about the game. The game is nothing compared to family loyalty. But some lines shouldn't be crossed — even by us — and family loyalty is nothing compared to dishonor." He paused. "I'm asking you to think about the future of our families, about whether this is what you want them to be or whether we want to retain some semblance of humanity."

Damn. Neo was sounding... eloquent? Convincing?

"And there's one more rule," he continued. "No one here says a word about this to anyone. If word gets out, we are all fucked and they'll start covering their tracks so we can never make them pay."

"What's the penalty for being a rat?" Alexa asked.

"We're a rat either way," Carlos, one of the Saints, said. "If we give up our families, we're a traitor to them. Now you're saying if we tell them what's going on we're traitors to each other?"

"No one said it wasn't complicated," Neo said. "I'm hoping to appeal to your sense of honor here."

"What if honor's not enough?" Alexa asked. "What's the penalty for warning our families you know what they've been up to?"

Neo scanned the crowd, letting his gaze linger on the leaders. "The penalty is death. Anyone who rats out our mission to their families dies, just like those girls probably died. Except this time it'll be by my hand. By the Kings' hands."

I expected the crowd to erupt again, but they were quiet, the gravity of the situation sucking all the protest out of them.

"The game begins now and ends when we have all the names," Neo said. *"Famiglia oltre il sangue."*

The crowd repeated it, albeit with less enthusiasm than usual.

I repeated it too, but in my head, I was thinking of Emma and repeating a different motto.

Sic Semper Tyrannis.

Down with tyrants.

Chapter 34

Willa

A week after the announcement of game four at the quarry, I woke up to the telltale cramping of my stomach.

Normally I would have cursed the powers that be for the inherent unfairness of getting my period. This time I was actually relieved. The Kings and I had been playing fast and loose with birth control, not just since Roberto's assassination attempt when it might have been an understandable oversight, but before that on the island.

We used it sometimes, but on other occasions we were too worked up to bother.

My brain cursed me for being irresponsible but another part of me, a part I didn't want to admit existed, wondered if I was intentionally playing with fire.

If the Kings were intentionally playing with fire too.

If I got pregnant, it wouldn't make sense to leave.

But I wanted to leave.

Didn't I?

Laying in bed, my stomach cramping, I tried to conjure the version of myself that had arrived at Aventine determined to find out what had happened to Emma and GTFO ASAP.

But that version of myself felt like a stranger. She was so naïve, not just about the evil lurking in her own family, but about her own desires — and not just her sexual desires either, although I was more than willing to admit I'd had no idea how much I would enjoy being fucked senseless by the Kings.

Back then, I'd thought my biggest desire was to find out what had happened to Emma and move on, maybe pick up my travels again.

Now leaving was the last thing I wanted to do. I couldn't imagine going a day without some smart-ass remark from Neo accompanied by his smoldering gaze, Oscar's hands on my face as he looked into my eyes, Rock's smile that lit up my world.

Was I rolling the dice on birth control to give myself an excuse to stay?

Did they even want me to stay?

I remembered the first time I'd fucked Neo after the cliff jump, the way he'd asked me if I wanted him to get a condom, the look in his eyes when he'd promised to always take care of me.

Except I wasn't one of those girls who'd been imagining a fancy wedding since I was five years old, a knight in shining armor to protect and provide while I baked cookies with a gaggle of kids. I'd never needed anyone to take care of me.

So why did the thought of staying with the Kings, who would insist on taking care of me in all kinds of ways, suddenly seem appealing?

I sighed into my empty bedroom. It was all way too heavy for first thing in the morning and definitely way too heavy for the first day of my period, which always sucked the most.

I went to the bathroom to take care of business and crawled back into bed. I just wanted to go back to sleep.

I texted the Kings in a group chat to let them know I was going to sleep in, then dozed off like it was midnight instead of first thing in the morning.

I woke up to the sound of my phone ringing with a video call from the nightstand. I had no idea how long I'd been asleep but it was rare for someone to call instead of text so I picked up my phone and looked at the display.

Mara.

Ugh. It wasn't that I didn't l want to talk to Mara. She was still my best friend and I knew from our texts that she was still struggling at Columbia.

But talking to her had become a kind of tap dance. I hadn't told her about Roberto trying to kill us when we'd left the island, and that meant I couldn't tell her about the time we'd spent at Daisy's house.

And if I couldn't tell her about any of those things, I couldn't tell her about game number four either.

I didn't want to worry her and there was no way she wouldn't be worried if I told her the truth because she wasn't a fucking idiot. She was part of the Alinari crime family through her parents, and she'd understand the danger we were in, even more now that we were on the hunt for the men from the other houses that were working with Roberto.

Still, she didn't call enough for me to justify not picking up the phone. That would worry her too, and right now, my biggest goal after keeping her from getting involved in my mess was to keep her from worrying.

I answered the call and waited for Mara's face to appear.

"Hey!" I said.

"Hi!" There was a note of false cheerfulness in her voice and she looked worse than I felt, her curly hair a tangled mess, dark circles shadowing her brown eyes.

"Long time no see," I said. I'd been leaning on texts as a way to avoid talking face-to-face. Mara knew me too well and I wasn't at all convinced I'd be able to assure her everything was cool.

"Right? That's why I decided to call," she said.

"I'm glad you did," I said. "It's so nice to see your face. I miss you."

"I miss you too, and I figured if I called you wouldn't be able to bullshit me anymore."

I sat up and leaned against the headboard. "What are you talking about?"

She looked insulted. "Seriously? I've known you my whole life. You've been texting me bullshit because there's something you don't want to say."

I considered my options and quickly came to the conclusion that they all sucked. I still didn't want to tell Mara the truth but I also couldn't continue to lie. At this point, it would be a form of gaslighting, and I wasn't down for that.

"There's just a lot going on here," I said. "And I really can't say any more than that."

"Is it about Emma?" she asked. "Did you find something out?"

"You could say that. But not enough to know what actually happened."

I was being vague but there was no way around it. Not if I wanted to protect Mara.

She rolled her eyes, clearly frustrated. "Whatever."

"What's that supposed to mean?"

"Just that ever since you went to Aventine it's like we're not best friends anymore," she said. "You go through the motions and everything but it's obvious you don't trust me."

"It has nothing to do with trust," I said. "This is some heavy shit. Girls have disappeared." I had to force myself to say the next thing. "Girls have died."

Her eyes widened. "Did you... did you find out more about what happened to Emma?"

"No, but come on, Mara. We all know she's probably dead. It's been two years. At this point, we're looking for her killer and probably the killer of all those other girls too."

I was relieved when she didn't try to argue the point. She'd probably come to the same conclusion a lot sooner than I had.

"I'm sorry," she said. "I wish I was there to give you a hug."

"Me too." I said it even though I didn't mean it. Until we figured out who was behind the disappearance of the girls, I didn't want Mara anywhere near Blackwell Falls. "Let's talk about something else. How are you? How is it being back at school?"

I knew from our text conversations that she'd had an excruciating holiday break with her extended family in Florida. She'd sounded miserable and she looked just as miserable now.

Actually, Mara had seemed miserable pretty much every day since the first day of classes at Columbia. In any other situation, I would have been on a train months ago to check on her in person.

Yet more proof that I'd been a shitty best friend.

She shrugged and looked down, a gesture I recognized as one she made when she was picking at something, trying to act casual to avoid a difficult subject. "You know, it's school. It's fine."

"Now who's bullshitting?" I asked.

"I mean, I don't love it. I said that. But I need to see it through this year and then maybe think about transferring."

"If you're not happy, you should transfer," I said. "Where are you thinking?"

My cramps had intensified since waking up from my morning nap and I was desperate for some aspirin, but the call with Mara was too important to put off, and I was afraid to start moving around in case she used it as a distraction to avoid a subject she clearly wasn't eager to discuss.

"Well, you made it pretty clear you don't want me to come to Aventine, so I'm not sure," she said.

I sighed. "I thought we settled that. I never said I don't want you here. I just said that things are weird here right now. It isn't safe for anyone."

"You're there," she pointed out.

"Because I have to be," I said. "For Emma."

"Your turn to bullshit again I guess," Mara said. There was an unusual bite to her words. Mara and I hardly ever fought, but I could feel her resentment through the phone.

"I think we both know you settled in there just fine. Just admit it and stop making it all about Emma."

I felt called out, and rightly so. "I've gotten used to being here, that's true. I didn't expect it and it's still hard to believe sometimes, but I've started to feel at home here."

"Because of the Kings?" she asked.

A few months ago she wouldn't have been able to mention the Kings without throwing in some sexual innuendo, but all the playfulness had gone out of our friendship.

"That's a big part of it," I said, wanting to be honest with her about something at least.

"So you're a thing now?" she asked.

"More or less," I said.

"With one of them or all of them?"

I covered my eyes with one hand, feeling weirdly embarrassed to admit my relationship with all three Kings.

Maybe it was because I'd sworn I'd never fuck Neo. Maybe it was because it still felt weird to admit to having a sexual relationship with three friends at the same time.

Either way, I could barely utter the next sentence.

"All of them," I said.

"All of them all at once?" she asked. "Or all of them separately?"

I peeked through my fingers. "All of the above?"

A smile finally broke through her gloomy expression. "You dirty whore."

"Guilty," I said, glad to be back on safer ground.

"Wow," she said. "So how does that work? Do they take turns? Is it always a group of you? Do any of them get jealous?"

I laughed. "That's a lot of questions. I don't know... It just works. Sometimes we're all together and other times it's just one or two of them. I think maybe they get a little jealous every now and then but it still works."

"Girl, I'm so jealous I feel like I'm turning green," Mara said.

"Nothing stopping you from finding a little fan club of your own," I said.

"Ugh," she said. "The guys here suck. And I know you think I shouldn't come for a visit, but I could really use it. I wasn't kidding when I said I miss you."

I saw it in her face and felt like the worst friend ever for what I was about to say next. "I meant it when I said I missed you too. But I'm basically not even allowed out of the house except for school. Too dangerous apparently."

It was depressing just to say it out loud. I had no idea how long it would take the other houses to name the psychopaths who'd helped Roberto. It had been one thing to be told I had to stay at the Kings' house after the week we'd spent at Daisy's.

Back then it had felt like being consigned to a five-star hotel compared to the drafty old house at the top of the falls.

But we'd been back for almost three weeks. It was almost February, the days long and dark, the sun still setting early. The thought of being stuck in the house for weeks or even months made me want to scream even though I objectively had the three hottest roommates known to man.

"We wouldn't have to go anywhere," Mara said. "I just want to see you, hang out a little."

I knew the Kings wouldn't go for it and I wasn't even sure I had the bandwidth to entertain Mara. So much had happened since I'd last seen her at my mom and Roberto's wedding, and it felt impossible to bridge the gap in the middle of what felt like a fight for my life.

"I want that too, I promise," I said. "But it's not a good idea right now. There's just too much going on and too much up in the air. Maybe we could talk more often? Have a standing video date on Sundays or something?"

"Sure." She was trying to be cheerful but the disappointment was written all over her face. "Sundays sound good."

"Great!" Now I was the one forcing myself to be cheerful, a pathetic cover for the guilt seeping through my body like an ink stain. "We can have coffee together or something."

"Sounds good." Her gaze drifted upward for a few seconds — like someone had entered the room — before returning to the screen. "I have to run, but I'll see you Sunday. Love you."

I started to tell her I loved her too but the screen went dark before I finished my sentence.

I stared at my phone. Shit. I was going to have to do some serious cleanup when I was done at Aventine. With Mara and the rest of my life, which was starting to feel like one big mysterious question mark.

Chapter 35

Willa

I was trying to decide whether to go downstairs and forage for food in the kitchen when a knock sounded at my bedroom door.

"Come in," I called.

The door opened and Rock stepped into the room carrying a tray loaded with covered dishes and a vase holding a single giant sunflower.

"Thought you might be getting hungry," he said, kicking the door closed behind him.

"Please don't tell me you did all that yourself with one hand," I said, eying his broken arm, still in a cast.

"I wasn't planning to," he said, setting the tray carefully on the bed with his good hand.

"You don't have to do all of this you know," I said.

"You know better than that, kitten. I don't do anything because I have to."

It said a lot about how much my life had changed in the past few months that I wasn't surprised to see a stack of books on the tray. The first time Rock had brought me food and books I'd been shocked.

I hadn't even realized the Kings knew I liked to read.

But over the past few months, they'd surprised me more than once with items from my wish list, and from looking at the titles stacked on the tray, this was one of those times.

"Do you keep some kind of closet stacked with my favorite things for times like this?" I asked.

"I'm afraid not." He seemed to think about it. "Although that's not a bad idea."

"So how did you know I'd be laid up today?" I asked.

An indignant expression crossed his face. "Babe, really? You don't think we know when you're due to get your period?"

I closed my eyes and shook my head, not sure whether to be embarrassed, mortified, or impressed. "Wow, that's... nice? Creepy?"

"Whatever you want to call it, we just want to make sure you're taken care of," he said, sitting carefully on the edge of my bed to keep the tray from tipping over.

I lifted one of the covers off the tray and was hit with a face full of steam and the delicious salty scent of chicken and broth.

"I brought you some of that chicken soup you like," he said. "With the curry. And there are homemade rolls with butter. And make sure to drink the tea. The ginger is supposed to help with cramping."

I noticed two small capsules on the tray and picked one up to read the tiny writing. "You brought me Midol?"

He rolled his eyes like I was silly for being surprised. "Eat the food, drink the tea, and take the Midol. Then you can sleep, and I bet you'll feel a lot better."

I sank carefully back onto the pillows against my headboard, wondering what kind of nirvana I'd stumbled into and how it was possible that getting my period was starting to seem almost enjoyable.

"You're the best," I said.

"I like taking care of you." His blue eyes were filled with sincerity.

I reached for his hand. "I want to make sure you're taken care of too."

He flashed me a roguish grin. "I'm more than taken care of by you, kitten."

I rolled my eyes. "You know what I mean."

"Just having you here is all I need." He reached out to tuck a loose piece of hair behind my ear. "I didn't realize how dead this house was until you came to live here."

"What do you mean?"

"There were people here and everything, lots of noise

and parties. But when I look back on it all, it just feels like one big distraction."

"Distraction? From what?" I asked.

"From the fact that you weren't here," he said. "It didn't feel like home until you walked through the door."

It was such a simple thing to say but it held so much meaning, and I swallowed the lump that had lodged itself in my throat.

"I feel the same way," I admitted. "I mean, obviously not about the house, but about my life. I was so busy traveling and meeting people. On the outside my life probably looked so exciting, but when I look back, I think I was trying to distract myself too. Not just from Emma's disappearance but from the fact that something big was missing."

He grinned. "Are you saying that something big was me?"

I laughed. "You, Oscar, Neo. All of you." I shook my head. "I just didn't expect it."

"It didn't come as a surprise to me. I've been in love with you for half my life."

I blinked in surprise. I was in love with him too — in love with all of them — but I still hadn't figured out the etiquette of telling them all. Should I tell them separately or in a group? Was there an advice column for this kind of thing?

I made a mental note to search the internet.

"You have?" I asked.

"I'm surprised you sound surprised," he said. "I thought it was pretty obvious."

I reached out to touch his face and he leaned in to kiss me. When he pulled away, he stroked my cheek with his thumb.

I stared into his sea-blue eyes and decided to go for it. "I love you too." I took a deep breath. I didn't want to mislead him. "Is it weird to say I'm in love with all of you?"

"Fuck no," he said. "You're entitled to your feelings, whatever they are, and I hope you never let anyone tell you anything different."

"I haven't told Oscar and Neo how I feel yet."

He smiled. "Are you saying I'm the first person who got to hear 'I love you' from those beautiful lips?"

I nodded. "I guess I'm just not sure how it's all done."

"It's done however you want it to be done," Rock said. "Although I'm not going to blow smoke up your ass. I'm pretty fucking happy to be the first one."

I laughed. "Don't go bragging. I don't want to hurt anyone's feelings."

"My lips are sealed." He leaned in to give me another quick kiss. "Now eat your food and get some rest."

He stood to leave, and even while crampy and on my period, it was impossible not to acknowledge the utter perfection of his tanned face and the perfect body on display in his jeans and T-shirt.

"Totally off topic," I said, "but how long do you think it will take the other houses to find the people involved in the disappearance of the girls?"

He thought about it. "If they work fast? A couple of weeks. But it could also be months. What we're asking them to do is dangerous and difficult, especially since most of their parents live in other cities. Why?"

I sighed, thinking about Mara, about how complicated it was going to be to manage my life without being able to leave the Kings' house. "I know going back to school was a big deal, but no offense, I'll go crazy if the only place I can go for months is school."

"I know it sucks," he said, "but it's for your own safety."

It wasn't like I could argue the point after what had happened when we'd left the island.

"I know," I said, hearing the dejection in my own voice. "I appreciate it. It's just hard."

"I'm sorry, kitten." He flashed me another grin. "If it makes you feel any better, we're determined to make it hella fun for you here at the house."

I laughed again. It was impossible to be depressed in Rock's presence. "I know all about your *fun*. Now get out and let me enjoy my books and food."

"You're the boss, kitten," he said. "For today anyway."

His implication was clear and I was suddenly counting down the days left on my period.

Because while I didn't love being bossed around on an everyday basis, when it came to being ordered around by the Kings in bed?

I was all fucking in.

Chapter 36

Rock

I headed down the stairs back to the kitchen, Willa's question — which amounted to, *How long am I going to be trapped in this house?* — echoing in my mind.

It was a reasonable question and one we probably hadn't thought about hard enough.

Part of it was because we were so preoccupied with keeping her safe. The other part was that it didn't seem like a big deal, because whether Willa knew it or not, the same rules didn't apply to us.

Neo, Drago, and I were confident in our ability to protect ourselves and willing to take the risks of leaving the house for a destination other than campus. We'd been having groceries delivered and asking Reva to bring us things, but we'd each been to Blackwell Falls for varying reasons while Willa had been stuck at the house. Not only was it not fair but eventually Willa would get wind of the fact that we weren't subject to the same restrictions, and then all hell would break loose.

"How's she feeling?" Drago asked when I returned to the kitchen.

He was sitting at the island and nursing a beer while Neo moved around in basketball shorts and a wifebeater, making his post-workout smoothie.

"Not great," I said. "Hopefully the tea and Midol will help."

"And the books," Drago said. "If she's feeling better later we can watch a movie."

"We can watch that one she likes," Neo said. "The one with the kissing in the rain."

I did a double take because was this Neo suggesting we watch *The Notebook* because Willa happened to love it?

He must have caught the shock on my face because his face turned red.

He turned his back on us to pour his smoothie. "I mean, it's dumb as fuck, but if she likes it..."

"Sounds good," I said, not wanting to put him off by making a big deal out of it. "But in the meantime there's something else we need to talk about."

Neo turned around with his smoothie in hand. "Willa?"

Fucker didn't give two shits about anything but himself except when it came to Willa. Then he was all ears.

"She asked how long it would take for the other houses to finish the game," I said.

"We don't know," Neo said.

"I know," I said. "And that's a problem."

"How so?" Drago asked.

"It could be months," I said.

Neo's gaze didn't waver. "So?"

"So we can't just keep her locked up here except for school for months on end," I said. "That's some *Flowers in the Attic* shit."

Neo's expression was blank. "What the fuck is *Flowers in the Attic*?"

I stared at him in disbelief. "The book? About the siblings who are locked in an attic and end up having sex and babies?"

"What the actual fuck?" Neo asked.

"It's a thing," Drago said. "An old thing. All the girls like it for some reason."

"Don't act all shocked by sibling sex," I told Neo. "Or babies."

We'd all been rolling the dice on birth control, Willa included, and I had the feeling Neo wouldn't exactly be disappointed if Willa got pregnant.

He scowled. "Willa and I are not siblings."

"I don't see that we have any choice but to keep Willa here," Drago said, returning to the point of the convo. "We already gave in on the school thing. Anywhere else is a risk."

"Unless we get help," I said.

Neo narrowed his eyes. "What kind of help? We already have Rafe and his men."

I wasn't surprised by the suspicion in his voice. There were a lot of things Neo didn't do and asking for help was one of them. Asking for help meant you owed someone a favor, and Neo didn't like owing people favors.

He liked it the other way around.

"The Blades and the Phantoms own Blackwell Falls," I said. "If they put out the word that we're under their protection, Willa would be safe in town at least."

"You've got to be fucking kidding," Neo said.

I understood why the idea was hard to swallow. We were usually the ones offering protection. Asking someone else for it felt a bit like handing them our balls in a designer purse.

"It's not the worst idea," Drago said. "I mean, do I love the idea of giving the Blades and Phantoms leverage over us? Fuck no. But Willa's happiness is more important than our egos, and Rock's got a point, we can't keep her locked up here for months on end."

"And they wouldn't have leverage over us if we wiped the slate clean on their loans," I added.

Neo finished the rest of his smoothie and turned to

rinse the glass. "Now I know you're high. "That's almost five hundred grand."

"Are you saying Willa's happiness isn't worth five hundred grand?" I was pushing his buttons but sometimes that was how you got things done with Neo. The only problem was sometimes his psyche was like a big giant control room full of unmarked buttons.

You never knew what you were going to get when you started pushing them.

He turned to face me, his expression tight. "Are you saying you want my fist in your pretty face?"

I shrugged. "If that's what it takes. I'm just saying, keeping Willa alive isn't enough. We want her to be happy too, right? If we wipe the slate on the loans in exchange for protection from the Blades and Phantoms, Willa can at least go into town for coffee or food."

"If you think I'll stake Willa's safety on the protection of the Blades and Phantoms you're fucking crazy," Neo said.

"We wouldn't have to bank on it," I said.

"We have Rafe's men," Drago pointed out. "We can make any outings into town contingent on Willa having a security detail. Between that and protection from the Blades and Phantoms, she'll be safer in Blackwell Falls than anywhere else."

I waited, letting the silence sit while Neo came around to the idea. I would push the issue if I had to, force a vote, and with Drago on my side, get my way anyway, but it was always better to let Neo think he was agreeing to something.

His expression was murderous, his arms crossed over his chest. "I don't like it."

"None of us like it," Drago said. "But I'm with Rock. It's not just about keeping Willa's heart beating, it's also about making her happy while we sort through this mess."

"And there are other advantages," I said. "You could go back to fight night."

A flicker of interest passed over his features. Keeping Neo from pummeling someone bloody for months was like locking up a feral lion and trying to feed it cat food.

It might keep him alive, but eventually he was going to go ham and eat everyone in sight.

"I'll think about it," he said, stalking from the kitchen.

"I think he's in," I said to Drago. "Good thing too because Valentine's Day is right around the corner and I'm running out of romantic ideas for the house."

Drago shook his head in disbelief. "Did you seriously do all of that so you could plan something for Valentine's Day?"

I tried to affect an air of innocence. "What? No."

Valentine's Day wasn't the only reason, but now that I knew Willa loved me, I planned to make it extra special.

Chapter 37

Willa

I lay back in the chair at Siren, the salon in Blackwell Falls, and sighed as Flame, my hairdresser, washed my hair. It had been ages since I'd had my hair trimmed, since I'd had any kind of maintenance done that I hadn't done myself, and it was absolute heaven to be in a salon.

I closed my eyes and sank into Flame's capable hands as she massaged my scalp, enjoying the brief moment where I wasn't thinking about anything else.

When she was done, she wrapped my head in the towel and helped me sit up and I crossed the room to a chair in front of one of the mirrors.

Claire met my gaze in its reflection. "I feel like I'm with a celebrity."

I glanced at the front of the salon and the extremely

large man standing there with his hands crossed in front of him, sunglasses hiding his eyes.

"The least he could have done was try to blend in," I muttered, getting settled in the chair.

He was one of Rafe's men, and my companion in Blackwell Falls for the day, a requirement of my freedom. It wouldn't have been so bad if he'd worn jeans and a T-shirt or something. Instead he was dressed in black from head to toe, his sunglasses an ever-present accessory whether we were indoors or out.

It was obvious to anyone but the most naïve that he was packing under his leather jacket.

Not that I was complaining. I was just happy to be free.

"At least he's pretty to look at," Claire said about the bodyguard.

One of the other hairdressers, a fashionably dressed older man wearing round eyeglasses, was snipping away at her damp curls.

"I'm glad you're enjoying yourself," I grumbled.

I was annoyed but didn't have the heart to complain to the Kings. I'd been shocked as hell when they'd given me the news that I was now allowed in town while accompanied by a bodyguard — but only in town.

Apparently they'd struck some kind of deal with the Blades and the Phantoms and the word had been put out that we were untouchable within the city limits of Blackwell Falls.

I had no idea what kind of relationship the Kings had with the gangs of Blackwell Falls, and honestly, I didn't have the bandwidth to try and figure it out. I was just glad to have a little freedom, and I'd jumped at the chance to have a spa day with Claire.

"Maybe you'll be able to come to the masquerade at St. Andrew's," Claire said.

I laughed. "That might be... out of my comfort zone."

"You've never been to a sex club?" Claire asked, raising her eyebrows.

"Does a hostel full of horny travelers in Greece count?"

"Ugh. No. St. Andrew's is wild. You have to come! It's over a month away so you have lots of time to convince the Kings." She glanced at Rafe's man, still standing like a statue at the front of the salon. "Maybe you'll even have to bring your bodyguard."

"You definitely need to get laid," I said.

Claire grinned. "I don't disagree."

Flame combed out my hair, studying the ends. Her gorgeous red hair fell in waves around her pretty face, a Blades tattoo peeking out from the side of her neck. "Just a trim? Long layers?"

"Yes please," I said. "It's out of control."

"Just needs a little cleanup." Flame smiled at me in the mirror. "Be a shame to cut off all this length. It's so pretty."

"Thanks," I said. I knew the Blades were rivals of a sort with the Kings, but they were clearly business partners too, and I was glad to have them on our side for now.

"I'm so glad you were able to come today," Claire said. "Even with your bodyguard."

"Me too," I said. "It's been ages since I've had a wax."

Claire smirked. "You're getting a lot of action. It's important to keep up appearances."

My face heated and I looked in the mirror.

Yep. I was blushing. "Oh my god, Claire."

Flame grinned. "No need to be shy with me, honey. Those boys of yours are legendary. We should all be so lucky."

Great. Let's just tell the entire town of Blackwell Falls that I was fucking all three Kings.

I was relieved when Claire started chatting with the hairdresser cutting her hair. It was nice to have a girls' day — we'd gotten facials and mani-pedis in addition to the waxes — but I had no desire to play out my sex life for everyone at Siren.

We spent the rest of the time making small talk with Flame and Claire's hairdresser, and I fluffed my hair in the mirror when Flame was done while she looked on, waiting for the verdict.

"It looks amazing," I said. "Thank you so much."

"Easy to work with such gorgeous hair," she said.

I paid with the Kings' credit card as they'd instructed, gave Flame a hefty tip, and Claire and I stepped out into the sunny but cold winter day.

"I feel like a new woman," Claire said.

"Same. Want to grab lunch on me? Or on the Kings I guess." I still wasn't used to having no money of my own but Neo had made it clear that I was never to use the card Roberto had given me and now I understood why.

Owing Roberto was the last thing I needed.

Neo had told me to use the Kings' card for everything instead. When I'd asked about the limit on the credit card, he'd smirked and said, "Just use it for whatever you need, Jezebel."

"What about your shadow back there?" Claire asked.

I glanced back at my bodyguard, following a few feet behind us. "I guess he'll just follow us there?"

I wasn't exactly sure how the whole bodyguard thing worked.

"Lunch sounds great," Claire said. "Have you ever been to Chasen's?"

"I haven't been hardly anywhere," I said. "The Kings barely let me out of their sight before they knew Roberto was trying to kill us."

"Chasen's has the best food," Claire said. "It's not far. We can walk."

We were halfway down Main Street, straddling the line Oscar had told me not to cross when he'd taken me to the drugstore that first day. I was curious about the other side of town — I'd only seen it at night when Neo had fights at the Orpheum — but we were heading in the other direction, towards Cassie's Cuppa and the other cute stores the weekend tourists loved.

We passed a couple boutiques and a Greek restaurant and came to a large gallery window showcasing a series of black-and-white photos.

I stopped, studying the pictures, a series focused on exotic doors, probably in Turkey or Morocco.

"Those are gorgeous," Claire said next to me.

"Oscar's pictures are just as good," I said, "if not better. His work should totally be in a gallery like this one."

"I've always wondered about that," Claire said. "I almost never see him without his camera. What does he do with all the pictures he takes?"

"What can he do? You know how our families are about that kind of stuff."

Looking at the pictures in the gallery made me sad. I wasn't just bullshitting. Oscar's pictures really were good enough to stand next to the photographs in the gallery window.

He had so much talent. I hated that it was wasted because of his family. If not for their part in the Alinari crime family, Oscar probably would've been a famous director or photographer.

"That really sucks," Claire said. "What about you?"

"What about me?" I asked.

"What would you do if you'd been born into a normal family?" she asked.

"I've never really thought about it." I felt dumb saying it, but it was true. "I was in high school when Emma went missing, and after that..."

Claire reached out and squeezed my hand. "I'm sorry. I hope when this is all over you'll be able to live your life the way you want."

I had no idea what that meant or what it would look like but it sounded pretty good. "Me too."

"It's just one more block," Claire said. "Wait a minute..."

I stopped to look at her, frozen on the sidewalk. "What?"

"Is that... Neo?"

I followed her gaze to the black Hummer parked across the street. The side windows were tinted but I could clearly make out the firm set of Neo's jaw, the broad sweep of his shoulders in the driver's seat.

"What the actual fuck?" I asked.

Claire laughed. "Looks like somebody doesn't trust his own bodyguard to protect you."

"Unbelievable," I said.

"Want to go talk to him?" Claire asked.

"No, I really don't." I didn't know whether to be annoyed or touched that Neo was following me around even though he'd assigned me a bodyguard, but I wasn't going to give him the satisfaction of thinking I appreciated his stalker tendencies.

"If you say so," Claire said in a singsong voice. "We're here anyway."

We'd come to an upscale bistro with a green awning and an outdoor patio that was closed for winter.

Claire opened the door and we stepped into a cozy, dimly lit restaurant, the walls painted deep navy, soft light glowing from the chic overhead fixtures.

Claire greeted the hostess with familiarity and we were led to a private booth near the back of the restaurant.

"Going to the ladies' room before we eat," I said, stashing my bag and coat in the booth. "Can you get me a water?"

"Sure," she said.

I looked for the restroom sign and followed it down a narrow hall, past the men's room, to a wood door marked *Ladies*.

One of the two stalls was occupied so I took the other one and emerged a couple minutes later only to come face-to-face with Alexa Petrov.

She was applying lipstick in the bathroom mirror, black jeans hugging her perfect body, her ivory cashmere sweater looking like it cost a million dollars and perfectly complementing her glossy chestnut hair.

I turned on the water to wash my hands and waited for the inevitable snide remark.

But when I looked at her in the mirror, she was focused on her lipstick and I noticed her hand was shaking.

"Hey," I said, because I might as well try and be nice if it was going to be awkward.

She met my gaze in the mirror but didn't say anything as she finished with her lipstick.

Fun times.

I washed my hands and started pulling paper towels from the dispenser, eager to get out of there. When I turned to throw the paper towels in the trash, Alexa was looking at me with an expression I couldn't define.

Probably because Alexa had only ever looked at me with disdain, and this wasn't that.

She opened her mouth to speak, then seemed to think better of it. By now, I felt like I'd landed in an alternate universe, one where Alexa was mute.

Or maybe not just a complete and utter bitch?

A few seconds later, she sighed and headed for the door without a word.

"What the fuck?" I muttered.

I finished drying my hands and headed back to the table where Claire was sipping water through a straw, the menus closed at the end of the table.

I scanned the restaurant for Alexa and didn't see her. I had no idea who she'd come to Chasen's with but she was gone now.

"Okay, that was weird," I said, sliding into the booth.

"What was weird?" Claire asked.

"I ran into Alexa in the bathroom just now," I said.

"I thought that was her!" Claire said. "She walked past so fast I only got a view of her perfect ass, the gorgeous bitch."

"It was her all right," I said.

"What insult did she try and decimate you with this time?" Claire asked.

"That's the weird part," I said. "She didn't insult me at all. Actually, she didn't even speak."

"Alexa Petrov passed up an opportunity to make you feel like shit?" Claire asked. "She must be coming down with something."

"Right?" I didn't know how to explain the strange look on Alexa's face, the moment when it had seemed like she was going to say something that wasn't critical or demeaning.

Maybe even something that was... important?

"Oh well, who knows what goes through her head?" Claire reached for the menus and handed me one. "They have the best steak-and-Gorgonzola salad here, but everything is good."

"Thanks," I said.

I scanned the menu but I wasn't really processing the words. I kept seeing Alexa's face in the bathroom, the way she'd opened her mouth to speak and changed her mind.

The way her hand had shaken while she put on her lipstick.

Chapter 38

Willa

The Orpheum was packed as usual, members of the Blades and Phantoms streaming into the crowded lobby for the upcoming fight.

I remembered my first fight, how intimidated I'd felt around all the townies dressed in leather, chains hanging from their clothes. Now they felt like our allies, the only people standing between us and Roberto and his partners in crime.

Neo, Oscar, and Rock surrounded me on the way in, clearly taking their bodyguard duties seriously. We'd discussed bringing one of Rafe's men as backup, but the Kings had decided showing up at the Orpheum with a bodyguard would make it look like we didn't trust the people who'd given us their protection.

It would also draw more attention to us, and that was

the last thing we needed, evidenced by the way everyone already stared at us on our way in.

It wasn't like no one had ever paid attention to us before. We were always a source of curiosity at the Orpheum, either because of Neo and his reputation as a fighter or because we were technically from Aventine rather than townies.

But this was different. There was tension in the air, the bearded bikers and street gangs in ripped jeans and leather jackets shifting on their feet when they saw us, their gazes skittering away, like they'd been told to steer clear of us too.

We came to Bear, the bouncer who guarded the Orpheum's inner sanctum, and he frisked Rock and Oscar before turning his attention to me.

"Arms up, thighs spread, girly," he leered.

"Touch her and you'll be sipping your meals through a straw for the next three months," Neo growled.

Bear scowled. "You're not in a position to negotiate."

"I can just— " I started.

"I'm not negotiating," Neo interrupted. "The rest of us will submit, as insulting as it fucking is, but you'll pay a price for touching her."

"Let her pass," a voice said from behind Bear.

The bouncer was so huge it took a second for the owner of the voice to become visible, but when he did, I saw that he was every bit as big as Bear. His blond beard did nothing to hide his rugged good looks and his cut was adorned with patches, including one that read *Vice President.*

So this was Hawk, Vice President of the Blades Motorcycle Club.

Bear immediately stood down, a look of fear passing over his face. "Whatever you say, boss." He stepped aside and muttered, "Fucking Kings."

Neo held out his hand to Hawk. "Thanks."

Hawk shook Neo's hand. "Be on your best behavior. I can't help you if you cause any shit."

"Just here to fight," Neo said.

He put a possessive hand on the small of my back and ushered me past Hawk and Bear.

A shiver ran up my spine. Four months ago I'd hated him with the fire of a thousand suns. Now he touched me and I turned into a puddle of goo.

What even was my life?

We continued down the hall, defunct theaters on either side, heading for the big auditorium at the end. The doors were open, multicolored lights sweeping the dark interior as the crowd got amped for the upcoming fight, music thumping, growing louder as we approached.

It was cold outside, but I knew from experience that the theater got hot, and I was glad I'd chosen to wear a silky tank with no jacket over my black jeans. I'd frozen my ass off on the way in from the car, but now I wouldn't have to hold my jacket the entire time, and a small gold crossbody bag made up for the lack of pockets.

Plus my heeled boots made my legs look hella long without the distraction of a jacket and the Kings had definitely noticed.

"Want company while you change?" Rock asked Neo as we approached the theater.

Neo was on edge — we all were — and it wasn't a good idea for Neo to brawl when he was distracted. Rock was the designated Neo whisperer, and it wasn't uncommon for him to accompany Neo to the makeshift dressing room before a fight.

"No." He was on me before I knew what was happening, pushing me against the wall next to the open theater doors. "I want you."

I looked up at him, my heart beating faster, my cunt wet just from the feel of his body pressed against mine, his dick hard in his jeans.

"I'll be waiting." I smiled up at him. "Assuming you win."

He glared down at me. "I'll have you either way."

"Says you," I said, breathless as he ground his dick into my stomach.

"You saying you won't fuck me unless I win?" he asked.

"I'm not a participation trophy," I said. "If you want to fuck me, you'll win."

His eyes flashed fire in the moment before he lowered his face to my neck, closing his mouth around my throat and sucking hard.

I gasped, pressing my thighs together to stop the throbbing that had started in my pussy, and when he lifted his head, he touched a finger to the wet spot on my throat just above my choker.

"A down payment on what I'm going to do to you later," he said.

Fuck me.

He stalked off, leaving me panting and breathless. I tried to pull myself together as I pushed off the wall to rejoin Oscar and Rock.

They both looked down at me, their gazes locked on my neck.

"He gave me a hickey, didn't he?" I asked.

"More like a fucking brand," Oscar said.

"Let's go," Rock said, taking my hand. "I don't know about you, but I need a fucking drink."

We headed into the darkened theater and my eyes were immediately drawn to the movie screen. This time an older movie was playing, a motorcycle gang sitting in a circle in the woods, their cuts worn over bare chests as a blonde woman sniffled off to the side.

Oscar's eyes lit up. "I love this movie."

"What is it?" I asked.

"*The Glory Stompers*," he said. "Dennis Hopper."

281

The title of the movie didn't ring a bell but it was always fun to see Oscar excited by a movie.

"Want a drink?" Rock asked.

"Is that even a question right now?" I asked.

"Grab me one too," Oscar said, taking my arm.

Neither of us had to tell Rock what we wanted. He would bring my new favorite, a Huckleberry Twist, and a whiskey, neat, for Oscar. One of many benefits of living with people who knew you so well.

The walls were a kind of safe zone, everyone congregating in the center of the theater which had long ago been cleared of seats, and Oscar led me through the crowd, some dancing in groups, others trying to have a conversation over the roar of the music pumping from the theater's surround sound.

There was hardly room to move and I watched as Oscar nervously scanned the crowd, the set of his shoulders making it clear he was on alert.

I didn't blame him. Weapons weren't allowed in the Orpheum, and that meant we were relying on the edict of protection from the Blades and the Phantoms.

I'd initially protested coming at all — it seemed like a bad idea given the whole crowd and no weapons thing — but Neo was wound tight after two months with no fights.

He needed to let loose on somebody's face.

Plus, he'd rendered any argument I had null and void

when he'd pointed out that if I was allowed to go into Blackwell Falls to get my pussy waxed and have lunch with Claire, he was allowed to fight at the Orpheum.

"Busy tonight," I shouted up at Oscar.

"Always this time of year," Oscar said. "Not much else to do."

I remembered what Daisy had said about the falls, about how townies liked to party there when the weather was good. It made sense they would need another way to let off steam when they couldn't congregate outside.

Oscar's gaze snagged on someone in the crowd and he leaned down to speak against my ear.

"I'll be right back," he said. "Don't move. I'll have my eyes on you the whole time."

He moved through the crowd toward a skinny guy in a leather jacket with the Blades' logo emblazoned on the back, then positioned himself so that he could see me.

I kept my back against the wall and nodded along to the music, starting to relax. It felt like any other night at the Orpheum and I took comfort in the fact that while we didn't have weapons, no one else did either.

I didn't know who owned the Orpheum or who made the rules, but whoever it was must've had a lot of power because everyone seemed willing to behave.

I watched a couple minutes of the movie playing out silently on the big screen, then returned my focus to the crowd. I'd just scanned past Oscar, his eyes on me like he'd promised even though he was still talking to leather-jacket guy, when I spotted a familiar head of thick brown hair standing at the edge of the crowd on the opposite side of the room.

Alexa Petrov.

What was she doing at the Orpheum? It didn't seem at all like her scene. Even Claire avoided the Orpheum.

Alexa wasn't alone. She was looking up at a giant blond guy that I recognized as one of the Knights.

And they weren't having a casual conversation.

They were arguing. It was obvious from their body language even though I couldn't hear a word.

Alexa wore an unfamiliar expression. Not the disdain or dismissal I was used to but a storm of anger and something I was sure was fear.

The giant blond — I couldn't remember his name — pointed at her, his expression wrathful as his lips moved in what appeared to be a serious smackdown.

Usually I would've been more than happy to watch Alexa take some shit, but after our weird encounter in the bathroom at Chasen's, I couldn't help feeling like maybe she needed help.

Okay, it was a bit of a leap. But it was definitely weird combined with her argument with one of the Russians — someone from her own crime family — and at the Orpheum no less.

I was debating whether or not to push off the wall and brave the crowd to check on her, knowing Oscar would be right behind me, when she turned to walk away from the blond giant.

He grabbed her arm, forcing her to spin and look at him.

Alarm bells rang in my head and I pushed off the wall and took a step forward, but a second later she shook him off with a glare and a couple words I couldn't hear.

Then she was marching toward the exit, the blond guy staring after her.

"Huckleberry Twist for the lady," Rock said, returning with my drink.

He was juggling it with a beer and Oscar's whiskey so I took my drink out of his hand.

"What's up?" he shouted, following my gaze to the empty spot where Alexa had stood with the Russian.

There was no point explaining what I'd seen with Alexa. Not now anyway. It would be impossible to convey with so much noise.

I shook my head.

"Where's Drago?" Rock asked, displeasure darkening his blue eyes.

He clearly wasn't happy Oscar had left me alone.

I pointed to Oscar, still talking to the leather jacket, and Rock nodded, his shoulders relaxing a little bit.

The volume on the music dimmed by half a decibel and a cheer rose from the crowd.

The fight was about to start.

Rock took my hand. "Come on, kitten. Let's go watch Neo ruin someone's face."

Chapter 39

Willa

I let Rock pull me toward the front of the theater along with the rest of the crowd, all of us ready for the fight.

It was like being at the center of a mosh pit, everyone shoving and jostling to get the best view, and I held on to Rock's arm, determined not to be separated.

"How do you know Neo will win?" I shouted up at Rock when we found a place to stop.

Neo had lost to someone half his size in a fight before Thanksgiving break. There must've been a reason — it was the only fight I'd ever seen him lose — but he hadn't wanted to talk about it when I'd asked.

"The look on his face after he cornered you on the way in," Rock said. "I'm guessing you promised him a prize but I'm trying not to think about it. Jealousy is such a turnoff."

Oscar joined us a few seconds later and Rock gave him the glass of whiskey, now only half full.

"Thank fuck," Rock shouted. "I'm wearing the other half so don't complain."

Oscar downed the drink in one swallow. I wondered what he'd been talking to the man in the leather jacket about. Oscar wasn't a big drinker.

I smelled Neo before I saw him — the scent of his expensive cologne combined with sweat and sex sending a current of lust to every nerve in my body.

And goddamn. Neo always looked good, but there was something about him wearing nothing but basketball shorts and sneakers, his bare chest already glistening with sweat.

Like his angel — me — was weeping.

A shiver moved through my body. Lust or dread?

With Neo, who knew.

The wound on his chest was no longer covered with a bandage and the stitches were gone, but I knew it was there, blending into the ink, a weakness that he couldn't afford when he was about to go toe-to-toe with some other sociopath who liked to get the shit beat out of him.

"Are you sure about this?" I asked him, shouting to be heard over the still-deafening music. I was suddenly nervous, the weeping angel lingering in my mind like a bad omen.

His grin looked evil as the multicolored lights spun over his face. "Worried about me, Jezebel?"

"Yes!" I said. "Yes, I am. Can we go home now?"

"No way," he said, bouncing on his feet. "I have a prize to win."

I cursed myself for giving him another reason — one he didn't need — to fight, then looked over the crowd, trying to find Neo's opponent. It was one of the rules of fight night.

No one knew who was fighting until it started — including the fighters.

I gave up almost as soon as I started. If we'd been at a boxing match I would have looked for someone dressed like Neo, but at the Orpheum, Neo was as likely to be fighting one of the bikers in leather pants and a cut as he was one of the preppies from the nearby community college or one of the Phantoms in their jeans and leather jackets.

"Here comes Marge," Oscar shouted.

The crowd parted as the older woman who emceed the fights made her way to the front of the theater, her platinum hair glinting in the lights.

I couldn't help wondering what kind of sway she held over the townies. She didn't even have to tell them to shut the fuck up. They got quiet as soon as she took up her position at the front of the crowd.

"Welcome to another fight night!" she shouted.

The crowd roared in response.

"Let's meet tonight's sacrificial lambs!" she said.

Next to me, Neo bounced on the balls of his feet, rolling his shoulders and cracking his neck.

"First up we have our favorite pretty boy, Neooooo!"

The crowd was a mix of cheers and boos as Neo bounded to the front of the theater to stand on one side of Marge.

He was fucking huge, his sheer size menacing. Add to that the still expression on his face, a mask for the reservoir of rage I knew lurked under the surface, and I would have been absolutely terrified to confront him at the Orpheum.

Or anywhere really.

"Fighting Neo is our very own Phantom Menace!" Marge shouted.

"Someone's a nerd," Rock shouted.

"*Star Wars* isn't nerdy anymore," Oscar said. "Haven't you heard?"

I watched the crowd, waiting for someone to peel away and head to the front, then felt a rush of fear when I saw a big man in jeans and a wifebeater join Marge and Neo.

"Fuck," Oscar said. "That's Caesar. He's a mean motherfucker."

"At least his boots aren't as big as Marvin's," Rock said.

The fight between Neo and Marvin had been the first one I'd attended at the Orpheum. Marvin had been a mountain of a man wearing giant black boots that looked like lead weights on his feet, and the moments before the fight had been a flurry of instructions from Oscar and Rock, mostly to avoid Marvin's boots.

Caesar had boots on too, but they looked like ballet flats compared to the ones Marvin had worn.

I tried to relax a little. Neo had won the fight against Marvin even with the boots.

He could do this.

"Okay boys," Marge said, looking from Neo to his opponent. "You know the rules. Don't be dicks. Time to fight!"

The crowd went wild and Marge moved out of the way, retreating to a group of townies huddled in the front.

She'd barely gotten out of the way when Neo charged his opponent.

I'd seen two fights at the Orpheum: Neo had won one of them and tied the other, but in both cases it had been a fight.

I'd expected more of the same but Neo was like a raging bull, charging at Caesar with the full force of his height and weight.

Caesar was surprised too. I could see it in his flinch when Neo landed the first punch, the way he tried to gather his wits afterward.

But it didn't matter.

Neo was on the warpath, punching and kicking like a rabid dog.

At first Caesar tried to fight back, but after about a

minute he gave up and danced around Neo, trying to dodge his kicks and blows instead, probably hoping to tire Neo out.

It didn't work. Neo stalked after him, a blank expression on his face as he punched and kicked until Caesar, dripping blood, collapsed on the ground.

The fight had probably lasted less than two minutes.

"What the fuck got into him?" Oscar asked.

Rock looked down at me with a knowing grin but didn't have a chance to say anything before Neo stomped toward us.

Marge hadn't even declared a winner when he grabbed my arm, rough enough to make me wet.

He dragged me toward the exit. "Your ass is mine."

Chapter 40

Willa

I was in my room doing homework a few days after the fight when I heard Oscar leave his room and head for the stairs.

I glanced at my phone for the time, and jumped up from my bed, and went to the door, listening for his retreating footsteps. This was the time of night when he, Rock, and Neo liked to play video games so I figured I had at least an hour before Oscar would be back in his room.

I'd never seen the Kings do homework or even talk about it but they were all still going to classes at Aventine, so whatever they were doing, I guess it was working.

And if there was one thing I'd learned about the Kings in the last few months it was that they were a lot smarter than I'd given them credit for.

I cracked open my door and eased into the hallway, then paused just to make sure no one was coming. When it remained silent, I hurried for Oscar's bedroom, let myself in, and closed the door behind me.

His scent permeated the room, causing a reactive heat to bloom between my thighs.

Fuck me.

These boys really had me wrapped around their giant talented fingers.

As always, Oscar's room was neat, his bed made, books neatly lining on one bookshelf while his favorite DVDs lined another. Soft light emanated from a single lamp on one of the nightstands, casting a cozy glow over the room, dark in the winter evening.

A TV stood dark in the sitting area, and I knew he rarely used it, preferring the big screen and surround sound in the media room. I felt bad encroaching on his personal territory but I hadn't been able to get the gallery in Blackwell Falls out of my mind. I knew he would never submit his photographs, but they deserved to be seen, and maybe when this was all over, he'd actually be able to live on his own terms.

Maybe we all would.

I looked around, trying to figure out where he might store his printed photographs, then headed for the desk set against one wall.

But it didn't feel right. I couldn't even imagine Oscar sitting at a desk to do homework.

Still, I had to start somewhere, and I opened the desk drawers, doing a cursory glance for his photographs.

I didn't linger, because I really did feel bad snooping. As soon as it became obvious the pictures weren't there, I closed the drawers and moved on, resisting the temptation to pick things up and take a closer look.

Oscar was an open book with me but I still didn't want to take advantage of his trust.

I straightened and looked around the room again, thinking about Oscar.

His photographs weren't work. They were... personal.

I crossed the room and headed for one of the nightstands.

I was about to pull open the drawer when I heard the door open behind me.

I froze, then spun to face Oscar, leaning in the doorway.

My face burned. He'd caught me snooping red-handed.

I expected him to be angry, but he was just leaning in the doorway with a sexy-as-fuck smirk on his face.

"Looking for something, tiger?" he asked, teasing his lip with his tongue piercing.

I scrambled for an explanation, then remembered that when you were trying to lie, a lie close to the truth always best.

"You caught me," I said. "I was looking for your pictures."

"You could have just asked," he said.

"I know," I said. "I was embarrassed."

This was good. This was working.

Being embarrassed about having an ego giant enough to prompt me to search Oscar's room for pictures he'd taken of me would explain why I was so flustered.

"Because they're all of you, you mean?" he asked.

"I'm sure they're not *all* of me," I said.

"You might be surprised." The amusement had left his eyes, his expression turned serious, maybe even a little pained.

"I'm sorry I didn't just ask," I said.

I wasn't sorry. I wasn't even looking for pictures of me. But I didn't want to tell him that yet.

He stepped into the room and shut the door behind him. It closed with a finality that sent a shiver of anticipation up my spine.

He walked slowly toward me, his gaze locked on mine. He moved leisurely, fluidly, and I wondered how someone could look so fucking sexy in ripped black jeans and a T-shirt that inexplicably featured an image of Yoda taking a mug shot (I didn't get it).

He stopped when there was only an inch of space left between us and looked down at me.

"You've been a bad girl," he murmured, reaching for the elastic that held my hair in a messy bun on top of my head.

He tugged and my hair spilled around my shoulders.

I could hardly breathe under the heat of his gaze, locked onto my lips like a homing beacon.

"You might need a spanking," he murmured.

"What about your video game?" It was becoming increasingly clear that I'd have to get the photos another time.

"You think I want to play video games now that I have you alone?" he asked.

"I don't know," I said.

He leaned down until his lips were almost against mine. "That would be a hard no, tiger. Emphasis on the word *hard.*"

Then his mouth was crashing into mine, his hands cradling my face like he never wanted to let me go.

Chapter 41

Oscar

She was so fucking beautiful it almost hurt to look at her. Even taking pictures of her was a kind of torture because I would inevitably spend hours poring over them, making sure I knew every slope and shadow of her face.

I touched my tongue to her lips, running my piercing along the seam, and she opened like a flower.

I groaned when our tongues met, the wet heat of her mouth making my already-hard dick even harder.

I had no idea what she'd really been doing in my bedroom and I didn't care. I kept no secrets from her, would never keep secrets from her again, and anything I owned belonged to her as well.

I tipped her head to take our kiss deeper, using every stroke of my tongue to brand her with my name.

She belonged to all of us.

But somehow, she belonged to me alone too.

She slid her hands up my T-shirt, her fingers mapping a course over my chest. When she touched my nipple piercings and tugged, I growled into her mouth.

"Watch it, tiger. You're playing with fire."

"Maybe I like playing with fire," she murmured against my lips.

I slid the sweater she wore around the house off her shoulders. "In that case, play away."

She tugged again and my dick responded like a good soldier.

I lifted the hem of her T-shirt and pulled it off, revealing her perfect braless tits. I took them in my hands, savoring the weight of her silken flesh, and rolled her nipples between my fingers.

It only made me more eager to touch the rest of her and I slipped my thumbs into the waistband of her loose boxer shorts and tugged them down.

"I need you naked," I murmured.

Her sweet little pussy was smooth as a baby's bottom after her day at the spa. I planted a kiss just above her clit and she threaded her hands through my hair and tightened her grip with a moan that made me want to dispense with the preliminaries, bend her over the bed, fuck a hundred of those little moans out of her perfect mouth.

"Don't you worry," I murmured, trailing kisses down

her inner thigh, "I'm going to bury my face in that perfect pussy of yours."

She lifted her feet and I pulled off her shorts and underwear, chuckling when I saw the word *Saturday* printed across the ass.

"Feeling nostalgic?" I asked.

"They're surprisingly comfy," she breathed as I ran my hands up her legs.

I spread her pussy lips, relishing the view as I knelt between her thighs. It was like looking into the center of a perfect rose, her folds pink and wet with the dew of her desire.

My mouth watered and I rose to my knees to run my tongue all the way through the petals of her sex.

She gasped, tightening her hold on my hair, and I spread her wider to get access to her already-engorged clit.

I circled it with my tongue, loving the easy access but wanting even more.

"Put your leg on the mattress, tiger," I said.

She lifted her leg that was closest to the bed and her pussy opened for me like a cave of secrets.

"Fuck yes," I said, running my fingers through her folds. "Don't you know by now that I want to see all of you?"

I smoothed my hand over her hairless mound and she moaned as I slid two fingers inside her.

"You're always so fucking wet, tiger."

I leaned in to flick my tongue against her clit, using my

piercing to stroke the swollen bud, and she tightened her hold on my head, making it clear I was right where she wanted me.

Lucky for me there was no place in the world I'd rather be than eating Willa's wet pussy while I finger-fucked her, except maybe burying my cock between her thighs.

I got harder thinking about it because that was the next order of business — just as soon as I made her come on my face. I fucking loved this position. I could see every inch of her, every sweet pink fold below the tiny seed of her clit.

She moved her hips with the rhythm of my fingers and mouth, grinding on my face, her hands still tangled in my hair.

I would've told her it wasn't necessary — that I had no intention of leaving until I'd made her come — but she was already close and I didn't want to break her momentum.

"Oh my god," she moaned.

I took my cues from the motion of her hips, working my fingers and tongue faster. Her channel was getting tighter, clamping down on my fingers as she got closer to climaxing.

I pressed against her G-spot and sucked her clit, drawing it into my mouth, and felt her fall apart against my mouth.

She cried out into the room, letting loose a string of dirty words that brought me close to creaming my jeans.

I sucked and fucked, lapping up every bit of her juices, savoring the moment when she was mine and mine alone.

Her fingers loosened in my hair as she came down from her orgasm, and I looked up at her, blonde hair falling in waves around her shoulders, nearly touching her tits. Her lips were parted and swollen from my kisses, her chest flushed.

A fucking goddess.

I stood and chuckled when she went straight for the button on my jeans. "Ready for more, tiger?"

"Always," she panted, unzipping my pants and shoving them down.

I sighed with relief as my cock sprang free. Nothing was more uncomfortable than making Willa come with my dick in my jeans.

Worth it, but uncomfortable as fuck.

I stripped off my T-shirt in a hurry, then bent my head to kiss her, stroking her mouth with long sweeps of my tongue, trying as always to make sure I left no part of her unexplored.

Her touch was light as a feather over my shoulders, across my pecs, down my abs.

She wrapped her hand around my dick and I mapped her back with my fingers, tracing the long length of her spine, the narrowing of her waist, the fullness of her hips.

I took her luscious ass in my hands and squeezed, and she sighed into my mouth as she stroked my cock.

It was too much. Not just the sheer physical pleasure but something else. Something that filled my chest until I felt like it was going to spill out of every pore in my body.

I fucking loved this girl. I loved her like I'd never loved anything or anyone.

It was so overwhelming I broke our kiss, wanting to get a hold of myself.

"Lay down, tiger," I said gruffly, reaching for the camera on my nightstand.

She obeyed, her hair spread out around her on the pillow like rays of sun.

"You'd rather take pictures of me than fuck me?" she asked.

"No, I'd rather take pictures of you and then fuck you." I kneeled on the bed between her knees and aimed my camera at her face, hoping to capture the post-sex flush that said I'd given her pleasure.

Usually she was shy when I took her picture, but this time she tipped her head and moved her shoulders, giving me different angles.

"Fuck yes," I said. "You have no idea how absolutely stunning you are, Willa."

I could take pictures of nothing but her for the rest of my life and be a happy fucking man.

Not that I would ever tell her that. Because no pressure. I knew she planned to leave after we dealt with Roberto.

I just couldn't think about it.

I took a few more pictures of her and then set my camera aside. The images of her naked and posing for me had only heightened my hunger for her.

I needed to be balls deep in her stat.

I positioned myself between her thighs and held the base of my shaft to rub my dick through her pussy, teasing her clit with the piercing on my head.

She wiggled her ass, dropping a few inches to try and coax me inside.

Like I needed any fucking coaxing.

"Want me to get a condom?" I asked.

I had no desire to get a condom. In fact, what I wanted was to knock Willa the fuck up and keep her with us forever.

But that wasn't my call and never would be.

Still, I wasn't surprised when she locked her ankles around the back of my knees to hold me in place.

"No," she said. "I want you to fuck me."

I didn't question it. We'd taken more than a few chances, alone and together, and I could only assume it had been the same when Willa was with Rock and Neo.

In any other situation, with any other girl, I would've been wrapped to the nines during every single encounter.

But fuck me if I didn't just want to make her mine — ours — in every way.

"Music to my fucking ears, tiger." There was nothing

better than fucking her bare, feeling the glide of her pussy walls against my cock as I drove into her.

I pushed her thighs open wider. I'd started out wanting to play, to spank her delicious ass and fuck her from behind.

But now that I had her to myself, all I really wanted to do was be as close to her as possible, to watch her face while she came for me.

I leaned down to kiss her, feeling her tits flatten against my chest. She lifted her head off the pillow, meeting me halfway, her tongue sparring eagerly with mine as our kissing grew more urgent, my dick ready to explode against the opening of her pussy.

"I fucking love you, Willa," I said, pulling away and leaving a trail of kisses along her cheek, her nose, her mouth.

She held my head in her hands. "I love you too. So much."

I froze to look at her, wondering if I was hearing things. "You do?"

She nodded. "I have for ages. I'm sorry I didn't say it sooner. I just didn't know how to go about it because of... well, because of all of you. I've never done this before."

"Can we make a deal?" I asked her, my heart singing.

She loved me.

She nodded.

"Do what feels right to you. Always. Let us deal with the rest," I said. "Sound good?"

She smiled. "Sounds great."

"And?" I prompted with a grin, just because I wanted to hear it again.

"And I love you, Oscar Drago. And..."

"And?" I prompted again.

"I really really *really* want you to fuck me now," she said.

So I did, long and slow. Like my life fucking depended on keeping her with me.

With us.

Because it felt like it did.

Chapter 42

Willa

We were sitting on the couch a week before Valentine's Day, the Kings playing video games while I read a book, when the Kings' phones dinged, announcing a visitor at the front gate.

Now that the new security system had been added to the smart phone app, their phones were always beeping with one alert or another, but it was unusual to have an unannounced visitor.

Neo scowled and looked at me accusingly. "Expecting someone, Jezebel?"

Somewhere along the way, his once-annoying nickname for me had started to sound affectionate. I should probably have asked for a new one, but I was weirdly attached to it, a symbol of our strange journey from enemies to... whatever we were now.

"Just because I had one unannounced visitor doesn't

mean they're all mine," I said, remembering our steamy moment in the kitchen when Claire had shown up.

Oscar picked up his phone and looked at the display. "Okay, this is weird. It's Alexa."

"Alexa Petrov?" I asked. I had a flash of memory: Alexa's hand shaking as she applied lipstick, opening her mouth to speak and then changing her mind, arguing with the Knight at the Orpheum.

"The one and only," Oscar said. "She told the gate guard that she needs to talk to us."

Neo stood. "Let her in."

"I'm not big on bingo, but if I were, I would *not* have had this on my card," Rock said.

I hadn't told them about my weird exchange with Alexa at Chasen's or about her altercation with one of the Knights at the Orpheum.

It hadn't been intentional — I just hadn't known what to say. In the moment, both situations had seemed undeniably strange, but when I tried to formulate the why of it, I came up empty.

It was just one of those *you had to be there* things and that didn't seem concrete enough to mention to the Kings.

A couple minutes after the message from the gate, the doorbell rang and Oscar headed for the foyer.

"This should be interesting," Rock said.

Neo turned off the TV and game console as Oscar led Alexa into the living room.

At first glance nothing seemed out of the ordinary. Alexa was flawlessly put together, her makeup highlighting her perfect features, snug pants hugging her shapely thighs under riding boots.

Oscar must've taken her coat at the door because she was wearing a sheer blue blouse and I knew for a fact it was, as Reva would say, cold as a witch's tit outside.

"Hey," Alexa said, her gaze taking us all in.

"Hey," Rock said. "Can I get you something to drink?"

She shook her head. "I think I just need to get this over with."

Okay, this *was* going to be interesting.

"Have a seat," Rock said.

I tucked my feet under me to make room on the couch, but she chose one of the chairs.

"What's up?" Neo asked.

Her gaze slid to me, and I sat up straighter, preparing to leave the room. "I can go upstairs if you want to talk in private."

She drew in a breath, as if gathering strength. "No. This is about you too. You should stay."

I settled back onto the couch, anxiety tightening like a fist around my chest.

"I know the identity of the Knights that are involved in the disappearance of those girls," she said.

We should have been happy. The Knights' house would be the first to name their killer and it had only been a couple of weeks since the kickoff of game number four. But something wasn't right, and the Kings must've felt it too because they weren't exactly celebrating.

"You want to tell us why you're here alone?" Oscar asked.

Alexa wasn't technically part of the Knights' house. She was a Queen, and while she'd been forced to work with her male peers at Aventine on game four, it was more than a little strange that she was here alone to deliver the news that they'd completed it.

She pressed her lips together like she wanted to keep the words from spilling out of her mouth. "It's my father," she finally said. "Or he's one of them."

"One of them?" I asked.

She nodded. "There are more. All alumni."

"How did you find this out?" Rock asked.

She rubbed her palms nervously on her jeans. "I've... had a feeling. After you announced game four, I went home and did some digging, and I found escrow papers from the purchase of the cabin belonging to Global Limited, the shell company that holds most of the bratva's property interests."

I was quietly reeling, trying to make sense of the fact that my arch nemesis at Aventine was giving up her own father as one of the men responsible for Emma's disappearance.

I forced myself to stay quiet, letting the Kings take the lead. I wasn't sure I even trusted myself to speak.

"I'm sorry," Rock said.

She shrugged, but I saw the grief in her eyes, recognized it as my own, because if there was one thing I had a lot of experience with, it was being disappointed in people who shared your last name.

She reached into her jeans, pulled out a folded scrap of paper, and held it out to Neo. "These are the other names."

"And they're all alumni of the Knights' house?" Neo asked.

She nodded.

Oscar glanced at Neo and Rock, some kind of unspoken communication passing between them. "Then why are you here alone?"

"They wouldn't come," she said simply.

"Because the ones involved are family?" Oscar asked.

"Their fathers mostly," Alexa said. "I found their names next to the names of missing girls from Bellepoint, plus a few I'd never heard of. It was like..." She exhaled slowly, like she was trying to keep herself calm. "It was like each of them had chosen one of the girls or taken her or... something."

"Fuck," Neo said.

Oscar and Rock moved closer to me on the sofa, taking up positions on either side of my body like they could provide shelter from an incoming storm.

And this was one hell of an incoming storm.

Because if what Alexa said was true, we weren't talking about one man from each family kidnapping and murdering girls but a coordinated effort between multiple members of each houses' alumni over a period of decades.

Alumni whose offspring now attended the same school.

And worst of all, those offspring — at least in the Knights' house — had elected not to come clean to the Kings.

"This isn't about the game," I said.

For the first time, Alexa really met my eyes. "No. It's about Emma and all those other girls. I just couldn't..." She looked down at her hands. "I just couldn't stay quiet."

Now I understood her shaking hand at Chasen's, the words she hadn't spoken, her argument with the Knight at the Orpheum.

"Do they know you're here?" Oscar asked.

"No. Yes." She sighed. "Probably. I mean, I wasn't followed or anything but I doubt any of this will stay a secret. They know I wanted to come clean."

"We can offer you protection," Rock said. "You can stay here or we can put you up somewhere else until this is all over."

She shook her head and stood. "No, thanks. I'm the East Coast pakhan's daughter. Hiding would be shameful, more shameful than what they've already done."

The pakhan was the head of the bratva, the Russian Mafia. Alexa's father was the equivalent of an Italian don. Expectations were high for his daughter.

I didn't know whether to admire her bravery or curse her stupidity.

I'd once thought blood family was everything, but I knew now that it was nothing compared to the fellowship of crime. I hoped Alexa knew her father better than I'd known mine.

"There's no shame in preserving your own life," Neo said.

She stood and lifted her chin. "I'm good. I just wanted to make sure you knew. I'll let you deal with the Knights."

Neo nodded, and I was suddenly overcome with fear for her.

And not just fear. Gratitude.

I stood and gave her a hug before she could blow me off. "Thank you."

I was surprised to feel her arms come around me to return the hug. "I'm sorry I've been a bitch. I just... I had a feeling. It was easier to treat you like shit than to look in your eyes and see Emma."

I pulled back to look at her. "It's okay. A little rivalry keeps things interesting."

She laughed a little. "I'm really hoping for less interesting next year."

"Same," I said. "But seriously. Thank you."

She nodded and headed for the door.

"Any idea who the others are?" Oscar asked. "From the other houses?"

She turned around. "Not a clue. But there was another name, someone who isn't one of us."

"What name?" Neo asked.

"Laszlo Nagy," Alexa said. "The guy who owns St. Andrew's."

Chapter 43

Willa

I was still reeling from Alexa's visit when I went into town with Claire, my bodyguard, a scary-looking guy named Dash, in tow. I'd objected on the grounds that I was Valentine's Day shopping — well, not shopping exactly — but my arguments had meant nothing to the Kings, who'd reminded me about the rules for going into town and told me to take Dash or stay home.

So I'd sworn Dash to secrecy, because let's be honest, my plan wasn't going to remain a mystery once we'd parked the car and he'd trailed Claire and me to Monsters Ink, the tattoo shop in town.

"Are you sure you want to do this?" Claire asked, peering in the shop's glass window.

Claire was terrified of needles. I'd had to beg just to get her to come with me.

"I'm sure," I said.

I didn't know what the Kings were planning for Valentine's Day next week, but they'd told me to dress to the nines and pack an overnight bag, so whatever it was, I was pretty sure it was going to be out of this world.

Unfortunately, I didn't have the Kings' bottomless pockets, and I wanted to get them something special, something that came from me and wasn't bought with their credit card.

So I'd looked in my bank account, mortified by the painfully low balance left over from my travels and a little scared too, because how was I going to start over after we brought Roberto and the other men to justice when I didn't have a cent to my name?

It wasn't like I could ask my mom for money after plotting to have her new husband sent to prison, or worse.

I tried not to think about the *worse* part. The Kings and I hadn't gotten far enough to talk about what would happen to Roberto and the other men once we knew who they were. In my pre-Aventine brain, I told myself that they would go to prison for a very long time.

But deep down, I think I knew the Kings wouldn't let it go at that.

They were out for blood, not just for Emma and the other girls, but for what Roberto had done to Neo for all those years.

"Come on," I said to Claire, determined to set thoughts of Alexa and Roberto and the missing girls and the absolute shit show that was Aventine aside for the next couple of hours. "Let's do this."

I reached for the door and we stepped into a large cozy room, drawings and photographs of tattoos covering the walls. There was a waiting area at the front of the shop with a couple of worn couches and a coffee table strewn with magazines, and a TV was mounted near the ceiling, playing some kind of baking show.

I approached the long counter that separated the waiting area from the tattoo area. A bearded guy in a Blades cut was leaned back on one of the chairs, a gorgeous woman with jet-black hair and several face piercings bent to his forearm, drawing something I couldn't see.

They were alone except for a blond guy in his twenties, with steel-gray eyes and a defined shadowed jaw, who was cleaning something under running water. He turned it off when he saw us and approached the counter, drying his hands on a towel.

"Can I help you?" He leaned his forearms on the counter and I saw that they were covered in ink.

I was fascinated but I didn't want to stare.

"I'm Willa," I said. "I have an appointment."

A smile broke out over his face. "I'm Adam. You're with me."

"Sounds good," I said. Claire had started flipping through a stack of binders with available tattoos.

"Ever had a tattoo before?" Adam asked.

"Nope, this is my first one."

He grinned. "A virgin."

I thought of the Kings and blushed. I was pretty sure there was some kind of law against calling me a virgin of any kind by now.

But I'd play along. "That's me."

"Great," he said. "You mentioned that you already knew what you wanted?"

"I do."

"Perfect." He fished around behind the counter and produced a clipboard with forms and an attached pen. "Just fill these out and then you can show me what you want. You said there would be three of them right?"

I nodded, thinking of the Kings.

My Kings.

"Yes. Three."

Chapter 44

Willa

I turned in front of the mirror, trying to get a view of my Valentine's Day outfit from every angle. I'd been nervous when the Kings had told me to dress for a nice dinner. Everything from my old life felt too casual and the dresses the Kings had given me for the Welcome Ball — still hanging in my closet — felt too fancy.

But I shouldn't have worried, because when I got home from getting my tattoos I'd found a giant gift-wrapped box in the foyer with my name on it.

The Kings had led me into the living and room and watched me unwrap a slinky red dress with a plunging back and a high neckline, the collar in a halter style that would reveal my shoulders.

So much for a bra, which was probably why they'd included only a scrap of lace that turned out to be a tiny Gstring, along with a pair of gold stilettos and a matching bag.

They'd said it was only part of my Valentine's Day present, which was way too much, and I'd suddenly felt insecure about my tattoos, which were hidden for now. I couldn't do the things for the Kings that they could do for me and I could only hope they would like their present as much as I liked mine.

As for what else was in store for me tonight, I had no idea, but as long as it involved spending the time with my three favorite guys, I really didn't care.

I took a last look at the dress in the mirror, marveling at how the Kings always got it right. The dress slid over my body in a sea of silk, the neckline wrapping around my throat in a way that made me think of Neo, the way he closed his hand around my neck when he kissed me.

It would have looked matronly if not for the bare shoulders, the fabric draping under my arms and over my waist to offer a generous view of side boob, and the back, which plunged to just above my ass.

Not to mention the slit that ran all the way to my hip on one side.

I'd left my hair loose and kept my makeup minimal except for a smoky eye, and I leaned closer to the mirror to check my lip gloss, then double-checked the gold cuff I'd worn to hide one of my tattoos until the moment of truth.

The others were strategically hidden by my hair and

dress, and I was relieved they'd peeled and become less sensitive in time for the reveal.

Satisfied, I grabbed my overnight bag and clutch from the bed and headed downstairs.

The Kings were waiting in the kitchen, chatting in low murmurs that came to a dead halt when they spotted me.

Oscar's eyes darkened with appreciation as he took me in, and he came toward me, relieved me of my overnight bag, and bent to speak near my ear. "Tiger, you look good enough to eat."

The whisper of his breath against my ear sent a shiver through my body and my nipples hardened under the dress.

"Thanks," I said, looking him over, gorgeous in a dark gray suit. "I feel the same about you. Maybe we should skip dinner."

"Not on your life," he said.

"It's way past time we take you on a real date, kitten," Rock said, drawing my attention to him. "But Drago is right. Not sure there's a meal in the world that would look more appetizing than you in that dress." He kissed my cheek. "Don't want to mess up your lipstick."

His navy velvet suit made his eyes appear even bluer, his teeth even whiter. He looked like a supermodel hawking couture, toothpaste, and self-tanner.

But none of that was what really got my attention.

"Where is your cast?" I asked.

It had become so ubiquitous over the past few weeks, Rock so adept at working with it, that I'd almost stopped thinking about it.

"I cut it off!" he said excitedly.

"Um... I'm pretty sure a doctor is supposed to do that," I said.

He shrugged and showed me his arm, making a fist like that proved he was healed. "It's all good, kitten."

I sighed. I knew a losing battle when I saw one. "If you say so."

I turned my attention to Neo, leaning against the kitchen island in a simple but perfectly tailored black suit that fit his frame so closely I could make out his muscled pecs and the significant bulge between his thighs.

He studied me with his amber eyes but didn't make a move toward me.

He didn't have to. His eyes said it all, like he was going to make a five course meal of me.

I walked toward him, my heels clicking on the marble floor, and set my clutch on the island. I ran a hand up the smooth fabric of his suit jacket, over his chest and shoulder, sliding my fingers into the short hair at the back of his neck.

Just a few months ago it would've been unthinkable to press my body against his, but I knew the truth of it now: he was mine.

He always had been.

I stretched to kiss his cheek but he turned his face

toward mine at the last minute and captured my mouth in a greedy kiss.

I only had a moment to be surprised before the primal desires of my body took over. Then it was just the fevered parry of our tongues, Neo's hand slipping into the side of my dress to cup my tit.

When I pulled away, I was breathless, glad his other arm had come around my waist to hold me up. My knees felt like jelly.

"I don't give two fucks about your lipstick," he said.

I smiled up at him. "Of course you don't."

There was a time when it would have annoyed the fuck out of me that I would have to redo my lipstick in the car, but right then, I didn't give two fucks about it either.

"I think we can all agree that we'd rather get Willa naked right here in the kitchen and forget the whole night," Rock said behind me. "But we have a reservation."

Neo reluctantly let me go and headed for the door to the garage. Oscar picked up my overnight bag and followed.

"Where are your overnight bags?" I asked as we filed into the garage.

Behind me, Rock armed the alarm.

"In the car," he said, taking my hand and leading me to the car. "Don't worry about a thing, kitten. We've got it all covered."

Chapter 45

Willa

W e headed through town in the Hummer, Neo driving and Oscar and Rock in the back while I took shotgun.

I was surprised when we left Main Street behind, continuing for another ten minutes until we turned onto a winding gravel road lined with old-fashioned streetlamps.

"I thought we weren't supposed to leave Blackwell Falls," I said.

The lamplight and winding road lent a fairy-tale atmosphere to the scene, especially with snow on the ground, but I wasn't eager to risk our safety, even for a magical Valentine's Day dinner.

And that was doubly true since we'd left Rafe's bodyguards at the house.

The Kings were never worried when they were with

me, it was when they weren't that they pulled out all the stops.

"We are in Blackwell Falls," Oscar said from the backseat.

"Really?" I asked.

"Really," Oscar said. "Right at the town limit, but still technically in Blades territory."

"Wow," I said as we emerged onto a circular driveway with a massive rock sculpture at its center. I hadn't realized the city limits stretched so far outside of town. What is this place?"

Beyond the sculpture, a beautiful stone house glowed with soft light from every window.

Neo stopped in front of the valet. "This is the Seneca Inn."

"They have amazing food," Rock said. "It's Michelin rated."

I didn't know much about fine dining, but I assumed a Michelin rating was a good thing.

"It's so fancy," I said.

The valet reached for my door, then took a step back when Neo shot him a glare that said, *Touch that door and you're a dead man.*

I didn't get it until Neo himself hurried around to open my door. His possessiveness knew no bounds I guess.

I stepped from the car, grateful for the Fendi coat Neo had sent for the Welcome Ball. I hadn't worn it that night but I was glad I had it now. It was freezing, and I tucked my chin into the gorgeous coat and took Neo's and Oscar's crooked arms like I was a fancy Victorian lady with two suitors.

I looked up at Rock."I wish I had a third arm."

He smiled and bent to kiss my cheek. "No worries, kitten. I have an appointment with the kitchen anyway."

"You're not going to eat with us?" I asked as we started up the steps to the inn.

Now that we were closer, I heard the strains of music playing softly from inside, the murmur of other diners and clink of silver on porcelain.

"I'll join you in a few," Rock said. "I've ordered a special menu and want to make sure everything's perfect."

Now I really did feel fancy.

He hurried ahead of us and disappeared inside while Neo and Oscar escorted me up the stairs.

It was hard to remember a time when I thought they were total brutes. Turned out, they were surprisingly gentlemanly and well mannered — except in bed, where Oscar to some degree and Neo especially liked to play rough.

Not that I was complaining.

The restaurant lay ahead, the scent of fresh-baked bread and grilled meat making my stomach rumble, but I was distracted by a bellhop who passed by with our overnight bags, heading for the stairs.

"I think that bellhop has our bags," I said.

Oscar chuckled. "I hope so. We're staying the night."

"Here?" I didn't know why I was surprised. It was called the Seneca Inn, which obviously meant there were rooms somewhere.

"We booked the honeymoon suite," Neo said. "Actually we booked out the whole place."

"The whole place? Why?" I asked.

He stared down at me and I felt something powerful move between us like an electrical current. "Because I don't want anyone to hear you scream when we spend all night making you come."

I had to suck in a breath at the raw hunger that came to life with his words, the dampness between my thighs.

"But first," Oscar said, "we're going to feed you. You're going to need the energy."

It sounded like a threat and a promise.

And goddamn.

I was more than up for both.

Chapter 46

Willa

Rock was right. The food was incredible.

After checking in with the kitchen, he'd joined us for a five-course meal and I relaxed for what felt like the first time in months over microgreens with a champagne vinaigrette, filet mignon so tender it melted in my mouth, cheesy scalloped potatoes with truffle oil, perfectly seared scallops, and lightly steamed asparagus with hollandaise sauce.

And the fresh-baked bread. My god, the bread.

I didn't think it was my imagination that the other diners stared at us and I knew it was because I was with three of the most beautiful guys alive. I felt like the luckiest girl in the universe surrounded by my three Kings, each of them uniquely gorgeous.

The table was immaculately set, fine porcelain and heavy silver on a heavy tablecloth, complete with linen napkins and candles glowing at the center, surrounded by rose petals.

After the main courses, Rock disappeared into the kitchen again to check on dessert. When he returned, the waiter presented us with an assortment of divine treats including tiramisu, crème brûlée, and a heart-shaped chocolate soufflé.

We shared them all, dipping our spoons into the sweet goodness, the Kings insisting on feeding me bites of everything.

I returned the favor and by the time we stood up from the table I was satiated with food and starving for the Kings.

They led me up the grand staircase to the quiet third floor, the sounds from the dining room muffled by exotic carpets, sconces glowing softly on either side of the private hall.

It was a little like being back in Daisy's house, except the Seneca Inn was gorgeously restored. I hoped someday Daisy would be able to do the same for the house at the top of the falls that had given us shelter when we'd needed it most.

Neo fished an old-fashioned key out of his pocket and bent to open the door. He pushed it open and stood back, indicating that I should go first, and when I stepped into the giant living room, I saw that there was a trail of rose petals that started at the door and led into the suite.

I turned to them. "Did you do this?"

"This is just the beginning, kitten," Rock said.

I smiled, hardly believing they'd gone to all this trouble just for me.

I followed the trail of rose petals into the living room, furnished with a complementary array of comfortable modern furniture and antiques. Flames crackled softly from a fireplace next to the sofas and two bottles of champagne peeked out from a large ice bucket on the coffee table.

Next to it, a silver platter held a bowl of fresh strawberries and an assortment of chocolate truffles.

I shook my head. "I can't believe this."

At one end of the living room a set of double doors was open to the bedroom, offering a view of the biggest bed I'd ever seen.

I followed the trail of rose petals into the bedroom and saw that they continued onto the bed where they were arranged in the shape of a heart. Soft white candles glowed from every surface, casting the room in a romantic glow.

Through another set of double doors I caught sight of a massive soaking tub and what appeared to be a luxury bathroom.

I turned to look at them. "I was so excited to give you my Valentine's Day present, but now I feel like it's going to pale in comparison to all of this."

Oscar grinned. "This isn't even your present, tiger."

"Yeah, the real present will come later," Rock said, disappearing into the bathroom and returning with a red silk robe. "Time for you to get naked for your massage."

"My massage?" I looked around, half expecting a masseuse to materialize out of thin air. "Do they have a spa here?"

"We're the spa," Rock said, moving to the nightstand next to the giant bed where a bottle of massage oil sat along with an assortment of sex toys. "And the after-party."

Heat rushed between my thighs.

Valentine's Day, the Kings, massage oil, and sex toys?

Happy Valentine's Day to me.

I took the robe from Rock's hand and headed for the bathroom. Clearly they were going to discover their Valentine's Day present sooner rather than later, but I hadn't decided how to give it to them.

I closed the door of the bathroom and slipped off my dress, folding it neatly and setting the lace panties on top of it.

Obviously I wouldn't be needing those.

I twisted the cuff on my wrist a couple times before removing it. It was still strange to see the tiny chef's hat on my wrist. The tattoo was still a little red but I'd taken the bandage off and had been careful to treat it according to Adam's instructions.

I'd chosen my wrist for Rock because he, more than anyone, had shown me what it meant to take care of people. Even when his arm had been in a cast, he'd insisted on cooking for us, and it was always him who came to my room with trays of food and books when I was sick or sad.

Moving toward the mirror, I touched the boxing gloves just above my left tit. I'd chosen the placement for Neo because it was close to my heart, and I wanted him to know that I saw his heart even when he was being a total dick.

It was harder to see my tattoo for Oscar. I had to sit on the edge of the bathroom counter and lift my hair, twisting until I caught sight of it in the mirror: a camera at the back of my neck, just under my hairline, because it was hidden and Oscar had a way of seeing all the parts of me I tried to hide and even the ones I didn't know existed at all.

They felt like meager testaments to my feelings for the Kings, especially compared to all they were doing for me, but I loved having them inked on my skin, knowing they would be there forever, even if we weren't always together.

I shook off my sadness at the thought and slipped on the red silk robe. I would let them find their Valentine's Day presents themselves. Maybe it would be the same kind of discovery I'd felt when I'd realized they were so much more than they'd seemed.

I hoped so. I had so little to give them but I wanted them to have it all anyway.

"What the actual fuck are you doing in there, Jezebel?" Neo asked from the other room.

I laughed softly. After five months with the Kings,

some things were as predictable as the sunrise and Neo being an impatient asshole was one of them.

I reached for the door. I didn't know what the future held, but tonight, locked away with the Kings?

It almost didn't matter.

Almost.

Chapter 47

Willa

T hey were waiting in boxer briefs when I emerged from the bathroom in the robe.

As if my night couldn't get any better.

Because if there was any present better than being wined and dined by three godlike men, it was being massaged by three godlike men in their underwear.

I dropped the robe and felt a thrill of satisfaction when their gazes feasted on my naked body. Like most girls, I had my insecurities. For one, I'd always thought my tits were a little too small for the size of my ass, my thighs a little too fleshy.

But the Kings made me feel beautiful and perfect. They'd never expressed anything but total delight at every aspect of my body and over the past few months it had worked to reverse some of my earlier insecurities.

Part of it was because it didn't matter anymore if anyone else liked my body: I literally only cared about the three men in this hotel suite.

But the other part was that I'd started to see myself through their eyes. Not as someone scared and weak with a moderately pretty face and mediocre body but as someone strong and powerful who was the most beautiful girl in the world to the only three men who mattered.

I was almost sure they would see the tiny tattoo above my left breast, but they'd turned out the lights, bathing the room in the glow of the candles flickering on every surface, and I climbed onto the bed and followed Neo's orders to lay on my stomach.

I settled onto the mattress with a sigh and felt the drip of warm oil on my back, followed by the glorious slide of Rock's hands on my shoulders.

I didn't know what Oscar and Neo were doing and I didn't care. I was ready to give myself over to their ministrations as the scent of crushed rose petals wafted into the room from under my naked body.

Rock's hands moved down my spine in one fluid motion, pressing and rubbing in all the right spots. He used his thumbs to rub circles into my hips, then slid his hands all the way back up my spine.

The pressure was glorious and I moaned again as he reached my neck.

I was lost in sensation, the room dim, music playing softly from the living room, Rock's soft breathing mingled with mine.

He scooped some of the hair that had fallen across my neck, twisting it to move it aside, then stopped moving.

"What's this?" he asked, his fingers stroking the back of my neck.

Valentine's Day present number one: found.

"It's my Valentine's Day present to Oscar," I said.

"Drago," Rock said, "come look at this."

I kept my eyes closed, suddenly feeling shy.

About the tattoos, not the fact that I was ass-naked and sprawled out on the bed in the presence of the Kings.

I felt the stroke of another finger, this time Oscar's.

"Did you... did you get a tattoo of a camera for me?" he asked.

I opened my eyes and saw that his face was close to mine, shock and something else I couldn't name in his eyes.

"It was the only thing I could afford that felt meaningful enough for..." I hadn't told Neo I loved him yet and I didn't want to make it weird by saying it to Oscar in front of him, "how I feel about you."

I twisted a little to look at Rock, still straddling my hips in his underwear.

"There's one for you too." I searched the room for Neo and found him leaning against the wall, his eyes magnetic as they locked onto my face. "And you."

I started to roll over and Rock rose onto his knees to give me room to move.

I was stretched out on my back now, Rock's aroused cock visible in his boxer briefs and tantalizingly close to my bare cunt.

I held out my wrist to show him the chef's hat tattoo. "This one's for you."

He took my wrist in his hand and looked at the tiny symbol, then pressed his lips against it. "I can't believe you got tattoos for us."

"I wanted you to be with me always," I said around the lump in my throat. Saying it implied that they wouldn't always be with me, physically at least.

I didn't like to think about that.

I met Neo's gaze across the room and reached out for him.

He hesitated, then pushed off the wall and crossed the room to take my hand.

I placed his palm over the tattoo above my tit. "This one's for you."

I wasn't going to tell them why I'd chosen the placements I had. I knew why and I hoped they could guess.

He lifted his palm and leaned in to look at the boxing gloves etched over my heart.

"I know it's not an expensive present," I said. "But it's from me, from my heart. I... I hope it's okay and that you like them."

Neo stared at it for a long time. "You had me inked on your skin?"

I touched the angel tattoo on his chest, tracing her face — my face — and lingering on the unicorn pendant.

His gaze was still locked on mine when Oscar eased onto the other side of the bed.

He leaned down to kiss me, long and slow, and desire sparked to life at the center of my body. His tongue swept my mouth, Rock still straddling my hips, Neo's hand covering the tattoo over my heart.

I wiggled my hips instinctively as all the blood rushed to my cunt.

"Fuck me," Rock said. "You better turn back onto your stomach or we're going to have to renege on the massage portion of your present."

I pulled away from Oscar's mouth. "I wouldn't complain."

"If you're saying you want to jump right to the part where you get fucked, I'm happy to comply," Neo said, his voice laced with a dark promise.

"Fuck that," Rock said to him. "If I can keep my hard-on in my shorts, you can do the same. We're going to give Willa a fucking massage even if it means you have to jack off in the fucking corner like the freak you are."

I laughed. "It's your show."

Oscar grinned down, letting his gaze travel over my naked body. "And what a show it is."

"Damn right," Rock said. "Now turn your ass over. The night has just begun."

Chapter 48

Willa

I settled back onto my stomach, even more relaxed now that I'd given the Kings their Valentine's Day presents. I mean let's face it: tattooing a guy's symbol on your body could kind of go either way.

Romantic or creepy? You decide.

How I'd gone from barely being able to stand the Kings to essentially tattooing them on my body, I'd never know, but now that the cat was out of the bag I was able to relax even more deeply as Rock's fingers worked their magic on my neck, shoulders, and back.

When another pair of hands started working on my feet, I knew instinctively it was Oscar. After months with the Kings and hours spent naked with them, I would know their individual touches blindfolded.

Oscar stroked lengthwise down the soles of my feet,

continuing up my calves as Rock continued massaging my back.

They hadn't so much as approached any of my erogenous zones and I was already crazy turned on.

I felt the release of Rock's weight from my body and he stretched out next to me, running his fingers down my back. Then I felt the trickle of something cold on my tailbone and I knew Neo was at play.

I gasped as the cool liquid trickled between my ass cheeks, then moaned when I felt the warm slide of a tongue licking it from my flesh.

"Lucky bastard," Rock murmured, kissing my shoulder. "The only thing better than champagne is champagne licked from your perfect ass."

I sighed as Neo's hands closed around my ass cheeks. He spread them wide, and I felt the heat of his tongue slither from my pussy to my asshole.

I writhed, unapologetically seeking friction on my clit from the mattress, then lifted my hips to give Neo better access.

A new weight arrived next to me, opposite Rock, and I turned my head to see that Oscar had joined us, making me the center of a Rock and Oscar sandwich while Neo licked my cunt from behind.

Oscar leaned in to capture my mouth, his tongue diving inside as Rock kissed my back and Neo drank champagne from my ass.

I was on ecstasy overload, the slide of my tongue against Oscar's mimicking the slide of Neo eating my pussy from behind. I was totally unashamed of the fact that I was lifting my hips to meet Neo's mouth, desperate for more.

"Fuck yeah," Neo murmured, pausing his feast to run his fingers through my now-soaking cunt. "Everything tastes better on your pussy."

A strangled moan tore from my throat and Oscar chuckled against my lips. "I think she likes it."

"That right, Jezebel?" Neo asked behind me. "You like it when I eat your pussy?"

I was on fire, too turned on to even answer the question, and a second later I felt the slap of his hand against my ass hard enough to sting.

I yelped. "Fuck!"

Desire roared through my body like a rogue wildfire.

"Answer me when I ask you a question," Neo said, closing his teeth around the flesh of my ass.

"Yes," I gasped.

He bit harder. "Yes what?"

"Yes, I like it when you eat my pussy."

"Good girl," Rock soothed next to me, stroking my burning ass with his palm. "You know how cranky Neo gets when you don't answer his questions."

"But when you do, you get a reward," Oscar said, kissing his way along my jaw. "Isn't that right, brother?"

"If I feel like it," Neo said.

But he must've felt like it because a second later he grasped my hips, lifting them off the bed until my ass was in the air.

He turned onto his back and wedged himself between my thighs and I felt the whisper of his breath against my throbbing cunt.

"Hand me that vibrator," he said to no one in particular.

Oscar reached behind him and handed something to Neo, and a second later I heard the soft hum of the vibrator from the nightstand.

He slid it inside me and circled my clit with his tongue, causing my body to jump like it had been given an electric shock.

I'd risen onto all fours almost without realizing it, some primitive part of my brain wanting to give Neo easy access to my pussy. Now he was between my thighs, my cunt over his face while Rock played with my tits and Oscar stroked my back.

The vibrator sent currents of pleasure from my core to the rest of my body, Neo lapping at my clit like a hungry wolf while Rock wedged himself under my hips and took one of my nipples into his mouth, sucking while he pinched the other one between his fingers.

"Oh my god," I moaned, on the verge of orgasm. "I'm going to come."

Neo's mouth was suddenly gone from my clit, the vibrator removed from my pussy.

"Not yet you aren't." Neo slapped my ass. "Lay on your back, Jezebel. I want strawberries with my champagne."

Chapter 49

Willa

I turned over onto my back, my body humming with the withheld climax. Neo was naked, his broad shoulders and sculpted pecs glowing in the candlelight.

I let my gaze roam down his washboard abs and the taper of his waist to the trail of dark hair that led to his enormous cock, jutting between his legs and making it clear I wasn't the only one who was turned on.

He stared down at me, his eyes greedily drinking in. "You're the most beautiful fucking thing I've ever seen, Jezebel."

I didn't know what to say, so I said nothing. I was surrounded by three exquisite naked men, like some kind of fever dream I never wanted to end.

On one side of me, Rock continued playing with my

tits, cupping them, rolling my nipples between his fingers as Oscar's hand slid down my stomach between my thighs.

He stroked leisurely through my pussy with his long fingers, like he had all the time in the world when my body was screaming for release.

I lifted my arm on Rock's side so that I could slide my fingers into his hair while he played with my tits and did the same with Oscar while he stroked my cunt. Their heads, one light and one dark, were in my hands, their hair silky in my fingers.

Between my thighs, Neo reached onto the floor and lifted a bottle of champagne, then poured some onto my tits.

I gasped in surprise, then laughed.

"We're having a party," Neo said. "There's enough for everybody."

He poured more into my belly button.

"Move that hand before I break it," he ordered Oscar.

Oscar's hand disappeared from my cunt and Neo trickled more champagne onto my smooth mound.

I assumed he'd lick it off, but then he lifted the bowl of strawberries off the floor and onto the bed.

He plucked one from the bowl and teased my clit with it, and I watched through my thighs, mesmerized by the sight of the ruby-red strawberry moving over my cunt.

He slid the strawberry between my folds, then pushed it just into my entrance.

And fuck me if I didn't love it. If I didn't love the thought of him eating it from inside me.

He reached for the floor again and lifted a small pitcher of cream that had been on the silver platter in the living room.

"Strawberries and cream," he said, dripping some onto each of my tit's and down my stomach, "my favorite."

Rock and Oscar were all over it, each of them taking one of my nipples in their mouths, licking and sucking the cream from my skin while I moaned, holding their heads in place, my whole body throbbing with the need to come.

Then Neo poured more cream down my stomach and into my belly button with the champagne, continuing to dribble it over my waxed mound.

I sucked in a breath when it trickled onto my pussy, the strawberry still wedged into my opening.

I didn't know what was hotter, the pleasure flooding my body or the sight of Rock and Oscar sucking on my tits, my thighs spread for Neo, his giant dick inches away from my desperate pussy.

He stared down at me with fire in his eyes. "I'm fucking hungry, Jezebel. I've been hungry for ages."

He lowered his face between my thighs and I felt his tongue slide from my ass to the opening between my pussy lips, loosening the strawberry he'd placed there. I watched as he took it between his teeth, hovering over my pussy.

He bit down on the strawberry, letting the red juice drip from his lips, down his chin and onto my cunt.

He looked at my pussy, covered in strawberry juice, champagne, and cream. "I've been starved for you. Now I'm going to eat."

He bent his head and lapped at my pussy, licking the juice from my folds and my clit while Oscar and Rock worked my tits with their mouths and fingers, their hard cocks pressed against the side of my legs.

I reached between my thighs and held Neo's dark head in place. This time I was going to come, and no one was going to stop me.

I moved my hips, climbing the peak of my orgasm, and Oscar removed his mouth from my tit to watch Neo eat my cunt.

"I'm so fucking jealous, tiger, but have to admit, it's a hell of a lot of fun watching Neo bury his face in that pretty little pussy."

His words only made me hotter and bolder.

"Don't you fucking stop," I ordered Neo, grinding my face on his mouth. "Don't you dare fucking stop."

Rock chuckled against my tit. "We have such a bossy little kitten."

There was no holding back my climax and I moved my hips faster, relieved when Neo met my pace, sliding two fingers inside me where the strawberry had been while he tongued my clit.

I fell into the abyss of my orgasm all at once, light exploding behind my eyes.

"Fuck yes," I cried out. "Eat my pussy. Eat it."

I was out of my mind with pleasure, determined to prolong it, pressing Neo's head to my cunt as his tongue stroked my clit, his fingers plunging in and out of me.

It went on and on, my body shuddering, filthy words streaming from my mouth like I was possessed by the spirit of a fucking porn star.

When the tremors finally stopped, I threw my head back on the pillow and gasped for breath, the tension leaving my body until I was as limp as a rag doll.

Neo rubbed my thighs and pressed a reverent kiss to my hairless pussy while Oscar and Rock gently stroked my tits and stomach.

"That was fucking hot," Rock said.

"Agreed," Oscar said. "And the night is young."

"Fuck yeah it is," Neo said. "Now get on your knees, Jezebel."

Chapter 50

Willa

I obeyed because who wouldn't? The Kings had proven that they knew how to deliver maximum pleasure.

I wasn't going to start arguing now.

I rose to my knees and Oscar rolled onto his back at the center of the bed. He touched one of my legs and I lifted it over his hips, straddling his granite-like dick while Rock moved to the head of the bed, stroking his erection near my face, making it clear where he intended to put it.

The pierced head of Oscar's dick brushed against my pussy, igniting my desire all over again. I loved everything the Kings did to me but nothing was better than having them at the same time, filling me in every way possible.

"Hand me the lube and that other vibrator," Neo ordered.

Oscar reached for the nightstand and picked up a clear

bottle of lube and an extremely large vibrator and the first hint of nerves hit my stomach. I half wondered if he'd rip me apart, his giant dick, an instrument of extreme pleasure everywhere else, potentially an instrument of destruction *there*.

I looked over my shoulder at him, lubing up his cock and then the vibrator. "Are you sure it'll fit?"

"Which one?" he asked with a smirk.

"Either," I said.

"Oh, it's going to fit, Jezebel." He must have seen the panic on my face because his expression softened. "Didn't I say I'd always take care of you?"

I nodded. It was something he'd said the first time we'd fucked in the shower, after the cliff jump. Back then we'd been talking about birth control, but he'd proven a million times over that he meant it in every way.

I tipped forward onto my hands, indicating my agreement, and reached for Oscar's cock between my thighs.

I positioned him at my entrance and leaned down to kiss him, my body opening at the pleasure delivered by his skilled tongue, and I heard the hum of the vibrator behind me.

I flinched as it touched the tight bud of my asshole.

"Just relax," Neo coaxed behind me. "Give it to her, Drago."

Oscar drove up into me and I gasped as he filled me,

the piercing at the base of his shaft hitting my clit. Near my face, Rock tucked loose hair behind my ear and offered me his dick.

"Trust me," Neo said behind me. "Suck Rock's dick and trust me."

Rock brushed the head of his cock against my lips and I opened wide, eager both to taste him and for the distraction as Neo eased the tip of the vibrator into my ass.

I moaned as he slid it in further, matching Rock's pace as he pushed into my mouth.

Oscar grabbed my hips and lifted me off his dick before pulling me back down, burying himself in my cunt, the barbell on his head sliding along my walls, the one at his base hitting my clit with every upward stroke.

I looked up at Rock, gazing down at me adoringly as I took him deep into my mouth.

"You're so fucking pretty, kitten," he said.

Behind me, Neo slid the vibrator back inside my ass, creating an erotic friction that seemed to travel to every nerve ending in my body. I could already feel another orgasm building at my center and I relaxed as he worked it, preparing me for his massive dick.

Rock reached down and stroked the top of my head, smoothing my hair. "Your mouth feels so fucking good."

I was overflowing with pleasure, Rock fucking my mouth while Oscar drove up into me, setting a rhythm with his hands on my hips, the vibrator in my ass the icing on the proverbial cake.

I was already close to coming when Neo withdrew the vibrator and I felt the thick head of his cock push against my ass.

My impending orgasm drove me forward, and I tipped my hips, getting an even better angle to stroke my clit with Oscar's piercing while giving Neo even better access.

"Goddamn you feel amazing," Oscar said, thrusting faster.

Neo pushed inside, and I moaned around Rock's dick in my mouth.

Neo eased in a little at a time, letting me stretch for him, amping up my pleasure before he slid in the rest of the way.

I groaned as he became fully seated in my ass. He was huge, completely filling me, and I loved every glorious inch of it.

"Fuck, Jezebel," he growled. "I fucking knew you'd be able to take it all."

"She loves it," Oscar said. "She's drenched."

He was right. I was soaked, burning for them, and I moved faster, reaching for the promise of my climax, using Oscar's dick to stroke my clit while Neo slammed into my ass and Rock fucked my mouth.

Oscar reached up and grabbed my tits, pinching my

nipples, and I moaned, taking all of them in a frenzy as I raced for release.

"You ready to come for us, Jezebel?" Neo asked.

I couldn't answer around Rock's cock but I moaned my assent.

"Good," Neo said. "We're ready to fill you up."

The orgasm washed over me all at once and I cried out, the sound strangled as Rock spilled his hot semen into my mouth with a groan.

I shuddered with pleasure, my mind empty as waves of ecstasy rolled through me.

"Fuck!" Oscar said as let go.

"Take it," Neo said slamming into my ass and coming with a groan. "Take it all, Jezebel."

My orgasm seemed to go on and on, and I rode the wave, grinding on Oscar's dick, my mouth and ass relaxed and fully open for Rock and Neo until we all collapsed in a heap, sweaty and breathing heavy.

Rock removed his dick from my mouth and bent down to kiss me while Neo eased out of my ass with a sigh.

I dropped onto Oscar's chest, completely limp.

He wrapped his arms around me. "I'll never get over how good it feels to be inside you."

I eased off him and rolled onto the bed, tucked into the crook of his arm. Rock took the other side, spooning me and draping his big arm over my waist while Neo went to wash up.

I was thinking about where he would sleep when he came back, wanting to be close to him too, wanting to be as close as possible to all of them, when my eyes grew heavy.

"Happy Valentine's Day, tiger," Oscar murmured against the top of my head.

It was the last thing I heard before I fell into sleep.

Chapter 51

Willa

I slept like the dead, wrapped up in the Kings' bodies until I didn't know where I ended and they began. The sun was high in the sky and bathing the suite in warm light when I woke to a knock at the hotel room door.

I sat up, naked and groggy, and wondered where the Kings had gone. I was alone in the giant bed, the sheets rumpled and smelling like cologne and sex, champagne and strawberries.

It was a fucking mess and I didn't care, not even a little.

Soft murmurs drifted in from the suite's living room, but I couldn't see anything because the Kings had closed the doors to let me sleep.

And thank god, because they'd fucked me senseless, making me come again and again until I'd fallen asleep, limp and exhausted in the best of ways.

It was still weird to look down and see the tattoo over

my heart. I touched it with my fingertip, thinking of Neo, then did the same with the other two tattoos, calling Rock's and Oscar's faces to mind.

I was glad I'd been able to give them something that no one else could.

I sat up and stretched, the sheet falling from my naked body, then went to the bathroom and cleaned up.

I brushed my teeth and returned to the room to hunt for my robe. I found it on the floor and slipped it on before opening the bedroom doors.

The Kings were lounging in the living room, looking like a bunch of underwear models on lunch break. Neo sat on a chair in front of the round dining table, laden with covered dishes from room service, reading the paper.

His dark hair was tousled, a sexy shadow darkening his jaw, and I had to say, only Neo could make manspreading look that fucking hot.

Rock jumped to his feet from the sofa and put down his phone when he saw me.

"Morning, kitten." He came toward me and wrapped me in his arms, kissing the top of my head. "How did you sleep?"

"Like I was comatose," I said. "Is there coffee?"

"You better believe it," he said, walking to the table to pour me a cup.

"Good morning," I said to Oscar and Neo.

"Yes," Oscar said with a grin that called to mind last night's fun. "Yes, it is."

"It'll be better when you get your sweet ass over here," Neo said with a growl, setting aside his paper.

I crossed the room and rested a hand on his shoulder, preparing to plant a good-morning kiss on his cheek, but he had something else in mind and snaked his arms around my waist, pulling me into his lap.

"I woke up craving strawberries," he said, pushing aside my robe to suck on my tit.

I inhaled deeply, remembering the way he'd fished the strawberry out of my cunt and licked the juices off my body.

Fuck me.

I was sore and wet again anyway.

I grabbed a handful of his hair and tugged. "I'm going to need sustenance if you want more playtime."

"Yeah, you fucking brute," Rock said, taking my hand and pulling me to my feet. He closed my robe chastely and led me to an empty chair around the table. "Besides, we need to give Willa her Valentine's Day present."

I blinked. "But... you already did that. The whole night was amazing. You gave me the dress and we had an amazing dinner with dessert, plus the night in this gorgeous suite. You even gave me a massage!"

Rock grinned. "It's true, I am a great masseuse, but none of that was your actual Valentine's Day present."

Oscar stood and dug around in his duffel bag. He produced a manilla envelope tied with a red ribbon and crossed the room to the table.

"Sorry it's not wrapped nicer," he said, setting the envelope in front of me. "We thought about dressing it up, but it seemed silly."

He kissed the top of my head and took one of the empty chairs.

"Open it, Jezebel," Neo said. Normally, it would have sounded like an order, but this time, it sounded like something else.

What? I didn't know, but I was suddenly nervous as fuck.

I didn't bother untying the ribbon. I went straight for the tiny metal clasp and the sealed flap.

I peered inside, half expecting something besides a sheaf of papers even though that was exactly what it felt like.

I pulled them out and scanned the first page, trying to make sense of what I was seeing.

... the sum of $500,000 transferred to account #MJL986272H in the name of Willa Russo effective February 14th...

I shook my head. "I don't get it. What is this? You're giving me... money?"

"We're giving you freedom." Neo's voice sounded funny. Thick and hoarse.

"We want you to have options when this is all over, tiger," Oscar said, his dark eyes filled with emotion.

"You... want me to leave," I said, wondering why tears were stinging my eyes.

Rock crouched next to me and reached for my hand. "That's not what we're saying, kitten."

"This money means you can start over however you want," Rock said gently.

The tears spilled from my eyes, because now I understood: they didn't want me to stay because I had to.

They wanted me to have a choice.

I brushed the tears from my cheeks. "It's too much."

"You deserve every penny and more," Neo said. "And it's already done. The other documents explain how to set up passwords and PINs so that only you can access the account." His gaze was penetrating from across the table. "Happy Valentine's Day, Jezebel."

There was something else. Something he wanted to say but didn't, and at that moment I would have given just about anything to know what it was.

I drew in a shaky breath. "'Thank you' isn't enough, but..." I looked at Neo, felt the words lodged in my throat: *I love you*. "Thank you."

"You're welcome," he said.

"I think it's time for breakfast," Rock said. "We gave you half a million dollars and you cried."

I smiled. "Sorry. I was just..."

"Hungry," Rock said. "And I knew you would be, which is why I got everything."

I laughed as he lifted the covers from the dishes. And boy, he wasn't kidding. There were omelettes and French toast, eggs Benedict and perfectly cooked bacon, an assortment of pastries and crispy buttered wheat toast, even waffles and pancakes with tiny bottles of maple syrup.

We spent the next hour feasting on food and mimosas and I ended breakfast with syrup in places syrup should never be, or maybe it should, because the Kings were determined to lick it off my body, and I have to admit, it was pretty fucking hot.

After that we were all sticky, so we piled into the shower for more steamy fun.

Emphasis on the word *steamy*.

We'd just gotten out and were drying off when Neo's phone buzzed from the bathroom counter.

"I have to check that," he said, stalking naked across the bathroom.

He didn't have to explain. Since Alexa's news about the Knights, the Kings had been working their closest contacts in every house, trying to figure out who was loyal to them and who was loyal to their alumni.

Everything was going to get a lot more complicated if the other houses opted not to name their killers.

Neo picked up his phone and scowled at the display. I knew something was wrong when he answered the call.

Neo almost never answered his calls.

"What?" he said into the phone.

For at least a minute, he just listened.

"Talk to the Queens," he finally said. "See what they know."

He set down his phone and turned to face us.

"What's wrong?" I asked.

"Alexa's dead," he said. "It looks like she fell from one of the cliffs into the river. And by *looks like*, I mean someone killed her."

Part Three

Part Three

Chapter 52

Willa

The Admin building had a completely different atmosphere than normal when Rock and I stepped through the doors Monday morning. It was still crowded, but rather than groups of people laughing, talking, and goofing off, huddles of students stood in groups, talking softly, some of them crying.

It had been that way all day. My classes had been nearly empty, minus the usual banter and casual atmosphere.

But that wasn't all. While some of our peers were clearly upset by Alexa's death, others had eyed Rock and I warily, something surreptitious in their gazes.

Maybe I was imagining that part, but I didn't think so.

I had a feeling our enemies weren't just alumni. They were among us too, kids who saw the Kings' determination to ferret out Aventine's killers as an opportunity to gain favor with their crime families instead.

The question was, how did we tell the difference?

"Fuck," Rock muttered as we headed for the cafeteria. "This is fucking weird."

"Definitely not a good vibe," I said, moving a little closer to him.

We were almost to the cafeteria doors when one of the Rooks tipped his head at Rock. "I talk to you for a sec?" He glanced my way. "Alone."

I could tell from the way Rock looked at him that he was trying to decide whether to tell the guy to fuck off and say what he had to say in front of me, but in the end he nodded and looked down at me. "Go ahead without me. I'll be right behind you."

The cafeteria was only a few feet away, my friends, and presumably Neo and Oscar, waiting inside. Plus, Interim Dean Garcia was at her post outside the cafeteria again.

Either the board of directors hadn't given her much to do or she was unusually interested in student affairs.

I peeled away from Rock and walked hesitantly toward the cafeteria entrance.

"Hey there," she said to me as I approached. I wanted to dislike her, or at least be wary of her, but her brown eyes held nothing but concern. "How are you holding up?"

"Okay," I said. I shook my head, deciding there was no

reason to lie about this at least. "That's not really true. I think I'm still in shock."

We'd just seen Alexa a few days earlier.

Now she was dead.

"That's perfectly understandable," Interim Dean Garcia said. She seemed to consider her words. "My door is always open, Willa. If there's ever anything you want to talk about, I mean."

I couldn't shake the feeling that there was a hidden message in her words, but I couldn't imagine what it was. She'd been installed by the board, and that meant she was one of them.

Like Roberto.

"Thanks," I said. "I appreciate it."

"Of course. You have an ally if you need one."

Jesus. If she'd been a cop, a jury would have acquitted me on the grounds of entrapment. Was she trying to get me to talk? Planning to feed information back to the board, half of whom were Aventine alumni?

I smiled and nodded. "Thanks again."

Then I tucked my chin and hurried into the cafeteria like I was fighting a strong wind, because that was how it had started to seem.

It was noisier in the cafeteria than in the hallways, but the volume was still muted compared to every other day. I got in line and grabbed an order of mac and cheese and a hot chocolate, because if this wasn't a day for comfort food I didn't know what was.

I made my way to the lunch table I shared with Claire, Quinn, and Erin, and now apparently the Kings because Neo and Oscar were already at our table, eating and talking to each other in low tones.

"Hey," Claire said when I slid into my seat. "Anything new?"

I shook my head. Claire assumed that because I was with the Kings I knew something she didn't, but other than the name Alexa had dropped of the owner of St. Andrew's, I didn't know any more than she did, and I wasn't sure the Kings did either.

"Well, she definitely didn't just slip right?" Quinn asked. "I mean, nobody goes out hiking this time of year."

"Actually, that's not true," Erin said, dipping a spoon into her yogurt. "Winter hiking is a thing."

Claire rolled her eyes. "It's not an Alexa Petrov thing."

"It's definitely weird," I said, shooting the Kings a glance.

It was an unspoken agreement that we wouldn't tell anyone what Alexa had said about the owner of St. Andrew's. I didn't know why, but I could only assume the Kings were keeping things close to their vests because of what Alexa had told us about the other Knights.

If some of the Knights wanted to stay quiet about their

murdering alumni, it was a safe bet that all the houses had members who felt the same way.

"I heard it was the Knights," Quinn said. "They didn't want her to talk."

"I bet it was her family," Erin said. "And by 'family' I don't mean her parents."

Claire looked at Neo. "What does this mean for the game?"

"Nothing," he said, his voice cold. "The game continues."

Claire tried to hide her surprise but it was written all over her face.

I didn't blame her but I didn't blame the Kings for keeping the game going either. It was way more dangerous now that Alexa had been murdered — and I was sure she'd been murdered — but if the Kings called it off, we'd be admitting we were powerless against whoever was behind her death.

This was a defining moment for every member of every house. They had to choose: stay loyal to their crime families or do the right thing, the honorable thing.

And in a lot of ways, the Kings couldn't have constructed a more perfect game. If the games were designed to prepare us for the world we would all be joining after graduation — a world of organized crime — this one was the ultimate test.

Except everything was upside down because in any

other situation, the winner would be proving their loyalty to their families.

We were asking them to turn traitor.

My phone buzzed in my bag and I reached for it and saw a text from Mara.

We'd had one video date since our last argument, but she'd been aloof and distant and her texts had been perfunctory. I glanced at the text, a three-word response to a question I'd asked, and sighed.

I'd hoped our standing video call would make her feel better, but apparently not.

I added it to my long list of things to worry about and slipped my phone back in my bag.

"Are we still going to the Spring Fever masquerade at St. Andrew's?" Erin asked Claire.

Claire was the unspoken leader of their trio, which was why Erin took it so personally when Claire treated her like shit.

"I don't see any point in skipping it," Claire said.

"I don't know," Erin said. "Out of respect?"

"Don't you think the rest of us are in danger?" Quinn asked Claire.

"Not unless you know something about the assholes in the Irish family who have been taking girls," Claire said. "Because that's what everybody's saying, that Alexa knew the Knights who were involved and threatened to tell."

"I don't know shit," Quinn said, "and honestly, I'm fine keeping it that way at this point."

"Same." Erin stacked her utensils on her empty plate, then looked at me and hurriedly added, "I mean, obviously I want to find out what happened to Emma and the other girls. I'm just saying I'd rather not end up dead myself."

"I get it," I said, trying to reassure her before Claire jumped down her throat. "No worries."

"So we're going?" Erin asked. "To the masquerade? Because it's only a week away and I need a costume."

"We're definitely going," Claire said. "I've been waiting all year for this and I need to blow off some steam. Plus I've been flirting with Rico for the past three weeks and the masquerade at St. Andrew's is my chance to get him naked."

Claire had been working her way through the Saints since the start of the year. I admired her stamina, not to mention her ability to juggle all those texts from different guys in the same house.

Quinn leaned forward to look past Claire. "You should come with us, Willa. It'll be fun and you can always bring your bodyguard."

It was hard to hide the fact that you had a bodyguard when he followed you everywhere you went.

I started to demure, already certain the Kings had no intention of going to the masquerade, but I was interrupted by Neo.

"She can't go with you," he said, "because she's going with us."

I did a double take. "Wait... We're going?"

He held my gaze and I knew he was thinking about the name Alexa had given us the last time we'd seen her.

Laszlo Nagy.

"Okay, then I guess I'm going to need a costume too," I said.

Oscar flashed me a sexy grin. "Don't worry about that, tiger. We got you covered."

Chapter 53

Willa

A week later I sat on my bed and opened the giant box Rock had brought to my room. I knew it was my costume for the Spring Fever masquerade that night, but as soon as I parted the tissue paper I started trying to figure out what the actual fuck was inside.

Because there were feathers. White feathers.

And a lot of them.

I'd spent the last week begging the Kings for hints about our Spring Fever costumes, but they'd been determined to keep them a secret.

I'd pretended to be annoyed, complaining that I wouldn't know how to do my hair and makeup, but it had been a bit of much-needed fun in the midst of a stressful and somber week.

There had been a candlelight vigil for Alexa, but it had

felt loaded with tension and unspoken animosity. Looking at my peers through the flickering candlelight, people I'd learned to like and trust, I'd felt among strangers.

Which of them were hiding the identities of the killers amidst their families?

It was impossible to tell, and despite the Kings' efforts, we had no more information on the culprits in the other houses. The Rooks and Saints claimed not to know the killers among their alumni, but after what had happened with Alexa and the Knights, it was impossible to know if they were telling the truth.

And we were still playing the game too, trying to figure out who in the Alinari family had been working with Roberto.

So yeah. I wasn't mad about getting a chance to dress up, drink, and explore my first sex club with the Kings.

I lifted the feathers from the box, surprised by their weight, and realized it was a set of wings.

Angel wings.

I was no angel, and sometimes I was embarrassed that Neo saw me that way, but that was how I'd been branded into his memory all those years ago, and I couldn't control the picture he'd painted.

And these were no party-store costume wings. They were luxurious and heavy, silky soft, and obviously custom-made to strap on my back with gold elastic that would fit around my arms.

I set them aside and removed a white lace bustier with feathered trim that matched the wings. It was held up by thin straps, with another set of even thinner straps diving into what would be my cleavage at the center. The bottom of the bustier was trimmed with lace that cascaded down either side to create an inverted V, and when I turned it around, I saw that the back was barely there, just a thin strap with a hook-and-eye closure.

Looking past it into the box I saw that there was something else, and I set the bustier aside with the wings and pulled out a tiny white skirt.

A tiny see-through skirt.

It was obviously meant to be worn over the accompanying lace garter and stockings, but the entire thing was probably only a foot wide.

It would barely cover my pussy, which was probably the point.

The Kings had thrown in tiny white underwear and a note in Neo's handwriting that read, *Wear the gold shoes.*

A bolt of heat rushed to my cunt at the thought of him writing the note, thinking about my outfit and deciding what he wanted me to wear.

My feminist friends would be mortified, but I couldn't help it. Neo usually left the details to Rock. The fact that he'd thought enough about my outfit to be specific about what I would wear to St. Andrew's made me all hot and bothered.

I stood up and laid everything out on the bed. I had to hand it to the Kings.

The outfit was hot.

I had no idea what one wore to a sex club, but the Kings probably had a lot more experience, something I tried not to think about because even though I'd never been a jealous person I wanted to stab through the heart any woman who'd ever touched them.

I had no doubt the outfit would be perfect and I was suddenly excited despite the fact that we were going to St. Andrew's to figure out how Laszlo Nagy was involved with Roberto and the others.

I would have been nervous to go to a sex club with anyone but the Kings, but I took comfort in the fact that any fun to be had would be had with them.

Because one thing I knew for certain was that the Kings would never let another man touch me in their presence.

I picked up my phone and looked at the time.

Shit.

It was time to do my hair and makeup.

St. Andrew's — and my Kings — awaited.

Chapter 54

Willa

For once I was the first one downstairs before an event and I used my phone to check my makeup, even though I'd already done that before I left my room.

This time I'd gone for polished natural makeup and a bright red lip, rationalizing that most of my face would be covered by my mask anyway.

I'd pinned up my hair, leaving a few wavy tendrils to fall around my face, and omitted jewelry altogether — except for my choker of course — to keep the focus on my magnificent costume.

It felt strange to stand in the kitchen in such a revealing outfit knowing we were going out, but I was looking forward to experiencing something new, and to seeing Claire, Quinn, and Erin.

Everyone else would be there too — the Spring Fever

masquerade had been the talk of campus for weeks — but I had no idea how we would be greeted. Everyone still seemed to fear the Kings, but there was something else in their eyes now, a kind of nervous anticipation that put me on edge.

As for the Knights, they'd created a wall of silence around their house, no one willing to talk about Alexa or admit to knowing who was involved in the disappearance of the girls.

They didn't know we had the list Alexa had given us the last night we'd seen her. That no one had come forward with the names was a massive disappointment. I'd wanted to believe that when push came to shove, doing the right thing for Emma — for all the girls who'd gone missing — would be more important than loyalty to the gangsters who ran and funded our families.

Obviously I'd been wrong, about the Knights at least.

We could only hope to get a break at St. Andrew's, where the Kings planned to split up, two of them digging for information while the third stayed with me, keeping an eye on Laszlo Nagy who apparently liked to participate in the Spring Fever masquerade.

I sighed, then heard the Kings descending the kitchen staircase.

Neo was at the front, wearing black silk boxers, no shirt over his chiseled chest, and a devil mask in shades of black and charcoal gray. It was a counterpoint to mine, Neo's adorned in glittering black jewels and sequins, trimmed with silky black feathers that alluded to the fact that Satan was a fallen angel.

His eyes looked almost demonic behind the mask, his gaze piercing as he took in my costume, and his angel tattoo made for a twisted addition to such a menacing costume.

Oscar stepped off the staircase behind him in a mask that was identical, except his had been crafted in glittering rubies winking amid scarlet feathers. His nipple piercings were on full display over corded abs, his red boxer briefs molded to his body, giving me a prime view of his perfect dick.

He was carrying his camera, and I had no doubt the night would net more than a few photographs.

I wasn't surprised when Rock came into view wearing a mask that complemented mine. Where Neo's mask had been trimmed with shades of black and Oscar's with red, Rock's devil mask was white with blue accents.

His ocean eyes glinted with amusement behind the mask, his flawless chest accentuated by white tighty-whities that highlighted the bulge between his muscled thighs.

I smiled as they filed into the kitchen, lining up as if for my approval.

"Damn," I said. "I've got to hand it to you. You look incredible. This is an amazing group costume."

"We've always got you, kitten," Rock said.

I couldn't argue the point. I'd never been so well taken care of in my life.

They eyed me lustily, and I gave them a few seconds to take in the costume. I had to admit, it was perfect. The bustier was somehow both innocent and alluring, the tiny see-through skirt giving a glimpse of my lace-covered pussy and bare ass cheeks.

Neo had been right: the gold heels were perfect, and the wings were surprisingly comfortable on my arms.

The mask was elaborate in design, the white feathers fanning out around the upper part of my face. Even the choker looked perfect, the slim black velvet band adding a slightly subversive element to the look.

"You're stunning," Oscar said, his dark eyes glued to my face as he lifted his camera to snap a picture.

I crossed the kitchen and kissed Oscar on the cheek, then Rock. When I got to Neo I went straight for his lips because I knew he'd settle for nothing less.

He took my mouth with a vengeance, pillaging and plundering with his tongue, his hand closing around my throat until I broke away, gasping and breathless.

His hand was still around my throat like he had no intention of letting go, his gaze locked on my lips.

"I'm going to have to redo my lipstick, aren't I?" I asked.

He gave me a steamy smirk. "You complaining?"

I reached down and pressed my hand against his bulging dick. "Do I look like I'm complaining?"

He grabbed my wrist with a growl. "Keep that up and we won't be going anywhere, Jezebel."

I stepped away, putting a couple feet between us, not trusting myself not to call his bluff.

"We can't have that," I said. "Not after you went to all this trouble." I started for the garage and cast a flirtatious glance over my shoulder, getting a view of the Kings around the feathers in my wings. "Besides, I've never fucked in a sex club before."

"Fuck me," Rock groaned behind me. "It's going to be a long fucking night."

Chapter 55

Willa

St. Andrew's wasn't what I expected.

And to be fair, I didn't know what I'd expected.

Maybe just something... nicer? Or maybe I'd just watched too many movies.

In any case, we'd driven to the outskirts of town in the Hummer after storing my wings in the back for the drive. Rock had taken shotgun next to Neo while I sat in the back with Oscar, his hand between my thighs, his thumb stroking my sensitive skin until I had to slap his hand away.

He grinned knowingly through the car's dark interior, like he knew he'd turned me on.

Cocky bastard.

If it wasn't for the crowds of people making their way inside the dilapidated old house, their faces masked, I might have thought Neo had another errand to run when we pulled up outside.

It was just an old white farmhouse, a wide porch stretching its length, costumed people congregating on its peeling floors. White lights winked from the eaves in an attempt to soften the neglect but I was willing to bet in the harsh light of day it looked hella sketch.

Club music sounded from inside, like it was some kind of rave instead of a private sex club on the outskirts of town.

"This is St. Andrew's?" I asked.

"The only game like it in town," Neo said.

"Sounds like you've been here before." I tried to keep the note of jealousy out of my voice but apparently I didn't succeed.

"Jealous, Jezebel?" he asked, meeting my gaze in the rearview mirror.

"I withdraw the question," I said, both because I didn't want to answer and because now I wasn't sure I wanted to know either.

He chuckled.

Dammit. I couldn't get anything past these boys.

Oscar opened his door. "Come on, tiger. I'll help you with your wings."

Five minutes later we were making our way up the creaking porch steps and through an open door.

We stepped into a large main room, lamps with red

bulbs glowing from an assortment of mismatched furniture. A large St. Andrew's cross rose almost to the high ceiling at the center of a room, a masked brunette strapped to its surface, a man kneeling between her thighs, eating her pussy as she moaned. There was a line behind her, men and women, waiting to take a turn as another man played with her tits.

I was shocked, but I had to be honest, I was turned on too.

Couples and groups, some in scantily crafted costumes and some ass-naked, congregated on the sofas and chairs, some of them just talking while others were making out or fucking like there weren't a bunch of strangers passing through.

"Drinks?" Oscar asked.

"Not for us," Neo said. "Looks like Laszlo is occupied."

I followed his gaze to where an older man with a hairy barrel chest over tiny Speedo-like underwear was getting a blow job from a redhead covered in tattoos.

"That's Laszlo?" I asked.

"That's Laszlo," Oscar said.

"Don't look so surprised, kitten," Rock said. "Who were you expecting, Timothée Chalamet?"

I didn't answer because my entire time at Aventine had been one big fuck-you to my expectations.

Why should it change now?

"Stay with Willa," Neo said to Oscar. "No matter fucking what."

"Like I'd let her out of my sight at St. Andrew's," Oscar said.

I knew they were edgy about having me here because the possibility of leaving me home had come up more than once in the past week, but in the end the Kings had decided I was safest with them, and whether it was true or not, it felt true, and that was all that mattered to me.

"Keep your eyes on Nagy at all times," Neo said. "Text us if he heads for the stairs."

Apparently Nagy's office was on the second floor, and the plan was for Neo and Rock to scope them out while Oscar and I kept our eyes on Laszlo.

"What about them?" Oscar asked, tipping his head at one of the men in dark suits that stood at the edge of the crowd.

There were two of them in the main room, clearly bouncers, but I had to assume there were others.

"Same thing," Neo said. "We'll make sure we're clear upstairs. You let us know if trouble is incoming."

"Roger that," Oscar said. He grinned. "I'm sure Willa and I will be entertained in the meantime."

Neo looked down at me and hesitated, like he had something else to say.

"See you on the flip side, Jezebel," he finally said.

"Don't do anything we wouldn't do," Rock said. "And by that I mean don't do anything until we come back."

He didn't have to worry. The sights and sounds of people fucking were definitely a turn-on, but the Kings were the only guys starring in my fantasies.

"Let's get a drink, tiger," Oscar said.

"What about Laszlo?" I asked.

"The bar's on the other side of the room. We can keep our eyes on him from there."

He led me through the crowd and I watched as the redhead stroked Laszlo Nagy's dick with her hand while she sucked. A blonde had cozied up to him on one side and he kissed her greedily while holding the other woman's head in place.

We came to the bar and Oscar ordered me a Huckleberry Twist and a double shot of whiskey for himself.

He handed me the drink and touched his glass to mine, then downed the shot in one go.

I was turning to follow Oscar's gaze, presumably still on Laszlo, when I heard Claire's voice behind me.

"Not to sound weird, but I'd know that ass anywhere."

I turned around and laughed, then opened my arms to give her a hug.

She pulled back to look at me. "Oh my god... The Kings really outdid themselves. You look fucking incredible."

"Thanks," I said. "So do you."

Her peacock mask was gorgeous, the feathers making her hazel eyes look bluer than usual, and her barely there teal baby-doll nightie showed off her amazing rack.

I looked past her at Quinn and Erin. They'd obviously come as a flock of birds, Quinn as a swan wearing white, Erin as a raven in black.

"You both look gorgeous," I said.

"You're one to talk," Erin said, looking over my costume.

Claire's gaze traveled the length of Oscar's body appreciatively. "You make hell look good, Oscar Drago."

It might have seemed like flirting coming from anyone else, but this was just Claire, and I wasn't at all worried.

He chuckled. "Thanks, Claire."

She returned her attention to me and lifted her eyebrows suggestively. "Have you been to the basement?"

"No, what's in the basement?" I asked, my eyes on Laszlo, who had just come all over the redhead's tits.

"All the kink," Claire said.

"What kind of kink?" I asked her.

"Whatever kind you want basically. We're heading down there now. Want to join us?"

I glanced at Laszlo, pushing himself to his feet from the sofa across the room while the redhead wiped off her tits.

"I'm going to hang with Oscar for a bit," I said. "But I'll look for you later."

"Try and find me before I find Rico, because I do not expect to be standing after I'm done with him," Claire said.

I laughed. "Understood."

They headed out of the room and I watched as Laszlo headed for the hall that ran toward the back of the house.

"That's our cue," Oscar said, pushing off the bar.

He took my hand and we trailed a naked Laszlo, dick swinging, as he made his way down the hall.

Along the way we passed open doors to various rooms, one pitch-black, another with a strobe light, and everywhere people kissing and licking and sucking and fucking.

I felt like I'd fallen down some kind of surreal and very horny rabbit hole.

We followed Nagy into a room at the back of the house that turned out to be the kitchen. A large counter was lined with an assortment of food — cans of whipped cream, cupcakes, bottles of beer, melting ice cream, pickles, clear bottles of milk, chocolate syrup.

Couples smeared each other playfully, licking off the food while others watched.

A dark-haired woman sat on the island with her legs spread wide, a man spraying his fingers with whipped cream and then plunging them into her pussy to finger-fuck her.

Laszlo grabbed a beer and twisted off the top, then leaned against the counter to watch, seemingly oblivious to his own nakedness and the paunch that hung over his dick.

I couldn't help feeling like Neo and Rock got the better

end of this deal. Sure, they were sneaking around upstairs looking for information on the missing girls, but Oscar and I were down here watching Nagy get off on all the hot young people fucking.

I felt like a prude, but piling onto the sofa with the Kings in our comfy clothes before a night of group sex — just the four of us — suddenly seemed extra appealing.

Oscar's gaze was homed in on Nagy, and I dared to skim the room, taking in the various interactions.

My brain snagged on a young woman leaning against a shadowed portion of the wall near the back of the room. One of the Rooks leaned into her, his hand trailing down her ample cleavage.

There was something familiar about her, and I looked closer, trying to place it behind her mask of gold sequins and green feathers. My mind tried to make sense of it, flipping through the possibilities until it finally clicked.

It was Mara.

Chapter 56

Willa

I wanted to deny it. There was no way Mara would come to Blackwell Falls without telling me.

Right?

I grabbed Oscar's arm to get his attention, glad the music was softer at the back of the house. "I think that's Mara."

He followed my gaze. "I think you're right. She didn't tell you she was coming?"

"No," I said. "And I think she's in over her head, especially if she's here alone."

"Fuck," he said.

"I have to go talk to her," I said.

He hesitated, obviously calculating the twenty feet that would be between us if I talked to Mara.

"I have to watch Nagy," he said. "But you go ahead. I'll have eyes on you. Just don't leave the room."

"I'll be right back." I crossed the room, past the woman getting finger-fucked with whipped cream and another woman bent over the counter getting fucked from behind.

I was hoping I would realize it wasn't Mara after all, but the closer I got the more sure I was. She'd been my best friend since we were kids.

It was her.

I slowed as I got closer, trying to think of a polite way to interrupt her conversation with the Rook, then thought of Mrs. Giordana and her good manners.

Fuck that.

I marched up to Mara without stopping. "What are you doing here?"

I expected her to be surprised, but when she turned to look at me there was satisfaction in her eyes instead.

"Oh, hi Willa. I've been hearing all about the Spring Fever masquerade," she said. "I figured I'd check it out for myself since my best friend didn't want to hang out with me."

"You know that's not true," I said. "I always want to hang out with you. It's just to— "

"Too dangerous?" She looked around with a shrug. "It doesn't look dangerous to me. And you're here with your Kings so it must not be dangerous at all."

She was slurring her words, way too drunk to be in a situation like this alone.

"No disrespect, Willa," the Rook said. I recognized him,

a nice-enough guy named Ilya, "but I think your friend here is old enough to know what she wants."

"No disrespect Ilya, but you don't know what the fuck you're talking about," I said.

He held up his hands in surrender, casting a glance at Oscar, who was glaring daggers at him. "I'm going to grab a drink." He looked at Mara. "Mara you said, right? I'll catch up with you later."

He ambled off and Mara glared at me. "Thanks a lot."

"I'm just looking out for you," I said.

"No, you're looking out for you," she said, her voice rising in anger. "That's all you care about now."

I shook my head. "That's not true." I hadn't told her about Alexa or the Knights because I hadn't wanted to worry her. "I'm just trying to protect you."

"Maybe I don't need you to protect me," she said. "Maybe I just need you to be my friend."

"I am your friend," I said. "And that's why I'm going to get you out of here."

"That's impossible, because I don't want to leave," she said, pushing off the wall and staggering forward. She really was hammered. "I'm going to the basement. That's where the kink is."

It sounded absolutely ridiculous coming from her drunken mouth.

"Yeah, you're not going anywhere but home with me." I

had no idea what to do with her while Rock and Neo finished upstairs, but I wasn't leaving her like this.

I put my arm around her waist, trying to steady her, but she shoved me off.

Now I was the one who stumbled in my four-inch gold heels.

Oscar lurched toward me, his attention torn from Laszlo Nagy by my altercation with Mara. He took two steps forward and I saw Nagy turn and leave the room behind him.

I shook my head, trying to convey the fact that our mark was getting away, Neo and Rock presumably still upstairs digging through Nagy's offices, but Oscar's gaze was pinned on me, the urgency on his face making it clear I was his priority.

Next to me, Mara was muttering, slapping my hands off her arms as I tried to usher her out of the room.

It was a moment of confusion — Laszlo leaving the room unbeknownst to Oscar, Mara fighting me every step of the way, Oscar working his way through the crowd of fucking — like literally fucking — people to get to me.

Then, as if things couldn't get any worse, the shriek of a fire alarm.

I covered my ears by instinct, then shook my head to try and clear it around the piercing sound.

Smoke had started to fill the room from an unknown source and Mara looked around, confused.

I searched for Oscar across the room but everyone else had started to panic, pushing and shoving as they tried to make their way to the narrow hall leading to the front door.

I grabbed Mara's arm but she shook me off and disappeared into the haze, too drunk to understand or care what was happening as the smoke grew thicker.

I coughed, the acrid smoke winding its way down my throat and into my lungs. I was frantic to find Mara and Oscar, but I couldn't see a thing, and a moment later I felt a gust of cold air as someone opened a back door off the kitchen.

I was carried toward it by the teeming crowd, and I swiveled my head in every direction, desperately hoping for a glimpse of Mara and Oscar, hoping they were already outside or headed that way, closer than I knew but hidden because of the smoke.

I thought about all the news reports I'd read of people being trampled in crowded clubs during fires. I'd never understood how it could happen, but now the possibility felt all too real, the press of bodies painful and powerful, forcing me along in a direction and at a speed over which I had no control.

It felt like an eternity before I spilled out the back door and into the freezing night air.

I staggered forward with the rest of the crowd, trying to blink the smoke from my eyes. It clouded my vision, made it hard to make out the features of the people milling around me in a panic, the fire alarm still shrieking.

I caught the sight of flames leaping out of the second-floor windows and a strangled scream rose from my throat as I thought of Neo and Rock.

No, I thought. *No.*

I rubbed my eyes, searching the crowd for their faces, for Oscar, for Mara and Claire, Quinn and Erin.

But I didn't see any them, and I stumbled around the side of the house toward a crowd gathering at the front, hoping they would be there.

I was almost to the front when someone grabbed me from behind.

For a split second I thought it was one of the Kings, but it was all wrong — not a relieved tug of my hand pulling me into strong arms, but someone pinning my arms to my side from behind, lifting me off the ground, pulling me away from the crowd.

"No! Put me down!" I was screaming, but the sound was barely a whisper from my throat, made raw from all the smoke.

The house and crowd were growing farther away as I was dragged backward, everyone too busy running for their lives to notice.

I couldn't see the face of the person who was taking me, but I thought of Emma, wondered if this was how she'd felt in the moments before she disappeared.

A moment later I was thrown into the back of a van. I scrambled for the door but it shut before I reached it. A black bag was pulled over my head and I felt the pierce of a needle in my neck.

And then, nothing.

Chapter 57

Oscar

I'd been watching Laszlo, the disgusting bastard, while keeping an eye on Willa, clearly having an argument with Mara. I had no idea what Mara was doing in Blackwell Falls but I knew Willa had discouraged her from coming because of Roberto and the missing girls.

Now Mara was clearly hammered, stumbling and pointing at Willa. In all the years that they'd been best friends, I'd never seen them fight, and I wanted to give Willa time to calm Mara down and get her to leave St. Andrew's, because while Ilya was a decent guy, there were plenty of not-decent guys on the premises and we didn't have time to babysit.

Then, the ringing of the smoke alarm, the confused expressions on the faces of everyone in the kitchen, most of them drunk on both alcohol and sex, not to mention the assortment of drugs that routinely circulated these kinds of events.

There was about five seconds when I thought maybe it was a false alarm, somebody breaking the rules and smoking inside.

But then smoke started to fill the room.

Fast.

And not a little smoke, like when Neo tried to cook something.

Thick, dark smoke, billowing into the kitchen all at once.

Panic descended like a shroud over the kitchen. Everyone shouted, rushing for the main hall all at once, but there was only one thought in my mind.

Willa.

The crowd had thickened between us, blocking my view of her and Mara.

I didn't even think about Laszlo Nagy. We obviously had bigger problems.

I tore off my mask and shoved through the crowd, working against the current of people shoving for the hall. It was like being carried down the Blackwell River and trying to swim upstream.

The smoke grew thicker, my eyes and throat burning. I coughed and kept shoving my way through, trying to calm my panic with the knowledge that Willa would have to come this way to get to the hall.

I would find her sooner rather than later.

Then a gust of cold wind blew through the kitchen and half the crowd halted their forward progress and turned toward the back of the room.

"There's another door!" someone shouted.

I'd never paid much attention to the layout of St. Andrew's, other than knowing which room housed which proclivity, but clearly there was another exit and half the crowd was now pushing in the opposite direction, away from me, hoping to escape the smoke without having to push through to the front of the house.

I tried to tell myself it was a good thing. Willa had been closer to the back of the room with Mara — she would be one of the first ones out — but I shoved in that direction anyway because nothing was going to ease my mind except laying my eyes on her face.

I finally reached the door and emerged into the cold winter night, the other patrons of St. Andrew's staggering around me, sucking in deep breaths of clean air, tearing off their masks, rubbing their eyes.

Angry flames licked from the second-floor windows and another slick of dread rolled through my body.

I shook it off. Neo and Rock could take care of themselves. Willa was my only responsibility.

I scanned the crowd frantically, disoriented by the costumes and looking for her fair hair.

I didn't see her, but I spotted Mara, standing alone and looking dazed, and hurried toward her. "Where's Willa?"

"Willa?" She looked around. "I don't know. She was..."

I grabbed her arm and hauled her to the front of the house where I saw Claire standing with Erin and Quinn, all of them coughing.

"Watch her," I said to Claire, giving Mara a push in their direction.

"Okay, but..."

I didn't hear the rest of her words.

The scream of fire engines cut through the night and I hurried through groups of people, some of them naked and shivering, scanning every face for Willa.

I turned my attention back to the house, terrified that she'd slipped away into some other room and not made it out, and saw Neo and Rock come through the front door sans masks along with a couple of other stragglers.

The house was engulfed in flames. It was hard to imagine anyone left inside would make it out alive.

And still Willa was nowhere to be found.

"Where the fuck is she?" Neo roared. His face was darkened with soot, his eyes bloodshot from the smoke.

"We were separated," I said. "I thought she made it out ahead of me, but I can't find her."

"Fuck," Rock said, turning in a circle and scanning the crowd.

"Split up," Neo said. "Find her."

"I'll take the back," Rock said.

Neo pushed through me to the left of the house where people were still staggering from the back. I headed in the other direction, the only direction I hadn't been, trying to hurry as I scanned the faces of every person I passed.

I thought about the first hours Emma had been missing, the way the cops had told us all that the chance of finding her diminished with every minute.

I told myself this wasn't the same. Willa was just lost in the crowd, probably looking for us just as frantically as we were looking for her. but as I made my way to the back of the house where Rock was combing the tree line, I knew it was a lie.

I hurried toward him and was joined by Neo, jogging across the snowy lawn.

The firefighters and EMTs had arrived, their flashing lights casting an eerie red glow over the scene from the front of the house.

"She's not here," I said, reaching into the waistband of my boxer briefs where I'd stashed my phone.

I opened up the app that was synced to Willa's tracker and felt my heart drop out of my fucking body.

I looked at Neo and Rock. "She's on the move. Heading towards the woods outside campus."

Chapter 58

Willa

The first thing I noticed was the ice pick driving into my brain. After that, it was the sound of shuffling feet on snow, deep voices murmuring in conversation.

I opened my eyes and the sky spun above me, inky and scattered with stars.

"Well well well," a male voice said, "it looks like our little rabbit is waking up."

A familiar face appeared above me.

Igor?

Sergei?

I couldn't pull the name from my throbbing head but he was one of the Russians, the father of someone I knew in the Rooks' house.

"Let's not be rude," another voice said. "Help the little rabbit to her feet."

I was hauled to my feet by two pairs of strong hands and then I realized something else.

I was cold. Like, fucking freezing.

My shoes were gone, leaving me standing barefoot in a shoveled clearing, the snow mostly gone, the ground frozen.

The costume that had been perfect for the masquerade at St. Andrew's did nothing to protect my body from the elements, and I shivered, wishing I could pull the wings around me for warmth.

I couldn't, because my arms were being held by two men, the Russian I recognized and an unfamiliar man with red hair and a beard.

I took in the scene around me, trying to get my bearings, and realized we were at the site of the cabin where Dean Giordana had died. Its charred remains stood cold and vacant to one side of the clearing.

A small fire burned, not that I could feel any of the heat from where I stood.

I was surrounded by four men: the Russian, the redhead, a dark-haired dark-eyed man, and Roberto.

My stepfather stared at me, his eyes burning with hatred every bit as hot as the fire that crackled in the clearing, embers drifting up into the dark night.

"I tried to warn you," he said, his voice cold. "You just wouldn't stop."

"You killed Emma," I said. "And all those other girls

too."

Somewhere in the back of my mind I knew that I should have been looking for ways to escape, but after two years of wondering what had happened to my sister, I finally had the chance to find out.

"We kill people all the time," Roberto said. "Don't pretend to have a conscience now. It's what we do, what all of us do, what your father did before he became a fucking traitor."

I was rendered momentarily speechless by the argument, because he wasn't wrong. Our families weren't good people. They stole and hurt and killed. It was why I'd wanted out.

But even knowing that, the killing of the girls from Bellepoint felt different.

"That was business," I said. "You killed those girls — you killed Emma — for fun."

I saw shades of Neo in Roberto's smile, but that was where the resemblance ended. I knew deep down Neo was terrified of becoming like him and I couldn't wait to tell him there wasn't a chance in hell it would ever happen.

Neo was nothing like his father.

The thought of him excavated a hole the size of the Grand Canyon in my chest.

Would I ever see him again? Would I get to tell him how much I loved him?

"Your sister died because she was nosy. Like you,"

Roberto said, clearly the spokesperson for the group of men, a group of men I'd realized were representative of all four houses at Aventine. "But yes, the other girls were entertainment. Men like us, powerful men, have to blow off some steam. You can't blame us for having a little fun."

"I do blame you, you sick fuck."

The other men laughed and Roberto stepped toward me and landed a hard slap across my face.

"You're going to find out how sick I really am, you little cunt."

... you little cunt.

It was like traveling through time, back to the moment when I freed Neo from the closet.

Full fucking circle.

I drew in a breath, tried to keep myself calm. My choker was still around my neck, the Kings' symbol pressed against my flesh like a caress.

They would find me.

"Is this what you did to her?" I asked. "To all of them? You brought them out here to hurt them? Kill them?"

I needed to know. After all this time, after everything I'd been through, I just needed to know.

"Is that what you want?" Roberto asked. "To know?"

I drew in a breath. "Yes."

"Then it's your lucky fucking night, little rabbit," the dark-haired man, clearly a member of the cartel family, said.

Roberto shot him a look that shut him up, and the other man looked down at his feet, clearly chastened.

"Carlos is right," Roberto said. "You're going to find out firsthand what happened to your sister."

Terror clawed at my throat, but there was something else there too.

Relief.

At least now I would know.

"Let me explain the rules of our little game," Roberto said.

"What game?" I asked.

The other men still had a hold of my arms. Their grips had loosened but trying to run now would be a mistake.

There were four of them. I had no shoes, no weapon.

I could only hope another opportunity would present itself or that the Kings would arrive on the scene soon.

"Let's call it... a chase," Roberto said, pacing in front of me. He looked up, as if searching the sky for the right words. "Like tag."

I narrowed my eyes. "Tag?"

He picked up a long stick. "Yes, tag. I'm even going to help you out by drawing you a map."

He scribbled in the half inch of snow that remained in the clearing. "You are *here*." He dragged three lines from the cabin in three different directions. "There are three other cabins *here*."

I watched as he scribbled at the end of each line and a

picture formed in my mind: the map in the binders from Dean Giordana's office.

Roberto was drawing the cabins owned by the four families, the trails leading between them.

"You will be given a three-minute head start," he said. "Then we'll start the chase, along with teams from the other cabins that will start their game at the same time."

Other teams... I understood now. He was talking about other members of the four families, all staging from the other cabins.

All prepared to chase me through the snowy woods.

"Sounds like a dumb game," I said. My feet were turning numb from the cold, my exposed skin stinging with it. "And definitely not a fair one."

Roberto shrugged. "I won't deny you're at a disadvantage, but that's life. It's a real bitch, isn't it?"

"Says the guy with every privilege who uses it like a coward to hurt innocent girls," I said.

The redhead laughed, stroking his beard. "This rabbit has bite."

"Your complaints are noted," Roberto said. "Nevertheless, these have been the rules for years. No special treatment for you." He walked toward me, stroked my cheek with the back of his knuckles, ran a finger down my neck, into the cleavage displayed by my bustier. "The good news is, if you can outrun us, we might let you live."

That was a lie. They were never going to let me live now that I'd seen their faces, knew about their little game.

But I wasn't going to bother arguing the point.

"And if I can't?" I asked.

"If you can't, we get a little playtime before you join your sister and the others out here," he said.

I had to force myself to keep breathing. They'd done this to Emma and the other girls. Buried them somewhere in these woods where no one would ever find them.

I didn't want to think about what these men had done to them before that.

I tried to keep myself calm. The Kings would already be tracking me. They would be here any second.

Then Roberto slipped a finger under the velvet ribbon around my neck and tugged.

The choker gave way.

He looked down at it with a sneer. "My son thinks he's the king. He and his friends. But tonight I'm going to show him who's really king."

He tossed the choker aside and stepped back, nodding at the two men still holding my arm.

For a few seconds, nobody said anything.

Then Roberto shrugged and simply said, "Run."

Chapter 59

Neo

I drove like a bat out of hell, my gaze switching from the road to the red light showing Willa's location on the tracker app.

I had no idea what had happened at St. Andrew's, but I smelled a rat.

It was too much of a coincidence that a fire had started right before Willa disappeared.

This had my father written all over it.

"How much longer?" Drago asked from the backseat.

"Another minute to the closest trailhead," I said.

After that it was anybody's guess. The trails weren't cleared in winter. We hadn't had a big snowfall in a while and I could only hope some of the existing snowpack had melted.

I pulled into the parking area at the trailhead and

slammed on the brakes, grabbing my phone and opening the door before I even turned the car off.

"Let's fucking go," Rock said.

I held up the phone, relieved to see that Willa was still near the cabin where Dean Giordana had died, where he'd tried to kill her.

That she was there again, alone and probably scared, made me feel like I was losing my fucking mind.

We'd found a list of names in Laszlo Nagy's office that had included prices next to them, a list I'd pocketed just as the fire alarm had gone off. Had he trafficked other girls to my father and the other alumni involved in the disappearance of the Bellepoint girls?

I didn't know, and right now I didn't care. Right now it didn't even feel like it mattered. All that mattered was her.

Willa.

Her name beat like a drum with every pump of my heart.

I'd never even told her I loved her, had never even told her about the ring I'd been screwing up the courage to give her.

It's not too late.

I didn't know whether it was a plea or a statement of fact.

I'm coming, Willa. I'm coming.

We hit the trailhead and I was relieved to see that there was only about six inches of snow, probably because of the trees that grew on either side of the trail, blocking some of the snowfall.

It was dark as fuck, no moon to light our way, and I held my phone up with the flashlight on to illuminate the path in front of us.

We'd covered up with some of the gym gear that I kept in the Hummer — sweats, T-shirts, and one hoodie currently worn by Drago — for emergencies, but it was nowhere near winter appropriate.

It was fucking cold and all I could think about was Willa in her angel costume, hoping whoever had taken her was keeping her warm but knowing they didn't give two fucks about her.

I stifled a scream of primitive rage and kept running.

We ran until my lungs burned, the path seeming to go on forever, like one of those dreams where you run and run and get absolutely fucking nowhere.

Finally, I looked at my phone and saw that we were close, the red light of Willa's tracker blinking just ahead.

"We're almost there," I said to Rock and Drago.

Less than a minute later I caught the flicker of a fire, the scent of wood smoke.

I stopped running and held out my arms to stop Rock and Drago. "Wait. The cabin's just ahead. There's a fire outside."

We were about ten feet back from a clearing. It was

quiet, but I couldn't be sure the clearing was empty through the cover of the trees and undergrowth.

We'd armed up with the handguns I'd started keeping in the Hummer — courtesy of Hawk — but I had no idea what we were going up against. Barreling into the situation out of desperation to save Willa could backfire if we were severely outnumbered.

I withdrew my weapon and watched as Rock and Drago did the same.

"Circle the clearing," I whispered. "Come at it from every side."

Rock and Drago fanned out in different directions and I waited a couple of minutes for them to get into position before advancing through the trees to the clearing.

The safety was off on my weapon, ready to fire, and I scanned the clearing, now visible.

It was empty.

I stepped cautiously from the trees and looked around, and a few seconds later Rock and Drago did the same on the other side of the clearing.

"Someone was here," Drago said, approaching the fire, kicking at a handful of cigarette butts. "Multiple someones. And not too long ago if this fire is any indication."

"Fuck," I said, advancing on the fire, stalking the area as if some clue about Willa's whereabouts would materialize out of the night.

"She has a tracker," Rock said. "Where is she?"

Right. The tracker.

I was out of my mind with panic and I forced myself to breathe deep as I looked at the app.

I looked up from my phone and scanned the clearing again. "It says she's here."

Rock and Drago looked around, pacing to the tree line and tracking it in the circle around the clearing, peering into the trees.

"Either I'm fucking blind or that app is a fucking liar," Rock said, his voice thick with frustration.

My heart was in my throat as I realized what was going on. "She dropped it. Or someone took it off her."

I didn't want to think about the latter possibility. I knew whoever had her could be hurting her, but the thought of anyone harming a single hair on her head, daring to touch her, made me want to go full psycho.

I wanted to spend forever with her — she just didn't know it yet — and I cursed myself for not giving her the ring when I'd had the chance.

"Wait..." Drago stepped out of the clearing into the trees on the other side of the fire.

"You got something?" I asked, crossing the clearing to where he stood holding something in his hand.

He held it up for me to see.

A white feather.

"Let's move," I said, crashing through the tree line and starting through the woods.

Chapter 60

Willa

I ran, wishing I'd had time to get rid of my wings. They snagged at low-hanging branches and made me feel like I was running with a parachute on my back.

At first I didn't hear anything, and I dared to hope I stood a chance of escaping them.

But then, up ahead, I heard the shouting of men and remembered there were others coming at me from all directions.

I called to mind the map of the woods surrounding Aventine — not the one Roberto had drawn in the snow, the one in Dean Giordana's binders. That one had been a topographical map and had included the cliffs and the Blackwell River.

I hoped to avoid one and potentially find the other.

If I stumbled off a cliff I was dead. If I could find the river I could follow it downstream into town.

If I didn't die of hypothermia first.

My feet were completely numb, causing me to stumble, and I knew there was a real danger of frostbite. The temperatures weren't extreme, but it was still fucking cold, and dying of exposure was a distinct possibility.

I swatted a low-hanging branch out of my way as I weaved between the trees, then felt it snap back and smack me in the face.

Blood trickled a warm path down my cheek, the least of my problems.

I thought of the Kings. Had Rock and Neo made it out of St. Andrew's alive?

I couldn't think about that because if any of them were dead I would want to die too. Then I would stop running and give in to the hopelessness that threatened to suffocate me as I ran and ran.

"That way!" a man's voice yelled behind me.

They were closing the distance on all sides, their voices growing louder.

I urged my legs to move faster, trying to ignore the burning in my lungs, the stinging of my skin as it froze in the night air.

And then, from another direction, the barking of dogs.

This wasn't a chase. It was a hunt.

Chapter 61

Rock

Hating myself was a welcome distraction from the fear that felt like a lead weight on my chest.

We should have left Blackwell Falls.

We should have taken Willa and gone far far away.

No amount of revenge was worth her life. Nothing was worth that.

I tried not to think about the vastness of the woods as we ran. Willa was a needle in a haystack and we weren't the only ones determined to find her. I couldn't even be sure we were running in the right direction. We seemed to be on some kind of trail but it was hard to tell with the snow cover.

The deeper we got into the woods the deeper the snow became, not the flattened snowpack that had been around the fire, but a good six inches of heavy wet snow.

I tried not to think of Willa, barefoot and half-naked, exposed to the cold and probably fighting for her life.

If I did that I was going to lose it, and Willa needed us all to keep it together.

Up ahead, a low-hanging branch blocked the path. I reached out to swat away and saw something snagged on its end.

I stopped running, panting from exertion, and reached for the branch as Neo and Drago came to a stop next to me.

A feather.

"She's been this way," I said, holding it up for them to see.

Drago reached into the hoodie he'd grabbed from the trunk of the Hummer and withdrew his gun. "If she's been this way, so have they."

"We should split up," Neo said.

I looked at him like he was crazy because he must have been if he was suggesting we split up with a bunch of killers roaming the woods, looking for Willa and all too happy to kill us before we got to her.

"He's right," Drago said. "If two of us split off we might be able to circle around, intercept Roberto and the other men."

"You take the path," Neo said to me. He looked at Drago. "You go north, I'll go south." He stared at us both, fury etched on his face. "We save Willa. Anyone in our way dies."

Chapter 62

Willa

I was running out of steam, the cold and constant running catching up to me as I crashed through the woods.

Voices sounded behind me. "Where are you, little rabbit? There's no point running. We can smell you."

They were close. Too close.

And up ahead, other male voices, their words indistinguishable. I didn't need to know what they were saying to know they were with Roberto, the men who'd staged from the other cabins seeking to cut off my escape.

I'd been running along some kind of trail, snowy and overgrown. It had been the path of least resistance when I'd run from the site of the ruined cabin, but now it seemed foolish.

I'd been making it easy for them.

There was no time to weigh the pros and cons. I was

surrounded on all sides. I would have to take my chance off trail.

I looked for a spot in the tree line along the path wide enough to get through with my wings and spotted it about ten feet ahead.

I waited until I was next to it, then hurled myself through the gap into the old-growth trees.

Unfortunately I hadn't thought about the downside to leaving the trail, and I was immediately forced to slow my pace without a clear path through the trees. There was no reason to the way they grew, some so close together there was no room for me to squeeze through, large gaps between others creating mini clearings that allowed me to temporarily pick up speed.

I was starting to feel hopeful. The voices of the men, on my heels almost from the moment I'd started running, had disappeared. I was steeped in the ageless silence of the woods, beginning to believe I might have lost them.

Then I passed through one of the small clearings and entered another thick copse, slowing my pace to avoid slamming into one of the thick trucks that rose into the night sky. I didn't even see the man hiding behind one of the trees until he grabbed me, locking his arms around my chest from behind and lifting my feet off the ground.

"I think I caught a rabbit," Roberto's voice said against my ear. "And she's going to make one hell of a dinner."

Chapter 63

Neo

Splitting up was the right thing to do, but running through the forest off trail was challenging as fuck.

The moonless night was no help, and I had several close calls, thick roots that rose from the ground, threatening to trip me as I ran, low-hanging branches I didn't see until they'd already smashed into my face.

I didn't care about any of it. All that mattered was that I stayed on my feet for Willa.

It was eerily quiet, the crunching of my footsteps on snow the only sound in the night. Even the animals that lived here were silent, hiding or hibernating for winter.

And then, barely loud enough to hear over my steps, a soft squeal.

I stopped running, holding still, listening.

I almost thought I'd imagined it, was gearing up to start

moving again, when I heard it again from the trees to my right.

I broke in that direction, heading for the sound, moving more slowly and carefully now, not wanting to tip off the wrong people if they were close by.

But in the end it didn't matter. I was almost on top of them before I spotted them: my father and Willa, my father holding the blade of a knife to Willa's slender throat.

Chapter 64

Willa

I almost couldn't believe my eyes. I'd been struggling against Roberto's iron grip, managing a couple of soft screams, my throat still raw from the smoke at St. Andrew's, before he clamped a hand over my mouth.

I felt the bite of a blade against my throat and knew I was finished. We were in the middle of nowhere, with not even Roberto's playmates nearby.

Not that that would have improved the situation.

I was thinking about Emma, hoping heaven was real and that I'd see her there when I died. Maybe there, this would all seem like a bad dream.

Then I saw a flash through the trees and a few seconds later Neo flew into the clearing, freezing when he saw Roberto with his knife to my throat.

Neo was holding a gun and I had a brief moment of hope before I realized our predicament.

To kill Roberto, Neo would have to make an impossible shot, hoping the bullet wouldn't hit me instead, that it would hit Roberto before the slide of his knife through my neck.

It should have filled me with despair, but instead I felt a strange kind of relief. I finally knew what had happened to Emma, to all the girls from Bellepoint, and now Neo would know too.

I would die, and because of that, Neo wouldn't let Roberto live to hurt anyone else. My mom would be safe, and at least she'd have my body to bury.

"If it isn't my dear old dad," Neo said. "And by *dad* I mean the psychopath who donated his sperm."

"Boo-hoo," Roberto mocked, dropping his hand from my mouth. "I was the best kind of father to you. You're just too stupid to know it."

"Yeah, they should've awarded you Father of the Year for locking me in the dark and beating the shit out of me," Neo said. "Maybe you would've gotten a special prize for all the girls you killed like Emma."

"They should have," Roberto said. "I was the best kind of father, the kind who taught you how to be strong, how to be a man."

He was getting animated, his knife digging deeper into my throat, and I felt a trickle of blood drip down my neck.

"How to be a monster you mean," Neo said. "You taught me that well."

I heard the bitterness in Neo's voice, and the sadness too.

"You're not a monster," I said to Neo, staring into his eyes across the darkness. "You never were. That's just another lie he told you."

"Shut up!" Roberto yelled, the knife scraping along my neck, his voice growing calmer. "Shut up, little rabbit. You're just like your sister. You never know when to stop."

Neo's throat rippled as he swallowed, trying to hide his nervousness as Roberto became more unhinged. "Put the knife down before I blow your fucking head off."

Roberto laughed. "You think I'm afraid of you? I'm not, and the reason I'm not is because you don't know yourself. You think you're a monster, but deep down you're still just a little boy crying in a closet."

I felt like my heart was being ripped to shreds. I wanted to take the knife in Roberto's hand and stab him until he stopped hurting the man I loved.

I wanted to tell Neo right now, wanted to shout it across the distance between us just in case I didn't get another chance, but I knew it would just distract him, and that was the last thing he needed.

Neo raised his gun and pointed it at Roberto's head. "Says you."

I stared into Neo's eyes, trying to send a message.

Do it. Put a fucking bullet in his brain and let the cards fall where they may.

And then, behind Neo, movement in the trees. I didn't know if Roberto saw it or if he was too fixated on Neo, but a second later a face came into view and I knew I wasn't imagining it.

It was Oscar.

Chapter 65

Oscar

I 'd run north like Neo had ordered, then looped back, crossing over the narrow path and back into the woods, hoping to find Willa, or at the very least to cut off some of the men chasing her.

It was like running through molasses, the cold slowing my movements, the dark making it impossible to see anything until it was right on top of me.

Which was why I was shocked to hear voices coming from the woods up ahead, and then, when I slowed my steps, I saw Neo's back visible through the trees.

I moved cautiously forward, and Roberto came into view.

But not just Roberto: Willa, held at the point of his knife.

Fuck.

Fuck fuck fuck.

If I tried to move around the area where they stood to get behind Roberto, I was almost certain to alert him to my presence, but if I stayed where I was, there wasn't fuck all I could do to help Willa.

I still had my gun, but my shot was worse than Neo's, and Neo's shot sucked.

I scanned the area around them, hoping for something I could use, anything that might at least act as a distraction for Neo to put a bullet between his father's eyes without hurting Willa.

I found it a second later when I saw Rock move slowly into position behind Roberto — and either Rock was as stealthy as a jungle cat or Roberto was distracted as fuck because he didn't seem to hear a thing.

I had no idea if Neo could see Rock but I hoped he could, that he would wait until Rock made a move rather than risk shooting Willa instead of Roberto.

"I'll tell you what," Neo said. "You let Willa go, I let you go."

Roberto laughed. "You must think I'm stupid. This isn't going to end until one of us is dead and you know it."

Somewhere in the distance I thought I heard helicopters, but I couldn't be sure and I didn't dare tear my eyes away from the unfolding scene.

"You're probably right," Neo said. When he spoke again, I knew he'd seen Rock. "And it's not going to be me."

Rock rushed through the trees, making a fuck-ton of noise that caused Roberto to spin toward him.

I held my breath, hoping his knife wouldn't slip against Willa's throat, that if it did it would slip out of his hand instead.

Willa took advantage of Roberto's loosened hold, ducking underneath his arm and moving out of the way as Rock crashed into Roberto with the full force of his body weight.

They fell to the ground in the snow, punching and grappling, making it impossible to see who had the edge.

Neo advanced on them as Willa scrambled back, wrapping her arms around her nearly naked body as Rock and Roberto rolled around on the ground. Neo was holding his gun over them, waiting for a shot when Rock gasped, rolled off Roberto, and clutched his stomach.

Blood seeped from between his fingers, Roberto still holding the now-bloody knife in his hands.

Willa rushed toward Rock, pulling his head in her lap as Neo took up position above his father, pointing the gun at his head.

"Ready to roll the dice on that theory about me?" Neo said.

Roberto grinned, then lunged forward with the knife.

Neo's shot echoed through the woods, and Roberto fell back into the snow, blood trickling from a hole in his forehead.

The sound of helicopters got louder, a spotlight trained on Neo and his father as the helicopter hovered above them.

"Drop your weapon," said a voice through the helicopter's broadcast system.

Neo dropped the gun.

Then the scene was swarming with officers in tactical gear, advancing on us with weapons drawn, Willa still sitting in the snow, cradling Rock's head.

Chapter 66

Willa

I shivered under the warming blanket the EMTs had wrapped around my body on the portable gurney. I hadn't had time to explain why I was in the woods in my underwear with a pair of wings attached to my back, but luckily they seemed more concerned about frostbite and hypothermia.

I peered out from inside the ambulance, parked at the trailhead near the Hummer, watching as Neo, Oscar, and Rock, spoke to the police.

I felt sick looking at Rock's bloodstained shirt. Grateful the knife wound had turned out to be less serious than it had looked, but sick. Of course, he'd refused to be transported by ambulance to the hospital, but he'd agreed to let doctors look at it when we got there.

I didn't know what would happen from here, but we

were alive, all of us. The same couldn't be said for Roberto, and that meant it was really over.

I peered through the darkness as a figure in a nylon police coat walked toward the back of the ambulance. From a distance the bundled-up figure looked like a man, but when they reached the ambulance doors I realized I'd been wrong.

I blinked, wondering if I was hallucinating from the cold. "Interim Dean Garcia?"

She climbed into the ambulance and sat next to me. "My last name is actually Rodriguez. Are you all right?"

She looked different, young and fit in jeans and her police coat, her hair loose around her shoulders, her face devoid of makeup.

"I think so. I mean, I might lose a toe or three, but they don't know yet," I said. "You're... a police officer?"

"Detective actually. I've been undercover on this case for a long time." She smiled. "Maybe you should join the force. You cracked the case before I did."

"Not soon enough," I said, thinking about Emma and the other girls.

"I'm sorry about your sister." She sounded like she meant it.

"Will you look for them now?" I asked. "For all of them? In the woods?"

She nodded. "Already on it. We have a team incoming now. We'll start around the cabins and fan out from there."

I tried to blink back my tears but they leaked down my temples anyway.

Emma was gone, and I was going to have to find a way to live with that for the rest of my life.

"She'd be proud of you," Detective Rodriguez said. "She is proud of you."

I stifled a sob and nodded because it was all I could manage. I didn't know what to say. Maybe I should've been surprised that she'd been undercover at Aventine, but I kind of thought I might never be surprised again. About anything.

Then again, as I watched the Kings break away from the police, Neo heading for the ambulance as Rock and Oscar started for the Hummer, I remembered that not all surprises were bad.

"Looks like your friend is coming," Detective Rodriguez said. "You're really lucky to have each other."

Didn't I know it.

She climbed out of the ambulance. "We'll be in touch," she said to Neo as he climbed in to take her place.

His face was pale and drawn. He took my hand in both of his and touched it to his lips. "Are you okay?"

"Depends," I said. "Will you still want to fuck me with seven toes?"

He started to laugh, but it turned into a sob, and he buried his face against my chest.

"I fucking love you, Jezebel."

I stroked his silky hair. "I fucking love you too."

Epilogue

Willa

I was disoriented when I first opened my eyes. I wasn't in my room in the Kings' house and I wasn't in any of their rooms either. The ceiling was made out of acoustic tiles, laid out in squares, the light dim.

Then I remembered: the chase through the woods, Neo killing Roberto, Detective Rodriguez visiting me in the ambulance.

Neo saying he loved me.

I'd been in the hospital for two days and had narrowly missed losing some of my toes. I was dehydrated and being treated for exposure. My voice still sounded funny from the smoke at St. Andrew's.

But I was alive.

I was comforted by the weight of Oscar on one side of my hospital bed and Rock on the other. It had been that way since I'd been assigned a room, the Kings taking turns staying with me, making sure I wasn't alone for even a second.

I made a show of complaining but I secretly loved it. There had been a moment in the woods when I'd thought I would never see them again. It still felt like a miracle to be alive and together.

I searched the shadows at the edges of the room and found Neo, staring at me from the chair across from the bed, his post whenever he wasn't lying with me.

We hadn't had a chance to talk about the fact that he'd killed his father. I imagined it would take a long time to process, and I hoped he would do that and not stuff it down under a bunch of macho bullshit.

Enough damage had been done in the name of macho bullshit. There had to be a better way.

He smiled at me across the room and I felt that same unnameable thing move between us. I'd once thought it was just physical chemistry.

Now I knew it was so much more.

Oscar and Rock stirred, like they'd sensed I was awake.

"Need anything, kitten?" Rock asked, his voice sleepy.

I had no idea what time it was but I knew it was the middle of the night, the hospital around us quiet except for occasional footsteps outside my door.

"My own bed would be nice," I said. "Or one of yours."

Oscar grinned. "Now I know you're feeling better."

News of Roberto's death and the arrest of several

infamous figures in the Italian, Irish, Russian, and cartel families had been broken in an exclusive scoop from Daniel Longhat in the *Blackwell Tribune*. The search was still underway for the missing girls, presumably buried in the woods, but Detective Rodriguez was hopeful one of the suspects would confess and point them in the right direction in exchange for a plea deal.

I hoped they would. My mom — and all the moms and families of the missing girls — deserved closure.

I wasn't looking forward to my conversation with my mom, but I hoped it would be the first of many that would repair our relationship now that Roberto was out of the picture.

Neo rose to his feet and wiped his hands on his jeans in an uncharacteristic display of nervousness, then walked toward my hospital bed.

"Move over," Neo said to Rock.

Rock shifted to give Neo room and Neo settled on the edge of my mattress.

He scratched at the shadow on his strong jaw. "I have no fucking idea how to do this."

I shook my head. "Do what?"

"This... thing I'm about to do," he said. "I thought maybe I should do it when we're alone, but these two assholes are basically my brothers, and I want to make sure everything's cool."

"What the fuck are you talking about?" Oscar said.

Neo looked at me. "Listen Jezebel, it's no secret that I'm a world-class prick. I don't think I ever saw a single good thing in anyone until the day you opened that closet door when we were kids."

I reached for his hand. "What is this?"

"Just... let me get this out," he said. "So anyway, as I was saying, a world-class prick. No need to protest."

I smiled. "Do you hear me protesting?"

He chuckled. "Brutal."

I smiled wider. "I learned from the best."

He held my gaze. "What I'm trying to say is that if my soul is a fucking black hole — and I'm pretty sure it is — then you're the one brilliant shining fucking star at its center. And if you really want to leave, well then, I want you to leave too because there's nothing I want more than for you to be happy, and that's because there's no one in the fucking world who deserves it more than you."

"A-fucking-men," Oscar murmured next to me.

"But I want you to know that I want you to stay. I want you to stay so that we can see your beautiful face and that smile that lights up my whole fucking world. And... I'm not just saying I want you to stay." He reached for something in the pocket of his jacket and held out a tiny black velvet box. He popped the lid, and a giant square-cut diamond in a platinum setting glimmered from inside. "I'm saying I want you to marry me, Willa. I want you to marry me and let me do my fucking best to make you the happiest girl on the planet with the caveat that I probably won't be able to *not* be a world-class prick overnight. But.... well, I'll work on it every day."

I was pretty sure my mouth was hanging open, which was probably why Rock chose that moment to mutter, "Fuck me."

Neo looked at him. "I'm sorry I didn't tell you and Drago. I wanted to ask Willa and I wanted you both to be here. I'm not trying to take anything from you. I love the way things are and I want them to stay that way. I just... I want to do this."

"I'm not mad you didn't tell me," Rock said, reaching into the pocket of his hoodie. He removed a white velvet box. "I'm just mad you beat me to the punch."

He opened the box to reveal a princess-cut diamond set in rose gold.

I covered my face with my hands. Because really?

What's a girl to do?

"I hope that's not a no," Rock said. "Because there's a lot I could say about how much I love you and how much you mean to me, but really, I just want you to let me take care of you forever."

"I can't believe this," I said.

Oscar shifted uncomfortably on the bed.

Neo glared at him. "Get it fucking over with."

Oscar shrugged and pulled a red velvet box from the

pocket of his jeans. "Fuck. I hadn't even decided what I wanted to say."

An emerald ring lay inside the box. It looked vintage, and I touched my finger to its surface, marveling at its depth.

"I chose this one because it made me think of your eyes, the way I feel like I found my soul there," he said. "That's a lot of pressure, I know, and I don't want to lay that on you, tiger. I just don't know if I can go the rest of my life without looking into your eyes and seeing my real self there. And your real self too."

I touched their faces one by one, marveling that they could be so dear to me when I'd started out hating them. "I love you. All of you. But just so I'm clear, is this a triple proposal?"

"I sure as fuck didn't plan it that way," Neo grumbled. "But that's what it looks like."

I drew in a breath. "How would it work?"

I asked because I wanted it to work. Because each one of them held an equal portion of my heart and soul.

"It works however you want it to work," Rock said.

"It works however *we* want to work," Neo said.

Oscar grinned. "Just say yes, tiger."

I looked from Rock, who took care of me like no one else, to Oscar, who saw every part of me.

And Neo. My twin flame.

Six months ago, I'd stepped into the unknown, and you know what?

It hadn't turned out half bad.

So I looked at the three guys who'd become my world, who'd reminded me who I was and shown me who they were too, and I said the only thing a girl could say under those circumstances.

"Yes."

Thanks so much for reading! If you enjoyed Willa and her Kings, you're going to love Daisy's story in **Gather the Storm.**

I owe them my life.

Or do I?

Five years ago I was falsely accused of killing my brother — until the three most important men in my life took the fall.

Now that they're being released from prison, I'm bringing them together to live in the abandoned mansion I inherited from my mother.

Otis: the devoted protector who worships the ground I walk on.

Wolf: my dead brother's best friend, forbidden to touch me.

Jace: the bully who wants me dead.

The newspapers called them the Blackwell Beasts. Were they used as scapegoats for someone else's crime?

Or is one of them a killer?

I think I'm prepared for the answers. What I'm not prepared for?

Falling for the three men who kept me out of prison — even if one of them is a murderer.

Did you enjoy this book? Please help other readers find it by leaving a review.

Want freebies, book news, and exclusive Aventine U content? Sign up for the Sadie Hunt newsletter and learn more about Blackwell Falls and the swoon-worthy Kings: https://mailchi.mp/1986196a4e5c/sadie-hunt

Find me online:
Instagram: @authorsadiehunt
TikTok: @authorsadiehunt
Facebook: authorsadiehunt

Share Kings & Corruption and tag me on Instagram and/or TikTok for a like, comment, and share!

Made in United States
Troutdale, OR
05/04/2024